CW00434733

Land Girls

and

Lovers

Hazel Stephenson

Second Edition Published 2010

British Library Cataloguing in Publication Data
A catalogue for this book is available from the British Library.

ISBN 978-0-9562863-0-7

Printed by Lintons Printers Ltd.
Unit 14B, Beechburn Industrial Estate,
Prospect Road, Crook. Co. Durham. DL15 8RA.

Cover Illustration - June Barton

CHAPTER 1

Ethel Harrison was on her knees, lighting the fire. She was thinking she would have to get this room warmed up a bit before she got Gran out of bed. Rosebud cottage was covered in snow. It was a two up, three down with a privy at the bottom of the garden. On a postcard, this cottage would look picturesque, but to live in it in winter was very different, as the hellish winds lashed the cottage, threatening to lift the roof off.

The snow was blowing down off the fells causing Ethel's hands to grip like claws. The fire was starting to burn through. Ethel would soon be able to get the kettle on for a morning cup of tea and take a cup up for granny, but first she would have to go to the spring and get a bucket of water.

"I had better get my wellies and coat on," she thought. Although the spring was just down the road the snow would have been over Ethel's shoes and the cardboard that Ethel put in her shoes to cover the hole would have been soaked. "They have been good shoes," thought Ethel as she changed into her wellies, as she had walked miles in them in the summer she would walk down the country lanes, gathering berries to bottle for the winter. She especially liked the brambles and blackberries. Also, she had plums, apples and gooseberries in her own garden but her hardest job in the summer was to walk four miles to the fell gates, then up on the fell, dragging her old bogey to get the peat, which she cut with a spade in to square blocks. After she had got the bogey loaded, she had it to drag home and stack it in the out house to dry out for winter so that granny and she could have a fire on, as they could not afford a lot of coal. They also needed to have the fire on in summer, as it was their only means of cooking and heating hot water. "By it's bloody cold this morning!" thought Ethel as she splashed back with her bucket of water I will go in to the house and set the kettle off on the fire, then I might as well keep my coat and wellies on and go and feed the hens."

Ethel had thirty hens. She knew granny and she had made the right decision when they had made up their minds to buy some hens. They always had an egg each for breakfast and plenty to give to Ethel's daughter, Eva for her and her family. "That is more than the poor buggers in them cities are having with this war on. someone told me they were having dried eggs. I couldn't fancy that". Ethel walked through to the scullery to get a dish to collect the eggs. As she opened the door to go into the hen house, the hens started clucking and flapping. "Come on you buggers, let me be having them eggs. My hands are bloody frozen." She collected the eggs. There were twenty and she would give some to her neighbours such as Grace Hughes, the local nurse and midwife, who lived along the road, and was very kind to her and Gran. She gave the hens some corn, before she fastened them in as she was keeping them in with so much snow about.

Back at the house, the kettle was boiling as she opened the door .She thought she would make a cup of tea for her and granny. "But first I'll have to take these wellies off and put my shoes back on, as the stone stairs are cold on my feet some day when I have some money to spare, I'll get a bit of carpet for them stairs".

As Ethel opened the curtains she saw granny just waking up. " Here is your tea Gran sit up and drink it while it's hot, then I will help you down stairs as it soon goes cold in this old house."

"Well, I am ready for a drink. You have always been a good girl to me, Ethel."

"Nothing of the sort gran. Where would I have been if you had not looked after me when Mam died when I was born? Now drink your tea then I will help you dress. Then we'll go down stairs where it's a bit warmer then. I will boil you and me an egg each."

After Ethel had buttered the bread and boiled the eggs, she sat down to enjoy her breakfast with Gran. After breakfast she would have to go down the road to the well, to fill six buckets of water, to fill the boiler on the side of the fire, as it was wash day. She would have to get the poss tub out and start doing the weekly wash. They did not have a lot of clothes, but Ethel was determined what they had would be clean.

Ethel saw through the window her daughter and two grandchildren, Margaret and Shirley, five year old twins, coming up the road. Eva often called round to help Ethel on washdays as all the whites were to poss, then the colours ,then they all had to be rinsed in clean water. They all had to go through the mangle, to squeeze the water out, which was a massive thing. It took strong arms to turn it. If it was a dry day, the washing would be pegged on the line, which was stretched between two posts in the garden. If it was wet it would dry on a line above the fire. As Eva and the two girls walked in, Ethel saw that Eva had brought them a rabbit. Eva said, "I thought you might like to make some rabbit stew for tea as I know you always have plenty of vegetables."

"That is lovely, Eva, thank you. I will make a big pan full then it will last Gran and me two or three days. But what will you tell Joe when he finds out you have given me one of his rabbits?" asked Ethel" I know he can always get more, but he is so bloody greedy."

"I know he has his faults but he is good in other ways Mam. Besides, you provide us with all our eggs and bottled fruit," Eva said. "Have you heard, Mam, we are going to be getting some more children in to the village? Some evacuees, Joe has heard about it, and does not think it is right bringing all these children in to the village. He thinks the school is not big enough to accommodate all the children. Joe had met one of the teachers last night as he was coming from work and the teacher had told him that once the evacuees arrive, the local children will go to school on a morning and the evacuees will go on an afternoon. Joe said our children will be missing out on their education, but I told him you can't expect the children to stop at home in the cities when they are getting bombed on a night."

"Just like Joe to think like that," though Ethel, "As he is always selfish Never did see what Eva saw in him." Ethel went in to the big cold scullery and brought out some bottled plums, bottled cherries and black currants. "You can make some pies with these, Eva, as you have been a good help to me turning that bloody handle on that mangle."

"That's alright, mam, I don't mind helping you, but I will make some fruit crumble tomorrow and bring some for you and Gran. It will be lovely after your rabbit stew."

After they had gone, Ethel went in to the scullery to skin the rabbit and chop the vegetables. They would have a tasty tea tonight and the next two nights. Gran would enjoy her teas .She was seventy six but she still had a good appetite and Ethel looked after her the best she could. Ethel had been born in this cottage and she had never lived any where else. There had always just been her and Gran, as her mother, Gran's daughter, had died when she was born and her grandfather died when she was a baby, so it had been left to Gran to struggle on.

When Ethel was fourteen she left school and started work. There were plenty of live- in jobs, like going in to service, at some of the big houses, but Gran disagreed with it and forbade Ethel to mention such jobs. Ethel was always curious as to why her Gran was so much against it. One night she was going down the road to get some water from the well. Gran had been doing the weekly wash and needed some extra water. While Ethel was fetching the water she met Hilda Dent who was a nosy and spiteful woman. She had grown up with Ethel's mother and knew all about her. She called to Ethel, "Are you leaving school soon?"

Ethel replied, "Yes, in three weeks time, but Mrs. Young, our teacher, said if any of us were offered jobs we could leave earlier."

"Well, have you not got a job to go to yet?" asked Hilda.

"No," answered Ethel, "I was born and bred here, so I

would like to stop around in the dales.Also, Gran will not allow me to work in one of the big houses and live in. I think Gran doesn't want to live on her own, as she would be lonely with out me and I don't want to leave Gran either."

Hilda Dent replied sarcastically, "That is not the reason! I think she will be worried that you do the same as your mother did!"

"What do you mean by that?" Ethel was starting to get upset. "My Mam was a lovely, trusting person. Gran said she died giving birth to me."

Hilda Dent was the same age as Ethel's mother would have been, if she had lived. Also, they used to go around together when they were at school. But Hilda loved upsetting people.

"Well, if your Gran thought your Mam was so good, go and ask her who your father was and why your mother was never married !I'll tell you why, because your mother had an affair with the son from one of the big houses where she was working and you are the result! So don't try pretending that Gran wants you to stay at home because she might be lonely!"

Ethel dropped the bucket and started to run back home to tell Gran what Hilda Dent had said. Gran knew there was something really wrong when the door banged open and Ethel ran in crying. "Gran, Hilda Dent has said some terrible lies to me! She said my Mam was never married and I have to ask you who my Dad is!"

Gran knew this would be thrown at Ethel some day. When you lived in the same place as people like Hilda Dent. It was bound to happen.

"Sit down, Ethel. Now we have to have a chat .Your mother went to work in one of the big houses. She fell in love with the son of the house. She was infatuated with him but he took advantage of her as she was so naive. She thought the lad loved her too and when she realised she was having you, she came home to give birth. Everything was going alright and the midwife delivered you. Then afterwards your Mam started to haemorrhage. By the time we had got an ambulance all her life's blood had drained away so we had a birth and a death, both at the same time. I was devastated to lose your Mam, so I thought the only last thing I could do for her was to bring you up the best way I could. I have always loved you, Ethel, and always will, you are so much like her, so dry your tears and go and fill the bucket. Then I will fill the paraffin lamp as it 'll soon be dark."

After Ethel had gone back to fill the bucket, Gran thought, "I know some thing about Hilda Dent but I will keep quiet until the time is right. Then she will get her comeuppance and she'll not know what 's hit her."

However, Ethel did find a job the next day. Having been sent to the farm for some milk, she was walking along, swinging the empty milk can. Just as she approached the little shop, Mrs. Watkins, who owned the shop with her husband, came bustling out and nearly knocked Ethel off her feet. Mrs. Watkins was a very pleasant woman, short and plump."Sorry Ethel! "exclaimed Mrs.Watkins," I wasn't watching where I was going. Mind, you seem to have grown since I last saw you. When do you leave school?"

Ethel thought "Not this again!" after what Hilda Dent had thrown at her.

"I leave school in three weeks time but I haven't found a job yet."

Mrs. Watkins replied, "The girl that helps me in the shop is leaving to get married and I am looking to replace her. Would you like to do shop work, Ethel? Because if you are interested you and your Gran should come along tonight after we close as I would like to have a replacement as soon as possible. Also, I have known you all your life and you have always been clean and tidy.

Ethel hurried away to get the milk then she could get

home and talk to Gran. Gran knew Ethel was excited about something when she burst in with the milk, cheeks like two rosy apples. Gran never knew what Ethel was going to tell her. "Gran I have been offered a job by Mrs. Watkins at the shop. Can we go along tonight after she closes and see her?"

"We'll just slow down a bit. Ethel is that what you would like to do? You know you might have to help in the bakery as well, if there is nobody to serve in the shop."

"I don't mind Gran at least it will be a warm job in the winter."

Gran had to laugh at Ethel; she had an answer for every thing. Ethel could hardly wait to go and see Mrs. Watkins. "I've never met anyone as impatient as you Ethel but I will go and get my hat and coat." Ethel's Gran, Mrs. Brown was never seen out without a hat and coat. By that seemed a long time ago now, thought Ethel as she prepared tea and put her mind back on the present situation,

Just as Ethel was going to help Gran to the bottom of the garden to the lav, the front door opened and Grace Hughes walked in. "I hope I haven't called at a bad time Ethel?" How are you Mrs. Brown?"

"Well I would feel better if I was at the bottom of the garden heading to the lav that is where Ethel was taking me when you walked in." Ethel looked at Gran, and knew she would have to take her straight away, as Gran had a way with words, and could upset anybody if she was in that mood. "I am just going to help Gran down the garden, her arthritis has been playing her up lately, with it being so cold, sit down Grace we wont be long I am bloody sure, I wont be any longer then necessary, "I never linger in that lav the bloody draught blowing up through that seat it blows straight off them fells.

"The bloody door doesn't even fit properly; there is a gap at top and bottom that I could bloody crawl through." After Ethel had taken Gran out through the door Grace thought.

By! They don't call Mrs. Brown an old battleaxe for nothing, but then she had always been good to Ethel. Grace Hughes was the local nurse and midwife, she travelled lots of miles on her bicycle and had lost count of the number of babies she had delivered. She got to know about every thing that was going on. She was a remarkable lady and had a genuine interest in people. Her husband was a boss down at the quarry, he treated the men, as he was heard to say, The same way as he liked to be treated ,Just then a cold drought blew around Graces legs, then Ethel and Gran walked in ,Grace got up and went to help Ethel put Gran back in her chair. "What I called to ask you Ethel was when we get the evacuees and woman with children, would you be able to let some stay here? you may of heard about it already as this village is very big .It is about three miles long and there is quite a lot of houses and out lying farms, so we should be able to accommodate a lot of people. The authorities want people, who have room in their homes to take in evacuees, and people such as mothers and small children. They are getting bombed out of their homes in some cities, you have two big bedrooms haven't you Ethel? "Well I have Grace but I have no spare bedding, I don't have enough for us."

"What would you say Ethel, if I can get you some bedding towels and things, would you take in woman with children and may be a land girl I would not expect you to take the children as you have your Gran to look after?"

"Well how many would you like me to take? I can always sleep with Gran, so there would be a big spare room and it would hold an extra bed, also if I could get hold of another bed there is room for it in Gran's room."

"That would be grand Ethel, but where would you and Gran sleep?"

"Well the sideboard opens up and there is a double bed in there."

"Have you thought Ethel?" Grace asked.

"When your Jack comes home, you will want a bit of privacy.

Between us Grace "I would rather Jack stopped where he is at, as I can live with out that. He only comes home when it suits him. He gets plenty shore leave to sit in the pubs near the dock yard and the tarts." Grace thought Gran might of dosed off she had been quiet, but she had been listening. She said "Don't you be thinking about that bloody Jack, He will be getting his oats where ever he's at, He could never keep it in his bloody trousers."

"Well Ethel said Grace" "I will be going, I will leave you to think about it and talk it over with Gran.

"Oh yes, Gran always knows what to do for the best, her legs and hands are crippled with arthritis but she still has all her faculties."

"Ethel is that rabbit stew ready yet because I'm ravenous?"

"It is Gran but I don't see how you can be so hungry" replied Ethel.

"Well if you had not talked all that time to Grace I could have had me tea."

"I'll dish it out now Gran."

After Gran had eaten every thing Ethel had put in front of her, Ethel went in to the scullery and Gran shouted through," By that tea was worth waiting for, I really enjoyed it

"You enjoy all your meals Gran, I don't know where you put it all at times, I am going to collect the eggs in and shut the hens up for the night. It might be an idea Gran to buy some more hens, as this village is going to need a constant supply of eggs once all these people arrive.

Although Ethel had said they needed more hens they still did not have a lot of money. Gran only had her pension and the rent she received for the fields and out buildings, including a byre, and Ethel had the little bit she made selling eggs. Ethel's husband Jack was a merchant sea man. It was very rare that he sent money home. Ethel was known to tell people rather than send money home; he would rather tip it down his throat. Never mind, summer wasn't far away then she would have one of her favourite walks through bluebell wood. Oh the happy memories she had of that place and bluebell farm. What Ethel didn't know was that she would have a lot more memorises of blue bell wood before this war was over.

As Ethel was walking along after closing the hen house door, all she could hear was the ice as it splintered and crackled beneath her wellies. Her hands were scrunched in her pockets as they were blue with cold and Ethel was shivering. As she was opening her house door, she saw Robert Lee coming towards her with his black and white collie dog named Meg. "I am just on my way to your house Ethel."

"Well lucky we have met out side Robert. Replied Ethel It saves opening the door twice and letting all the bloody heat out.

As Robert opened the door to let Ethel in first, Meg rushed in, nearly knocking Ethel off her feet in her rush to get to Gran. As Gran loved animals, she always stroked and cuddled Meg with her swollen misshapen hands. Gran had suffered with arthritis for a long time.

As Robert walked in Gran asked him what he was doing out on a night like this. ,"Well I came tonight Mrs. Brown, as I have something important to tell you. Also I have brought you a present. He opened his coat and handed Ethel's Gran a tiny pup." "I hope I have done right bringing you this pup, only I have received my call up papers so I will not be seeing you very often I will call from time to time when I get leave. I know how you like to see Meg and this is one of her pups. She only had three. My sister got one of them and my mother is going to look after Meg and the second pup I thought you might like this one she is black and white just like Meg."

"Well she is gorgeous isn't she Ethel? "She will be company for me when you are busy" said Gran I am going to call her Jess. What do you think Ethel?

"I think that would be lovely Gran, "said Ethel Now sit yourself down Robert until I make a cup of tea, then we will see what's to do about the fields and out buildings.

Afterwards when the three of them were sitting around the fire with a cup of tea each with Meg asleep on the prodded mat, stretched out in front of the fire, Jess on Gran's knee Robert said, "I need to talk to you Ethel, as I don't know if you would like to accept my present .I will explain what I have for you, then you can decide if you would like it, Ethel was wondering just what the bloody hell he was going to give her. But first I came to tell you I will no longer want to rent the buildings and fields off you after next week as I will be going away. That is why the pigs in the sty behind this cottage are going to the mart tomorrow as I will not be here to look after them. I would like to give you one of the pigs as a present, Ethel, as after a while you would be able to make money off it.

Ethel was astonished she had never heard of any one getting a pig before as a present. Her first instinct was to refuse. Then she thought, "I might as well listen to what he has to say first of all."

"Ethel if you would like a pig you can choose one in the morning before they go to the mart."

"But I don't know a bloody thing about pigs Robert and you are going away so I will have nobody to ask."

"Course you will Ethel, you live in the country. Everybody has animals. You are surrounded by farms."

"I know that Robert, but if I have to go and ask someone they might think I am bloody stupid."

"No they won't Ethel, there is only your son-in-law and old Dent the gamekeeper that like humiliating people. Besides, I will be here until next week to help you so would you like a pig?"

"I will then Robert", replied Ethel. "Thank you. If I make another cup of tea, will you tell me what I should do?"

"Well first of all Ethel, them pigs are twelve month old. Your pig will have to go to the boar so you can have some piglets. I will arrange that for you tomorrow. The boar will be brought here. It will stay for twenty four hours .She has to be served twice in that time to make sure that you get some piglets. They have two litters a year. After she has been served it takes three months, three weeks, and three days, for her to produce piglets. Then they are weaned after three to four weeks. Four to six, days after weaning the sow comes on heat again. You will learn as you go Ethel," explained Robert.

"Before I forget Robert, what breed are they?"

"Well mine have always been large whites. It is one of the most popular ones other popular ones are. Yorkshire, Berkshire, and Hampshire, Well! I had better be going. I will be along in the morning. By the way Ethel, what will you call it?" Ethel already had a name for it." I will call her Alice.

Ethel felt quite excited as she climbed the stairs to bed. No one ever gave Ethel presents. Robert was as good as his word and he came along bright and early next morning.

As Ethel was kneeling down on the prodded, mat, raking the ashes out, she could see Robert through the window. She shouted, "If you are still about after I get the fire lit and a bucket of water from the well, you can have a cup of tea with us." Ethel put her hands on the brass fender and pushed her self up off the floor, the sooner she got Gran up and her jobs done, the sooner she could choose Alice It was not every day that you got a pig given.

Robert thought he had never seen any one look as happy as Ethel as she chose her pig, "Don't worry about food for it yet, Ethel, as I have a small building at home full of turnips. I would've gone along and got you a barrow load, only I don't have a lot of time. I would like to re-felt this sty roof today."

Ethel said, "I can barrow some turnips along, after all they are for my pig. I will go along for them Robert. I don't mind popping out as much now that Gran has Jess to keep her company. She loves that pup."

When Ethel got back with the loaded barrow and a bucket of potato peelings that Robert's mam had given her, she asked Robert how long the turnips would last.

Robert replied, "There is a lot more at home, I will get the rest along for you." Robert was working and thinking about Ethel, feeding her pig and future pigs. The boar had been this morning to do his job. Then he thought she could may be have the pig swill from the big hall, so he hollered across to Ethel as she was about to step through the stile.

Ethel was a short, thin, country woman; she used to tell people I never have time to get bloody fat. "Come in to the house Robert and have a cup of tea to warm you up. It's bloody cold out here. I've. Some jacket potatoes in the oven. I scrubbed them clean this morning and put them in for dinner before I fed the hens. You're lucky today. You can have a bit of butter on them. Usually, we have run out of butter in the middle of the week. Isn't that right Gran?"

"Aye, it is," said Gran, "but then our Ethel looks after me. Are we having that crumble for tea Ethel? Will you put plums in it? I like plums"

Ethel got up and went in to the scullery for the big enamel dish and the bottled plums. It didn't take Ethel long to tip the plums into the dish and mix some sugar and marg. into crumble and cover the plums. "Gran, which will go in to the oven now for tea, I am sure all you think about is food!"

"When you get to my age, Ethel that is all you have to bloody think about." Gran chuntered. Ethel got back up and reached for the big, brown, earthenware tea pot. Hopefully, she would be able to drink her tea in peace. Before Robert went back out side he asked Ethel if she had thought any more about the pig swill from the hall. "Ethel said," I would like it; only Hilda Dent would not let me have it."

"It's not up to her Ethel", Robert said indignantly, "I will sort it out for you and get young Sam to drop it off on a night when he is passing here to go home, after he has finished working at the hall."

Ethel thought Gran had dozed off but she had been sitting listening."That's right lad, you sort it out for our Ethel, because we don't want to ask that malicious bitch for anything, do we Ethel? By God I will see the day with her!"

"Before I go back out side to finish off," said Robert, "have you heard that old Sid is giving his milk round up. His daughter can not do as much as she used to, with looking after her crippled mother. Sid is getting old. He said he is selling two cows in calf shortly. It seems shames for you're out buildings and byre to stand idle".

"Well, me and Gran could not afford two cows in calf," Ethel sighed.

Gran said, "If we got one that wasn't in calf, we could maybe afford it, but it would be Ethel that had all the hard work to do."

"Well I'm not afraid of hard work." Ethel replied. "I have worked out in all weathers. Do you think I should ask Sid about a cow Gran?"

"Well if you don't go and ask, you will never find out, our Ethel!"

"I will go in the morning Robert. It's a pity our Eva's husband isn't as helpful as you. I don't know how she puts up with him. Still we should be thankful for small mercies. He never comes here; I think he is frightened of Gran."

"Yes, well, I will frighten that arrogant bugger before I'm finished with him. He can not look you straight in the eye. I have always said that bugger's hiding some thing. But truth will out. I might sit here all day not saying a lot. I don't miss much."

Robert thought Ethel's Gran all ways had plenty to say, but he would not upset Mrs. Brown, Ethel's Gran Some people said you could slice bread with her tongue.

Next morning arrived fine and dry, with a low winter sun. After Ethel had got Gran fed and dressed and helped in to the rocking chair beside the fire, she remembered that she used to love to sit on Gran's knee in that rocking chair when she was small . Now she hadn't time to reminisce. She had to go and feed the hens, gather the eggs, then go to the sty and see Alice the pig.

Ethel could hear Alice as she approached because Alice was grunting and snorting for her breakfast. Ethel poured a bucket full of water in to one trough and a bucket of pig swill in to the other. She stood and stroked Alice for a while. She was thinking, "This is the best present I have ever had."

As Ethel walked back to the house she was beginning to think it was pointless going to see Sid as she had no idea how she could get some extra money. When she opened the door to go back in to the house, a cold wind blew in making the curtains flap, and waking Gran, who had dozed off in front of the fire, with Jess on her knee.

"Have you been to see Sid yet Ethel?"Said Gran, half asleep.

"No Gran and I don't think I will. We have no money to buy a cow let alone one in calf."

"Well I've got some money, Ethel. It is upstairs under me bed in a tin. You can have that, but you will have to put it back when you can, as it's me burial money."

Ethel was shocked. "I can't use that!"

"Course you can Ethel, I don't think I will need it for a long time yet, so go and see Sid," insisted Gran.

CHAPTER 2

Ethel enjoyed her walk along the path to Sid's as the buds were just starting to come on the trees because the snow had arrived later this year. Just as Ethel was going to climb on to the stile, she noticed Eva, Joe and the twin Granddaughters walking towards her. Ethel thought the girls looked as pretty as a picture .Joe was the dominant one in that relationship .However, Eva had stood her ground when she said she was not having any more children. He had wanted a son. He did not bother with the two children that he had. Ethel thought, "Eva and Joe will never grow old together. They will go the same way as me and Jack. He was never much of a husband to me or a dad to Eva."

The grand children ran to Ethel as soon as they saw her. She bent down and hugged them. "Where are you going mam?" asked Eva as she caught up to the girls.

Her mam replied, "I'm going to buy a cow off Sid."

"What ever for mam?"

"Well Eva I am hoping to start a milk round as Sid is going to retire shortly."

"Well I thought you had enough to do with out getting any more work, but if you ever need a hand, mam, I will come and help you. Have you heard from Dad lately"? Enquired Eva.

"No," replied Ethel, "I never hear from that bugger, never get no money neither

"The girls are asking, Mam, when you get your cow can they come and help you?"Said Eva.

"Yes, 'course they can, you know they can come and see me when ever they want."

After Ethel had walked a way Joe said, "Your Mother is getting dafter as she is getting older. Buying a cow indeed!"

Eva was getting sick of his comments lately. "Well Joe, at least she does not sit on her backside all day doing nothing like your mother." They carried on home, arguing as they went.

Ethel walked away down the path. She knew Joe would have some thing to say about her going to buy a cow. The clever bugger she would see her day with him.

As Ethel approached the farm she could see old Sid sweeping the yard. He turned around and looked as he heard Ethel's booted feet coming towards him. "Come away in," he shouted as he walked over to open the house door for Ethel, "and have a bit chin wag to my Gertie. She does not see many folk". Ethel was just about to step in to the farm house as Grace Hughes, the nurse and midwife, was coming out.

"I am pleased to see you Ethel, I was going to call and let you know that there is a meeting, in the school hall at 7 30 on Wednesday night," Grace informed her. "Will you be coming? Some villagers are against taking evacuees, especially children, in to their homes so we need as many willing people as possible. I heard that Joe does not want them in his home. He has been telling who ever would listen."

"Well he would, that bugger! He does not like his bloody self at times, I don't know how our Eva puts up with him, I really don't. I will definitely come to the meeting. I just wish I knew how to get Gran there", puzzled Ethel.

Grace stood and thought for a minute. "I tell you what Ethel; I will ask Tommy Gibson to give your Gran a lift up with his motor bike and sidecar. Lizzie his wife is going to look after the pub. I don't think the pub will be very busy, as everyone will be at the meeting."

"That will be lovely, thanks Grace."While Ethel had been talking to Grace, Sid had made a cup of tea for Ethel. As she was drinking the tea, she told them she would like to buy a cow in calf.

"How much money have you got there?" asked Sid?

"I have got fifteen pounds," replied Ethel. "I thought it would have been enough."

"There is no way you can buy a cow in calf, for that amount of money!" scoffed Sid. Ethel looked down cast Sid was an old skinflint he would rob his own granny. "I'll tell you what Ethel; I've got a cow I'll sell you. She is getting old and slower, but you will be able to get the amount of milk you are after for now."

Ethel thought the cow looked fat and healthy when she went outside to take a look."I will come back tomorrow for it," she said, "as that is the only one I can afford and I am using Gran's funeral money for that."

"I 'll have some rope ready so you can lead it away," Ethel heard him say as she watched his retreating back going over the yard .She walked despairingly along the lane. Coming towards her was Wilf. Now there was a bugger that was rotten with money.

"Hello Ethel," he called, "have you been for a walk?"

"No I've been to buy a cow."

"Well you don't look very happy about it. If you care to step in to my house, I will put a smile on your face," grinned Wilf.

"I wanted a cow in calf," grumbled Ethel, "but I don't have enough money."

"If you would like to warm my bed up I would not see you stuck for money. Just think Ethel, we could make my bed springs squeak. It would just sound like music to your ears."

"Get away with you. You dirty old bugger! I am a married woman."

"Yes, but he's never at home is he? Think about it Ethel."

Ethel did think about it all the way home She was using Gran's burial money, she didn't want Gran to go yet, but what if she did Ethel thought I would have a cow, but I wouldn't be able to bury Gran. As she walked in to the house the pup ran to meet her, she was very boisterous now and was spoilt by Gran. Ethel patted the dog before she moved the pan of rabbit stew over on to the fire to warm through for tea.

"Have you got a cow then asked Gran?"Yes, answered Ethel. But I didn't have enough to get one in calf."

"Never mind Ethel, we will get the cow, then we will have plenty of milk, so we will be able to have porridge, with thick cream, and rice pudding. I can hardly wait. You will be able to make some butter to sell, so we will be able to buy another cow .Before we start selling milk. It will work out all right Ethel just you wait and see"

"Oh by the way Ethel, Robert is here" Gran said, "he has brought you a few things along on his barrow, go and see him." Ethel was shocked when she saw what Robert had brought". There was straw for bedding, some hay, a milking stool, and a ten gallon steel churn.

"You're a good lad Robert. Come in to the house and I will give you some vegetables for your mother. You can have a cup of tea as well while you are here."

"Sit down a minute Ethel, until I tell you about a few things you can have," declared Robert. "There is a hand cart and another steel churn behind the engine shed where your son in law works, you will need them when you get your milk round going. I have been told I can have them, but I go back to camp tomorrow, so could you bring them up yourself?"I know Joe will not help you."

"That's all right lad, our Eva will help me with it." Next day with money in her pocket Ethel set off again. "I hope I am doing the right thing," she thought, Gran all ways said "nothing ventured, nothing gained." As Ethel approached the gate way to the farm she could see Sid with the cow, she had bought and come to collect, although Sid was an old skinflint, he always seemed to feed his animals well enough, in fact this cow she was getting and going to call Buttercup was fat.

"How much longer are you going to be delivering the milk Sid?"Ethel asked him as she approached.

"Oh it will be a few months yet Ethel, so if you can save your money up you might be able to buy a cow in calf off me."

"What bloody money, Ethel thought I've had to use Gran's burial money to get this one." Sid went to get some rope so Ethel could lead the cow home. Ethel thought who knows I might be back here soon for a cow in calf if I take Wilf up on his offer." As Ethel walked along the cow amber ling along beside her Tommy Gibson saw Ethel as he was busy cleaning his pub windows .He had lived at the shoulder of mutton now, the local pub for a long time. "He shouted just a minute Ethel."

"Grace asked me if I could take your Gran up to the meeting on Wednesday night, I thought if I came for her about 7 o clock, would that be alright Ethel? Then we can make sure she get's a seat at the front because I'm sure your Gran will have plenty to say about the evacuees we will be able to help her in to the side car, you can come on the bike with me. Ethel." "Thanks Tommy that will be grand." "Mind that looks a fine beast you have got there Ethel, I heard you were after taking over Sid's milk round." "Yes I am, but I wanted a cow in calf." Is this one not in calf Ethel? It looks canny fat to me." "No it isn't." Sid said it had not been with the bull".

"Be funny if it was Ethel, and Sid had missed it, you would be the first person to get one over old Sid. If it isn't in calf what will you do with all the milk until you take over the round."

"Well to tell you the truth Tommy. Every thing has happened so fast, first of all young Robert, who has been renting Gran's fields, and buildings, including the byres, has been called up for the army. He told Gran and me the other night he no longer wanted to rent them, he suggested I should use them, because when we get the evacuees in to the village, I will be able to sell more eggs, and milk."

"Tommy thought, "by heck you couldn't blame Ethel for trying, he had gone to school with her, he remembered when she had pig tails, and she still wasn't a bad looking woman now.

24

They were nice pleasant woman in Ethel's family, shame the same could not be said of the men. Take that that husband of hers, he never seemed to come home much, and when he does he sits in my pub drinking ,all his money and getting legless, while poor Ethel, and her Gran, were trying to get by on now't. He had told Ethel once that he had thought of barring him, but Ethel had said."

"You might as well have his money Tommy. He will only go along to the dog and whistle to spend it." Ethel was looking up the road said "here's Joe coming I could of done with out seeing him today, I wonder what he has to say for his self."

"Tommy said he's another clever bugger, or thinks he is, I would say he's very dubious, I would never trust him Ethel."

"Joe walked up towards Ethel, and Tommy, he sneered at Ethel, and the cow."   "What's that you've got there? Ethel?"

"What does it look like? It s a bloody cow retorted Ethel."

Joe was dressed immaculate; as usual he still had his uniform on he had just finished. Work for the railways in the signal box.

"Ethel thought the sooner he gets called up the better, as he intimidates Eva, my daughter, she would have a better life with out him." Joe walked around the cow with a smug look on his face.

"Well it does not look like it's up to much to me said Joe and you don't know any thing about cows. The bloody thing could be dried up." Just then Tommy spoke up.

"Ethel might not know a lot, as you have enjoyed pointing out, but there's plenty about here that does me included, so if she needs help she won't have far to look.",

"Joe stood behind Buttercup with his arms folded, just then the cow lifted her tail and splattered Joe from head to foot."

"Tommy looked at Ethel, and they both roared with laughter.

"Tommy whispered, to Ethel. It could not have happened

to any body better, the big headed bugger." Tommy got along with every body, but he did not Like Joe, there was some thing about him, but time would tell.

"Well I had better go Tommy, I can't stand here all day admiring your garden, Eva and the twins are waiting with Gran, to see buttercup."

"Right Ethel, I will pop along after tea to see how you are getting on, and I will bring you that separator, and barrel churn, so you can start and make the butter." Ethel felt very content as she walked down the road with Buttercup, she couldn't help thinking of Tommy's garden, one side of the path was a mass of crocuses, primroses and snowdrops, on the other side of the path was a carpet of daffodils.

Ethel's Gran was sitting in the rocking chair facing the window, watching for Ethel. Eva and the twins were sitting with her they were going to help Granny out side to look at the cow

"It's a long time since we had cows here Gran was telling Eva, I had to get rid of them when granddad died it was too much for me to look after on my own."

"The twins heard Ethel talking to the cow", "They started shouting." come on mam let's go out and see the cow.""You had better wait a minute until I help Gran out of the chair Eva shouted after them." Gran placed her hands flat on the chair arm to help herself up as Eva held the chair still for her,then Eva asked Gran if she was sure she could manage, Gran said,

"If I don't keep going, I'll seize up altogether, so just give me your arm to lean on then I'll manage."

Once Gran was outside she had a good look at the cow and said

"I thought you told me Ethel, that cow was not in calf.

"Old Sid told his daughter to let all the cows run with the bull, except this one."

"Gran said known her she probably let them all out together, because I don't think she is very bright." "Eva started to laugh."

"What are you laughing at our Eva, asked Gran?

"Oh Gran nobody could ever describe you as tactful."

"No Eva I don't suppose they could, I've all ways said what I think and I will continue to do so. I like to let people know where they stand with me and while we are on the subject of standing up for our selves, I expect you will come to the meeting on Wednesday night. Don't let that husband of yours try and stop you, because he is so fickle. As for that cow I will bet two shilling of anybody's money that Buttercup is in calf, by that will be one in the eye for old Sid. He is a greedy old bugger."

"Are you going to help me back in to the house Eva, Gran asked "While our Ethel takes Buttercup in to the byre, The twins can go with Ethel as they are happy as Larry with that cow, you could make us a cup of tea Eva as my mouths is as dry as a bone. Have you heard what I said Eva? "As Gran gave her a poke in the ribs,"

After the cow was taken in to the byre, Eva and her daughters called to see how Alice the pig was settling in, she came snorting and grunting over to the children, to see if they had brought her any thing to eat, she was in luck, Eva had put her daughters a bag of food up so they could feed Alice. Just as well Joe didn't know Eva thought that she had taken food for the pig, or he would be furious. Alice guzzled it down as quick as the children gave it to her, then she thundered across to the other side of the sty and stretched out.

"Come on girls" Granma, Ethel said. "If we stay out here much longer that cup of tea your mam made a while ago will be cold". As Eva and the girls were leaving Eva asked Ethel if there was any thing she could help her with. "Ethel replied, "I was just going to ask you, if you would come along tomorrow, to help me make some butter."

"Gran hollered after them."

"You want to hope it is a bit on the cold side tomorrow then it won't take long to make that butter. If it is a warm day it will take bloody ages, I have made a lot of butter in my time. While I'm thinking about it Ethel we could have porridge, for breakfast, and Jacket potatoes for dinner with butter on, and a rice pudding, to finish off with. I will look forward to that, now don't you think you should go and milk that cow?"

Ethel was pleased she had got a jersey cow they had a good temperament, and gave very creamy milk Ethel was talking to Buttercup, as she picked up the three legged milking stool and pail, ready to milk her.

At the same time Tommy at the pub, said to his wife Lizzie. "I think I will pop along to Ethel's to see how she's getting on with that cow."

."Tommy stood at the byre door watching Ethel. She was sitting with the milking stool, between her boney knees. Tommy could hear the milk swishing as it was being squirted in to the pail. Ethel turned to look at the door, at the same time Buttercup lifted her leg, and kicked the milking stool out from under Ethel. Tommy rushed to Ethel. "Are you all right Ethel?"

"Oh aye Tommy, I think Buttercup knows she's in unskilled hands."

"Well you go in the house and get those wet clothes off Ethel, and I will milk her for you, as you didn't get much out of her." As Ethel lifted the sneck to go into the house Gran said. "I didn't expect you being so quick."Ethel told her what had happened while she had been milking Buttercup so she had come in to get changed "Gran started to grumble. "I hope there is plenty milk for my meals tomorrow our Ethel. Before Tommy left to go back home, he called to remind Ethel, and Gran, that he would pick them up at 7 o clock, the following week for the meeting.

"Well! As long as Gran gets a lift in the side car, I can walk said Ethel".

"Tommy said nothing of the sort .You can get on the bike with me, you will be able to get your leg over Ethel." "In that case, I will look forward to it. By but you are a cheeky bugger Tommy said Ethel laughing."

"Next morning Ethel was up bright and early. After she had finished her work in the house, and Gran, was seated in the rocking chair in front of the fire, as it crackled in the grate. Ethel let out the hens and gathered the eggs, next in the queue for food was Alice. She was always ready for a bite to eat, a bit like Gran, Ethel thought, last but not least was Buttercup, Ethel was hoping she would manage the milking better then she did last night. She decided to fill the hay rack first it might help to keep Buttercups mind, on something else until she got her milked. As Ethel went to get the three legged milking stool Buttercup turned and looked at Ethel. As if to say I hope you can manage better this morning, than you did last night, as I don't fancy standing here all day.

"Ethel was a true country woman she thought to her self, "I will not be beaten by a bloody cow." It wasn't long before Ethel had a steady rhythm going, and the pail was filling up nicely.

"As Eva walked in to the byre, she was pleased to hear the splish, splash, of the milk". "Will we have time to make some butter today mam, I hope you haven't forgotten the meeting tonight as I am coming with you and Gran "

"Joe said I should stop at home, but I am coming with you and Gran. I think all the children should be away from the bombing. But you know what Joes like. "He said. We are not taking children into our home." Later in the day as Eva walked home, carrying her pats of butter, her arms ached from turning the handle on the butter churn. She was thinking about the lovely sound, as the cream was turning in to butter she had heard it flip flopping against the churn. From now on, she was going to help her mam every day. She liked being along at mam and Gran's and what a lovely walk back along home as the birds were twittering, she thought spring is in the air and. "I'm going to the meeting tonight at 7 o'clock." Tommy had arrived on time Gran and Ethel were ready for there outing they were both dressed in their shabby best, wearing their threadbare coats, but as Ethel was heard to say to any one that would listen.

"We might be a bit shabby, but we are bloody clean, I drag the tin bath tub in on a Friday night, then we share the water. Gran all ways says "waste not want not"

"I agree with her, especially when I have all the bloody water to carry."

Tommy was all ways pleasant. "Come on then girls, let' be having you. Are you alright in the side car Mrs. Brown.?"

"Yes I'm grand thanks Tommy."

"Come on then Ethel." Said Tommy as he waved her over Get your leg over this bike", "Then we will be away to the meeting." Tommy helped Gran in to the hall old Sid was standing talking to a few blokes including Joe when he saw Gran and Ethel he shouted over are you pleased with the cow?"

"Gran shouted back." "She is a bloody good milking cow she has some grand tits on her."

"Joe did not acknowledge his wife and family it was embarrassing being related to them scruffy buggers."He wished Sid would stop shouting over to them."

"It's a bit breezy tonight Mrs. Brown" Sid was saying. "But it hasn't stopped you coming out. I am pleased to see you."

"I put me long bloomers on tonight Gran was saying. They come over me knees and stop any draughts going up to me bits."

"Joe said." "I couldn't imagine anything wanting to go near her bits. Not even a bloody draught." Joe turned around to look at the door as Eva walked in, and went straight over to her Mam and Gran, she did not give Joe a second look he could not believe it. All them three buggers here tonight,

"He was thinking if I had a gun I would shoot the buggers." He turned to Wesley Dent and said.

Look at them three Wesley. Sitting cackling, like three

bloody witches, I might see about joining up. Eva has turned in to a cold fish in bed, and she might end up looking like them two old battleaxes. Well you wouldn't want to tackle them would you?"

Wesley started to laugh, look! Joe Gran is screeching at you." Joe had been trying to ignore all three of them. Then Gran shouted again 'Oi! Joe this chair is not very comfortable go and find me a cushion." Joe said if you didn't have such a skinny backside you would not feel it." "Ethel stood up." Surely you don't mind finding a cushion for Gran. You miserable get." Just then Grace Hughes walked in and saw Ethel. So she went to sit with them.

Grace said." "I wanted to see you Ethel". "I have arranged for you to have some things, which include two iron bedsteads, and mattresses. So is it alright if I call tomorrow?"

Yes that will be grand replied Ethel."

Joe sent Sid over with the cushion.""He told Sid rather then putting the cushion under her backside he would rather put it over her bloody face. Look said Joe they have got Grace reeled in now."

"The vicar has arrived, so should we get started Asked Lillie?" the wife of one of the quarry men, who was helping to organise the meeting."

CHAPTER 3

"Joe was not enjoying this meeting, "He looked across at his family and Grace. They were all cackling now and looking at him. I bet they are talking about that bloody cow covering me in shit and bloody old Granny sitting there lapping it up. By Ethel's Gran really is a vindictive old bitch. Joe was nervous when Ethel's Gran was around he some times felt that she could see straight through him with them little beady eyes. Joe knew that Eva trusted him when he said he liked to have a walk out on a night. But he all ways waited until the twins were in bed at night in case Eva suggested having a walk with him"

"Little Barbara, who he had been seeing lately, was going in to the W.A.A.F." "Helen who he had also been seeing had a bun in the oven so he has been trying to keep out of her way."

He would have to call in and see Mable tomorrow night, to give her some money, as she has two nasty brothers Joe thought "Just my bloody luck for her to have a bloody kid, She is all very nice when I call to give her some money, and all sympathetic when I tell her". "I am frightened Eva finds out." Then she says as long as I keep taking her some money to keep my baby Eva will not hear nothing from her." "Joe was thinking she had turned out to be a heartless bitch."

Just then Frank, who had come along to the meeting with his wife, asked Joe if he was feeling all right, as he had been mumbling to himself." Joe blinked and brought his mind back to the present "Oh sorry Frank, I was miles away." Well Frank said. "If you carry on like that, some bugger will be coming for you, and taking you to the nut house." Just then Joe heard raised voices.

Wesley Dent and Hilda were talking now. The vicar stood a side to listen to them. "They were saying." They did not have the space to take any one into their home, As Hilda's sister and her husband, were coming to live with them." Hilda said she felt very sorry for the people, and children, but families must come first". "We were never blessed with children If we had been, we would have been eternally grateful."

"Gran could take no more." She shouted. You are a bloody liar Hilda Dent. You went away. When you were just turned sixteen and got rid of a bairn, then things went wrong and you ended up in hospital. That's why you are bloody barren now." "Hilda Dent looked as if she could faint.

Wesley her husband was looking at her and said

"Tell me this isn't true Hilda?" as sweat broke out on his brow. Hilda just gave him a resigned shrug of her shoulders then she started pointing at Gran and shouting

"I want that old gossip monger thrown out."

"Gran shouted it is the bloody truth, standing there with all your airs and graces."

"Just then Hilda Dents sister turned around to Gran and said."

"You just can not keep you mouth shut can you?

"Gran shouted don't tell me what to do," "You were known as dirty Gertie. You used to sell your body and you gave your baby away."

Her husband Burt was a big florid faced man, he was as red as beetroot he turned to Gran and said,

"I bet you have really enjoyed this you bloody old bitch."

"Gran picked up her walking stick, and brought it straight down on his head, I only speak the bloody truth shouted Gran. "I told you years ago I would see my day with you." "I am just pleased, I have lived long enough to see it."

"Wesley left Hilda standing on her own as he went and sat down with his head in his hands."

"Lily Rain was sitting across from Gran, she shouted it's all true what Mrs. Brown has said. "I have lived in this village all my life they are all fur coat and no knickers and Hilda Dent is a nasty piece of work.

"The vicar coughed, and asked. Could we get back to the matter in hand?"

"Wesley got up and walked out, then Hilda went after him, so did Gertie and her husband. Burt was holding a handkerchief to his head as it was bleeding."

"Joe looked across at Gran." "He thought." She has caused all this bloody trouble, and never batted an eye lid."

"Tom who was standing next to Joe said to him." If you don't fancy taking kids in, how about taking a nice young teacher, or a land girl

"Joe perked up on hearing that." He would go across to Eva now, and tell her they would take a teacher in." "He could feel it in his loins, why hadn't he thought of that?"

"Eva looked up as Joe went across to her."

"Well! Eva said."You have changed your mind earlier tonight you did not want any one staying."After Joe explained to her how concerned he was now I thought, we should all do our bit Eva as I have been thinking about them poor people

"Gran looked up at Joe, and asked him." What are you getting out of it because you don't do any thing for anyone?" Gran looked again at Joe. He was on with some thing." "There was some thing about that bugger she had all ways said it. Her words would come true one day."

"Just then Robert walked in, so did Sid's daughter Mary Robert was home on leave How is the cow doing he asked Ethel before Ethel had time to draw breath Gran said it is in calf then Gran not content with all the bother she had managed to cause hollered over to Sid.

"Did you know that you sold our Ethel a cow in calf? I bet this is the first time somebody's got one over you, because you are know as a greedy old get. But it was money well spent if we get a calf out of it, although it was money put away for my funeral. But hopefully I won't be going yet."

Joe whispered to Wilf who was standing next to him.

"What a bloody pity, I would like to bury her now."

"Just a minute Mrs. Brown. Sid was saying. My daughter Mary let the cows out to run with the bull, so any mistakes will be her fault."

"Well I always thought she was not quite with it, retorted Gran". Just then Sid's daughter Mary shouted at Gran.

What do you mean I'm not quite with it you cheeky old bitch, I am run off my bloody feet, me father, leaves me to look after mother and the farm, so he can go along the village to that bloody woman's at woodbine cottage, dirty old get Sid looked shocked, he did not know that Mary knew what he had been doing.

Bill was a neighbour who was sitting at the front with his wife Margaret he turned to Sid and said." You are never away from there. I can see Doris's door at woodbine cottage from my front window."

Sid was feeling uncomfortable he was wishing he had not come, how many more knew about his goings on.

The vicar felt he would have a lot to think about tonight, although this meeting was open to any one in the vicinity, he couldn't help thinking it would have been a lot better if Mrs. Brown had stopped at home. Also would this be such a good place to bring woman and children, as he had heard some of them land girls that were coming were, quite promiscuous, and there was a lot going on here outside marriage. This was not his area he had agreed to help out as the other vicar was ill. He was beginning to wish he hadn't come he knew a lot of underprivileged people but none were bad compared to this lot tonight He had never heard anything like what he had heard tonight these people were all most primitive, that voice of Mrs. Brown would stay with him for a long time. When he first saw her being helped in, he thought she looked like a frail old woman, but he supposed any one could make a mistake, she had looked forlorn in that coat that was too large for her, she must of shrunk with old age, but the same could not be said for her mouth. People were getting up to go he knew he should of a said a prayer with every one, but then he thought this lot needed more then a prayer. He was watching Ethel and the other woman helping the old bat up. Then he heard her voice again.

"Are you coming along after we get home Grace, because I want to go home now .Our Ethel will you warm me that rice pudding up,? Me guts are rumbling, I didn't have time to eat all me tea with coming here, but I've had a good night .Are you taking me home now Tommy?"

The day had been dry and bright but now it was bitter cold and there was a cover of ice on the road, Gran had Ethel, Eva, and Grace helping her in case she slipped. The vicar was watching them go he thought he had never had a night like it. Now he would go and get his bike, and peddle home he just hoped he wouldn't fall off as the road was covered in ice, and he didn't think he could take much more tonight as he wobbled away down the road

As Gran stepped in to the house Jess came bounding over yapping and wagging her tail, it was the first time Gran had ever left her on her own. Ethel and Grace held on to Gran as the dog was big and would've knocked her off her feet. Once they had got Gran's, coat off and her settled in the rocking chair Gran's leg's were soon stretched out and her stocking feet were resting on the fender as Ethel had banked the fire down before Tommy arrived for them Ethel had poked the fire in to life when they came home and now it was roaring up the chimney.

Gran said later "This dog has more sense then a lot of people as her thoughts returned to the meeting." As she watched the kettle, sing and splutter on the fire while she waited for her rice pudding to warm,"

Back at the pub Tommy had parked his motor bike and side car in his out building He was thinking he had done Ethel a good turn tonight giving Gran a lift ,but after Gran had said all them things tonight there would be a lot of lives that would never be the same again. But he had to chuckle about old Sid, who would of thought it of Sid.

Tommy pushed his pub door open he could not believe the amount of people in the bar. The last time it had been as full as this it was New Years Eve, even then a lot of these people were not here. He hurried behind the bar to help his wife Lizzie, Tommy was thinking, we might as well of had the meeting here, and as far as the vicar was concerned, Tommy thought he looked as though he could of done with a drink. He looked over to where Wesley Dent and his brother in law were sitting, deep in conversation, and looking very unhappy, he thought they were drowning their sorrows. He told Lizzie about it when the pub closed. He said "who would, have thought it of Hilda Dent and her sister? I tell you who else didn't have a very good night. Eva's husband Joe not that I like him, as he is a clever bugger", Lizzie looked at her husband "I think there is trouble brewing there. Joe will have a guilty conscience, and if he hasn't he should have, he's neither use nor ornament to Eva .I have seen him down the town chatting to different lasses, one of them I think is called Barbara she looks pregnant to me, I bet it will be Joes."

Tommy thought. How the hell had she come to that conclusion, all she had seen them doing was talking, but thought better then say anything to Lizzie, as he could never win an argument with her, she never seemed to stop to draw breath ,she could just go on and on."

"Tommy." Lizzie said I hope you are listening to me, if ever you go astray I will chop your manhood off and feed it to Ethel's pig, not that it would get much."

"Tommy thought one woman giving him earache was enough with out any more, and they got worse when they got older, you just had to look at Ethel's Gran.""Now there was a force to be reckoned .with."

Along at rosebud cottage Ethel and Gran were having their last cup of cocoa of the day before going to bed, the fire was still glowing in the grate, it gave Ethel a contented feeling, as the wind had started to blow a gale making the glass rattle in the window frame, and the draught made the cobwebs sway against the oak beamed ceiling.

Gran looked across at Ethel "Don't you think we did very well tonight, I didn't think we would have been given all them things through Grace."

"Yes Gran, but Grace did say the daughter of the old lady that died didn't want or need any thing out of the house, and I suppose with her living so far away she is getting the house emptied, so it's helping her as well."

"I just wish I could help you Ethel, as you seem to get lumbered with all the work," "It's alright Gran, Eva is coming with me tomorrow and bringing the twins, it's only a couple of miles each way and we are taking a barrow each then we will be able to bring the blankets, and eiderdowns back with us. Grace said the old lady had a cupboard full of bedding, so we will bring as much stuff back as we can, then I will ask Harold when he comes up with his horse and cart to bring the rest up, I think we will go up to bed now Gran, I need to go to bed at a reasonable time, as I want to be up earlier in the morning, Eva and me are meeting Grace at dinner time, and I have the animals to see too in the morning before I can go anywhere."

"But if you are meeting Grace at dinner time, our Ethel what about my bloody dinner? I will be bloody famished by the time you get back."

"Its all right Gran, I will feed you before I go." As Ethel was helping Gran upstairs, Gran said. "Will you sleep with me and Jess tonight Ethel? My bloody feet were frozen last night, so I thought if you were on one side and Jess on the other I might be warm."

Ethel thought. "It's like sleeping with a bag of bones

sleeping with Gran, she has a boney backside and legs like twigs, but Ethel thought if they were both in the same bed, with the dog, they might keep warm and get some shut eye." Ethel awoke next morning to the black bird singing on her bedroom window ledge, and being a country woman, she knew it would be very early, as the black birds are up at the crack of dawn. Ethel swung her bare feet out of bed on to the cold bare floor."

Happen I might get me self a mat today to cover a bit of this bloody cold floor she thought as she opened the curtains, to let the early morning sun stream in, it would warm the room up. There was nothing like a bit of sun coming in to help warm a room. Ethel felt a sense of foreboding as she walked through the scullery on the flag stone floor. There was always a lot of condensation, and the distemper flaked off the walls, she would have to get some thing done about it, before the two land girls arrived, there was such a lot of work to do. Her first job this morning was the same as every morning, she would be on her knees, raking the ash out of the grate and, getting the fire laid, with paper, sticks, and coal ready to put a match to it. But while she was on her feet she would open the kitchen curtains, to let the weak winter sun shine in, she stood for a couple of minutes watching the rooks, gathering twigs to build their nests. It didn't take Ethel long to get a blazing fire going, then she hung the kettle over it Ethel and Gran looked forward to their first mug of tea of the day. Ethel hurried upstairs to help Gran down safely, before the kettle began to spit and splutter over the fire. Back downstairs with Gran, Ethel helped her in to the rocking chair so she could feel the warmth off the burning coals, as she held her mug of tea, with her gnarled arthritic hands".

"I 'm just going to pop to the sty, Ethel told Gran to give Alice the big pail of potatoes peelings that Roberts dad, dropped off last night for me."

"Don't be bloody long Ethel, because I'm hungry now."

As Ethel approached the sty she could hear Alice

stomping about and making noises, Ethel lifted the sneck and went inside, she felt a bit afraid of Alice, the way she was looking angry and going round and round the sty. She would have to leave her for now though, as Gran would no doubt be making noises in the house if she didn't get fed. Ethel hurried back to Gran and put some dried oats, and milk, in to a pan over the fire, then Gran could have her porridge, and Ethel could go back out side, to see what was wrong with Alice as she had Buttercup to milk. Mind when Ethel thought about Buttercup. She wasn't giving as much milk as she used to. Ethel thought "I have more to do then I can cope with at times." As the porridge was simmering before coming to the boil Gran said

"What is wrong with you this morning Ethel?" You look as though you have the problems of the world on your shoulders what ever it is it's no good moping."

"Well Gran," Ethel replied. "Its Alice, there is some thing wrong with her this morning, she is stamping about and she's looking wild eyed."

"Funny you should say that Ethel, I was reckoning the dates up yesterday, I think she will be about ready for farrowing."

"Oh Gran with so much going on, I had completely forgot she was so near having them piglets."

"Well all you can do Ethel, is milk and feed Buttercup, then let her out, when Eva comes along, she won't mind mucking out for you just this once. Then after you have fed the hens, and gathered the eggs you'll have to go and see that Alice doesn't sit on her piglets, or eat them, when they are born. But finish making my porridge first, as I could eat a bloody horse, put plenty of sugar on and cream off the top of the milk."

As Ethel went back out side she thought about Gran, "what ever problems arose, Gran always tackled them on a full stomach."

As Ethel opened the byre door buttercup turned

awkwardly, and looked at Ethel with her big brown eyes. Ethel picked up the three legged milking stool, and with the clean wet cloth and towel in her hand she started to wash Buttercups udders, before she started to milk her. Buttercup was getting big. As Ethel started to wash her udders she felt a movement on Buttercups belly. Ethel stopped rubbing Buttercup straight away "no wonder she is so bloody big, she is with calf Gran was right", the first time she saw Buttercup she said she was with calf. Well she would not be milked again until the calf arrived". Ethel walked out of the byre, leaving the door open incase buttercup wanted to go out side. Ethel knew what Gran would say. "Don't be so bloody soft our Ethel." "Gran was a tough old bird."

The noise from the sty made Ethel hurry, as she stepped in side Alice was laying on her side, Ethel looked at her and saw her eyes, flashed fire, just then the first of eight piglets popped out. Ethel ran over and picked the first one up and put it in a bed of straw in the corner. Robert had told her that some pigs ate their piglets, while they were giving birth. Ethel hoped there would be no complications, as she was no bloody midwife, just as another piglet popped out. There was a noise behind Ethel, it was Eva.

"I have just been in to see Gran, and she sent me round to give you moral support."

"Well I am bloody pleased to see you Eva, as Alice is having them piglets I am putting them in that bed of straw, then we will see if her tempers any better after she's had them. After an hour had gone by the last of the litter were born and alive. Ethel was so pleased it was all over and she had eight live piglets you would of thought she had given birth her self.

"I can see the after birth coming out mam,"

"That's all right Eva, we will pick it up. Then we will try putting the piglets on to her to see if she will let them suckle. Just then the afterbirth plopped on to the straw. Alice promptly turned around and ate it. And Eva went out side to be sick As Ethel gathered the piglets up, she laid them, all side by side at Alice's milk points. The fire had left Alice's eyes now, and she seemed happy with her little family. So Ethel walked quietly out and shut the door, she would look in later. As Ethel walked from the pig sty with Eva, she called at the hen house to collect the dish of eggs she had left earlier this morning she noticed how the cockerels were strutting about with their head held high, while the hens walked sedately along, with the tiny chicks.

"Ethel asked Eva if she and the grandchildren would like to stay for dinner?" as she had a big pan of stew to warm up. Its mince as well, not rabbit as it usually is."

Eva asked. "How have you managed to get some mince mam?"Ethel said.

"Well it's like this Eva, when someone wants to buy our spare butter, and they have no money, I swap them for some thing. Yesterday the butcher came around, and I fancied some mince, or some thing for a change. So I asked if I could swap some butter, he said his wife would enjoy the butter, so I swapped him for mince and sausage."

"In that case mam the girls and I will stop for dinner and after we have eaten we'll take the twins round to see the piglets." "Yes alright Eva." "Ethel just hoped, Alice would of not of eaten the buggers."

As Ethel and Eva walked back in to the house, the girls and Gran were eagerly awaiting them, the girls had eaten all the sweets that Gran had given them she saved all her sweet rations for Shirley and Margaret, Ethel always thought Gran was an old softie at heart, but nobody else would agree. While Eva told Gran and the girls about Alice, Ethel put the stew pan on the fire. It was full of vegetables, Ethel grew them herself she kept them in straw in the winter, in an outbuilding. The stew didn't take long to warm through, as Ethel had cooked it the night before. Later she pulled it aside, so the plum pudding could boil. Gran wanted clotted cream with hers. "Well Ethel", thought "Gran would not be getting as much cream from now on as she couldn't milk Buttercup." Ethel always made clotted cream, because Gran loved it. She always boiled a big pan of milk then allowed it to cool the cream rose, then Ethel skimmed it off before putting it in a jug and placing it on the stone shelf in the scullery. Ethel asked Eva to go in to the scullery and bring the jug of clotted cream through. The plum pudding was simmering nicely. Ethel's hands were covered in flour, as she dropped the dumplings in to the simmering stew pot. They would all sit down together, at the big scrubbed table that dominated the room, and enjoy a good dinner. After they had all eaten and Gran had guzzled hers down."

Ethel went to check on Alice and took the girls with her, while Eva washed up and put some more coal on the fire for Gran, as Eva was going with her mother to meet Grace.

Ethel carried with her a bucket of pig swill, she wasn't sure if Alice would eat the bucket of potato peelings, with her just farrowing this morning, and it would save her having to walk all the way back for them. Ethel looked at the bucket, it was empty and thought, Alice must be like Gran, nothing puts her off her food.

Alice lay on her side snoozing, while her piglets were lined up at her milk points, Shirley, and Margaret, Ethel's granddaughters, thought they were lovely. They asked if they could hold them. Ethel said no not until the piglets were a bit older. As they walked away from the sty Ethel looked across at Buttercup, who was stretched out in the afternoon sun. "Ethel thought just as well I realised she was in calf, as she has enough to do carrying that big bulk around with out getting milked" Ethel and the girls went back in to the house for Eva, and to see if there was any thing Gran needed.

"Gran said I am bloody busted, with all me dinner, you had better take me to the lav before you go, I wont be able to keep me legs crossed all afternoon." After Gran was finally settled Eva, Ethel, and the Girls set off with two barrows, the girls were riding on the barrows.

"Ethel said, you can have a ride now as you will have to walk all the way back." As they walked down the road towards the wood, Ethel said.

"Let us stop and have a look, I love this wood when all the blue bells are in flower, it won't be long now, as the green shoots are just poking through the leaves." As they walked on down the quiet road, they were screwing their eyes shut against the glare of the warm afternoon sun after they had walked for a while.

"Eva said, let us sit down and enjoy this afternoon sun for ten minutes mam, you never have time to enjoy it, so we will sit on this seat, also my neck and arms are aching pushing this barrow. The girls were enthralled, by the assortment of wild flowers growing in the hedgerows so they were walking around looking at them.

"Ethel shouted at them I don't know why, you are making such a fuss about them flowers, as you see them every day."

"Yes Gran but these are all together and they smell lovely." After a while Ethel got up "Come on Eva, or we will be late." Ethel wasn't used to sitting about. "Just as well Grace's dinner time is2 o clock or we would have been late Ethel was saying, but as it is we will make it in time. As they moved closer to the house they could see Grace standing at the door.

"It's a lovely day Grace called out to them, so I thought; I would stand out here and enjoy the sun. Now you are here, come in and see if there is any thing that you would like."

"Ethel's eyes nearly popped out of her head when she saw all the things that was on offer if they wanted them"

Grace saw the look on Ethel's face and said. "You can have it all if you want, or if there is any thing you want Eva? You can take it."

"Ethel took one look at the piano and said. "If I don't get any thing else, I want that."

Eva said "but mam no one can play a piano in our family."

"I know that Eva, but it's a lovely piece of furniture and I've always wanted one, if that's alright with you Grace?"

"Yes it is Ethel, there is all so a wardrobe and a set of drawers upstairs if you would like them.

"Could I have the wardrobe please Eva asked?" "The school teacher, who is coming to stay with me, will expect some where to put her clothes."

Grace said. "That is upstairs sorted now, we agreed earlier that you would have the beds and the drawers, didn't we Ethel?" "When we go back downstairs I would like that rocking chair." Ethel explained. "Then Gran and I will have one each, as my backside gets stiff as a board, at night sitting on that hard chair."

"Yes just take what you want Ethel." Grace knew, they would take every thing as both Ethel and Eva didn't have a lot, as they both had husbands that liked to keep their money. "There is a settee and two chairs." Grace told them.

"I would like the two chairs mam." "That's alright Eva."Ethel replied, as I will have the settee."

Grace said. "You might as well take the plates, cups, and all the kitchen utensils. You could take them now, and share them when you get home. All so Ethel takes this small table, and put the aspidistra on it you will look posh."

Ethel said. "You can not go by looks, the cottage will look a lot better, but I still won't have a farthing to scratch me backside with." Grace started to laugh at Ethel she might be a bit rough, but she said what she thought Grace supposed, that was with living with Gran, as Mrs. Brown was never stuck for words.

Right Eva was saying. "Let's get these barrows loaded, there will be one full of bedding." Ethel thought." It would be lovely to be warm in bed; there would be no need to lie so close to Gran's boney backside". At last they were loaded up with as much stuff as they could manage. Harold would bring the rest of the things when he came to the village to pick up some things with his horse and cart. They were walking back up the road pushing their barrows when Shirley started shouting "I have seen some hares Gran."

"The last time we walked down here they were running, and jumping about also they were fighting and hissing cried Margaret."

"Mammy said they were bucks."

"Yes they were explained Eva, they were sparring up to each other as all the bucks were after the does, that was in March that's why they are called mad March hares."

"Ethel told Eva, "I've known them start in February." Ethel's hair was wet with sweat

"I wish we were home with this lot." Ethel muttered as she trudged wearily along" Mind you. "When we get home there, will be no bugger about to help us."

"Joe will be on his way shortly to start his shift replied Eva."

"Well if he had been at home Eva he is no bloody good." Just then Ethel looked up and saw Joe coming down the road. "Look whose coming Eva. Talk of the bloody devil."

"Joe saw them about the same time as they saw him. By he thought. "They looked like two bloody tramps." But he was in a hurry; he was seeing Barbara, before he started work. The thought cheered him; he would have a bit of how's you're father. As he approached them he heard, Eva telling her mother "pushing this barrow has taken all my energy."

Joe thought. Well she will bloody have plenty of it, as she never uses it in bed."

"Eva turned to Shirley and Margaret her daughters and said, here's your dad say hello to him" "are you off to work now Joe?"Eva asked him.

"Where do you think I'm going? Out for a bloody stroll?" "And I made me own dinner he complained."

Ethel gasped. "It will do you good to fend for yourself, instead of having our Eva running about after you."

As Joe started to walk away he shouted "I hope you enjoy pushing them bloody barrows." Ethel shouted back

"We can do with out your bloody sarcasm."

"Eh I don't know how I'm going to manage all the bloody work I have to do Eva." Ethel remarked.

"It will be all right mam I will help you." But I don't know yet Eva, where I'm going to put them pigs once they are weaned."How long will that be mam?

"It takes three, to four weeks then they are off their mother's milk, but they will have to be moved."

"Your little out house isn't very full now mam, so they could go in there for a time until all your vegetables are ready again."Eva suggested.

"I know Eva but I don't have a lot of room when all the vegetables are ready I even hang carrots and onions from the roof beams to get a bit more space."

"When Harold delivers the furniture Eva, I have asked him to drop me some straw off for bedding. Once the eight pigs are moved, I will have to muck them out every week, or they will be up to there knees in muck." As they were approaching the seat they had been sitting on earlier Eva said, "Let us have a sit down mam as we are both jiggered."

"Well I won't say no to a sit down Eva, these barrows are heavy." As they were having a rest, Ethel was thinking about all the work she had to do when she got back home."

Shirley and Margaret were sitting quite on the seat eating the paste sandwiches that they had taken with them, after they had finished eating them they started climbing on the seat looking over the wall in to the field.

Margaret saw the fox first, lying in the field. "Look Shirley, Margaret shouted excitedly over there, look there is a fox, and it's got four cubs, look, they are jumping over each other."

Margaret turned to Ethel and said. "You don't like foxes do you Gran? You said you were sick of them screaming."

"I think there are bonny with their red coats and long noses, replied Ethel it's just that I get sick of them screaming, in December, and January, but that's their mating season, so we have to put up with it."

"Those little cubs said Eva, as she pointed at them, Are only 8 weeks old. In late August, beginning of September, they will leave their mother as they will be six months old."

"Oh I think that's awful, leaving their mother said Shirley."

"Yes I know, nodded Eva but, they are animals, and that's the way it is. So come on we have sat long enough. It will soon be your bed time." Ethel thought. Gran will be waiting for her tea, she would be, quarrelsome if she was hungry" As they were walking up the road Eva said.

"The day after tomorrow when Harold brings the furniture, who are we going to ask to give us a lift with it? And, how are we going to manage that bloody piano? It's a daunting thought. I don't know why you wanted it, none of us can play It." little did Eva know that once the land girls arrived, they would have many a good night having a sing along around that piano.

"I am so pleased mam that you talked me in to, having that sideboard like yours, with the bed in. I have a bed now for when the teacher arrives."

"We are finally home now Eva," Ethel was relieved; as she felt weary. Should we have a cup of tea Eva, before we take my stuff off the barrow? Then I will walk home with you, to help you to unload your things."

Gran said. All this talk about unloading the barrows, have I missed some thing?" "No Gran" replied Ethel

"Well I haven't heard you mention my tea. I am bloody starving. It's past me tea time and all you two can talk, about is unloading them bloody barrows." Eva knew her mother Ethel was tired, so she said

"You make a bit of tea mam for all of us. Me and the girls

will fasten Buttercup in for the night, and give her some food same as Alice, and the hens."

Ethel was pleased she had put plenty of potatoes in the oven, before she had gone out, so they could all have jacket potatoes, and there was a big enamel dish, full of rice pudding. Ethel went to the scullery and carried the big jug of milk through and a big pat of butter. She was just dishing it out as Eva walked in with the girls carrying a pail of coal."

Ethel beckoned them over "Come on, have some tea and after a sit down, we might all feel better, then we will both push the other barrow along to your house Eva."

Later as Ethel left Eva's house, a keen wind started blowing the branches, but the birds carried on singing, and twittering, high up in the trees. The sky was darkening as Ethel walked back in to the house, so she lit the lamp, and drew the kitchen curtains, the fire was burning brightly. Ethel was just going to flop down in her new rocking chair that she had brought home today, when Gran said. "Are you making the cocoa now Ethel? And can I have some biscuits? It makes me hungry sitting here on me own."

Later as Ethel lay in bed she thought. "I am knackered. I've had a hard day, but Gran and me have plenty blankets on our beds now, and eiderdowns, each full of feathers and there is plenty to spare for them land girls, that are coming to stay with us."

CHAPTER 4

Morning dawned warm, and bright. Ethel had risen earlier to get a lot of jobs done before Eva came along; Just then she heard Gran calling for her, so Ethel went through to the kitchen and asked. "What do you want Gran?"

"Quick. Ethel looks through that bloody window. Do you see who that is walking down with our Eva and the girls?"Yes Gran its Joe, but he won't be coming here." Just as Ethel turned round to lift the big black kettle, that hung over the fire Joe, Eva, and the Girls walked in. Ethel was astonished to see Joe.

Ethel said. "I am just going to scold the crowdie, for the hens then; I will make you a cup of tea."

Gran turned round in her chair and looked at Joe. "What have you come begging for? Because we have nothing, you've never bothered calling before. You walk past here twice a day, so you might as well bugger off now."

Joe was thinking "I would love to strangle that bloody old bat."

"I have come to give Harold a hand with the furniture." Before Joe could get another word in Gran said.

"Well you're too bloody early, he isn't coming till tomorrow. I told Eva when she was going to marry you. That you were no bloody good, and you're very bloody deep. I know you have not come down here for our good; I wonder what's in it for you?"

"Eva said. "We were told this morning, that the school teacher is coming tomorrow to stay with us, so we had to ask Harold to bring the things today." Ethel came back through the kitchen, and filled the old black kettle out of the bucket of water that was standing near the door.

Eva said. If you wash the beams on the ceiling in the scullery this morning mam?, I will distemper the walls, as I will not be able to pop along as much until the new teachers settled in."

"Joe looked up nothing of the kind, you can call a long as often as you like, and I can keep her company some times for you, as your mother needs help." Oh Aye and how bloody safe will she be with you? Gran said as her gaze scrutinised him."

Joe could feel his self starting to stutter. "That evil old bag, was making him flustered, he knew she could see straight through him." Ethel was handing round the biscuits Joe picked one then he saw Gran glowering at him so he dropped it back in the dish.

Gran told Joe. "I should think so as well, you get pheasants, and rabbits, given all the time off Wesley Dent. But you never bring us any thing along you greedy bugger, so don't sit there thinking you are going to eat our bloody biscuits."

"Joe heard the clip clop of the horses hooves out side, what a bloody relief he would go and help Harold to carry this furniture in, as the old witch was getting ready to say some thing else."

Ethel got up and started to wrap a blanket around Gran's legs, "I hope you will be warm enough Gran, as the door will have to be open a while, until they get the furniture in.

"Are we stopping for dinner asked Shirley, because I'm hungry now?"

"Ethel thought. They are spending that much time along here, I hope they don't end up like Gran, because she has a appetite like a bloody horse, Yes you two and your mam are stopping for dinner, but your dad seems to be in a hurry to go some where."

Ethel asked the Girls. To move over, out the front of the fire, while she put the big black pan on, it was full of potatoes, she had put the bit of mince she had left in the oven with some onions earlier, she would now go to the out buildings and bring in some vegetables. This was another cheap dinner, as she had swapped the mince for a pat of butter, off the butcher and she grew her own vegetables and potatoes. Ethel all so had a rhubarb crumble in the oven, which she had made with rhubarb she had grown in her garden, all she had to do now was make a jug of custard.

After dinner, when they had all eaten their fill, Eva said. "You make some good meals mam, and you don't have much money."

Ethel said. I've done it all me life, and Gran did it before me so it's nothing new."

Eva thought about Joe .It was bad enough trying to get food with out him being so picky, she just hoped the school teacher would not be so awkward, she would go back through and finish the scullery for mam as she would not be along tomorrow.

Morning arrived with a light drizzle, it had rained during the night. Gran was asking Ethel, "When was she going to see Sid? And find out when his cows where due to calve, as Buttercup would calve about the same time."

Ethel thought. "I will go this morning as soon as I get my jobs done."

Mean while at Eva's. Joe did not seem able to sit still; he kept going to look out of the window. Eva thought "Joe seems excited, and yet at the meeting he was against any one staying with us. Eva was thinking. Gran's right, Joe can not agree with his self. Most of the time he does not seem to know what he wants." just then the girls started shouting, that a car had stopped. Before Eva had time to get out of the chair, Joe was opening the car door for Miss Breaker. The first thing he saw was a fat booted leg, followed by an enormous backside ,he then saw her thighs like tree trunks, as her skirt rode up he could see that her stockings were just above her knees, and the rest of her legs were the colour of raw dough. On her head she wore a felt hat the same colour as her coat. Joe could not believe his eyes he just stood staring at her. She brought his mind back to the present, when she stared at him with her cold grey eyes and shouted.

"I am Miss Breaker, I have heard of sex pests like you, starring at my body. Well I am nobody's play thing. So pick my bags up then you can introduce me to your wife." as Miss Breaker took off her hat, Joe had never seen hair like it, he thought she looked startled, her steel grey hair was scraped back tightly in to a bun, at the nape of her neck. It made her look as if her eyes were popping out. Joe was in for a bigger shock as Miss Breaker took off her coat, he didn't know who had the biggest tits Miss Breaker or Buttercup? He thought, if she swung them around, they would knock a man off his bloody feet. He was wondering; how he could get out of the house until it was time to go to work? All the desire had left him, as soon as she had put that fat booted leg out of the car. Just his bloody luck she would be like that other indestructible old bat along the road. He saw Miss Breaker or Prudence as she had told Eva to call her, in full flow, they would probably talk all bloody day blathering woman.

"Well Joe had met someone else, whom he had started going out with. She was a young woman with a three year old child; her husband was in the army, so Joe had been spending a bit of time with her. And now that bloody school teacher had arrived, he would spend more time .Eva thought he was working extra hours but as she didn't get much money off him it was very easy to tell her lies and get away with it. He was not bothered about Eva or the twins; in fact he would set off now, and see Freda before he went to work. He set off down the road then he met Ethel coming towards him. Bloody hell Joe thought, news travels fast round here, she would likely be on her way to meet that bloody school teacher.

Ethel was on her way to see Sid; she opened the farm gate and looked along the bank side it was covered in primroses, and cowslips. Ethel loved the country side. Jack her husband always said it was the back of beyond, and he could not wait to get away from it. Ethel thought, in all fairness Jack had been brought up in the city. She had met him through her friend Winnie. Jack had been a friend of Winnie's brother, and when Winnie's brother came home on a weeks leave, Jack had come with him. After they had gone back to the docks to sign on for another ship, he had written to Ethel. Then the next time he had come up he had left her expecting Eva so he had to come back as soon as possible to get married. It was not much of a romance. "

Gran had said. "It's a sorry day this. "Thou has tied a knot Wi' thee tongue thou'll niver loosen w.i' thee teeth." Ethel jumped as old Sid came along beside her

"What's matter Ethel?" "Oh nothing Sid, "I was just thinking about the past."

"Well Ethel. I have often heard it said, you should never look back at the mistakes you made then. Because it's too bloody late to alter them now, Sid lifted his cap and scratched his bald head. Now Ethel I bet you have come about that cow you bought off me. So we will go into the house and talk, over a pot of tea. As they walked in to the house, Sid's wife was sitting in a chair near the fire. Ethel thought she looked ill she was very thin, and pail. She looked a lot worse since the last time Ethel had seen her. Sid's daughter, Mary was kneeling on the prodded mat putting some coal on the fire. Ethel could feel the heat coming off it as it was not a cold day out side, and Ethel had a brisk walk so she was sweating. Sid looked at Mary, and said.

"Put the kettle on for a pot of tea, and then you can start fettling my dinner." As Ethel talked to Sid's wife .Sid broke in to Ethel and his wife's conversation. "Now first of all Ethel, you wanted a cow, in calf, so you got one which is my fault and nobody else's. As he said it he looked across at Mary he would not blame her again, he'd had more then he bargained for, off her, that night at the meeting. I should have let them out my self, to run with the bull instead of leaving it to our Mary. Sid was saying although they will all calve roughly with in a fortnight."

"Well I don't mind telling you Sid, I am excited but I am also dreading it as I will be on my own."

"You will be alright Ethel, Sid was trying to reassure her, Buttercup has calved before, and been no bother, and it isn't as thou it is her first calf."

Ethel left Sid's house, and as she was approaching Eva's she thought she might as well call In. As she walked up Eva's garden path, she noticed Eva had abundance of daffodils, Eva loved flowers, just then she opened the door, she had seen her mother coming along the path.

"Hello mam come in and meet Miss Breaker." As Ethel walked in Prudence Breaker got up off the chair and shook hands with her. It wasn't long before they were chatting away like old friends. After a while Ethel looked at the clock, and realised she had stayed longer then she should have done. But she had met Prudence, and they had got on well together, and she was coming to meet Gran tomorrow. Ethel thought there would be two of a kind with them two. Ethel doubted if a younger girl might not have been safe where Joe was at. But Prudence would not take his slaver. She knew he had met his match with Prudence. Ethel thought Eva and Joe could do with spending a bit of time together, as they were not getting on, and having Prudence there would make things worse.

As Ethel walked along the quiet road she was thinking about buttercup having her calf. But as Gran said, "There was a first time for every thing." and as Ethel thought about it she had managed, when Alice had her piglets and now when she looked in to feed them she could not help feeling proud, as they were fine healthy piglets. They were always squealing, grunting, and climbing, over one another. All Ethel could hear as she walked along was the rustle of the trees, until a voice shouted.

"You look sexier every time I see you." Ethel looked up to see Wilf. She thought you have to laugh at Wilf he never gives up trying. "I bet you have been to my house Ethel, pity I was out we could have made my bed springs squeal, but you can come back with me if you want? You know you fill me with desire."

"Bugger off Wilf. "I have been to see Sid."

"Well you have never been making his bed springs squeal have you Ethel?"

"No I bloody haven't Wilf you randy old goat. I have been to see when Buttercup will have her calf.

"What's that you have in that bag Ethel?"

Well its a bit of liver our Eva, has given me to go with mine for tomorrow's dinner, as the school teacher who is stopping with Eva is coming for her dinner, and so are Margaret and Shirley.

"Well I still have my bit of liver I haven't used it yet. If you are short Ethel you can have mine, this rationing is getting harder to make a meal, and I living on my own I don't have a lot." Ethel thought poor Wilf, but she was never sure how serious he was about making his bed springs squeal. Ethel quickly made up her mind and said.

"Bring your liver along in the morning Wilf and come and have your dinner with us." "Well if you're sure Ethel? I will look forward to it. I'll see you in the morning Wilf. Next morning as Gran and Ethel were eating their breakfast Wilf arrived. He was loaded down with bottled fruits, and vegetables. "Come in Wilf, Ethel called to him. What have you there? Well Ethel I bottle all my fruit and it seems a shame to let it go to waste, I also grow all my own vegetables. But living on my own I don't use much, so I thought I would bring them along. I am sure you will be able to use them."

"Mind you have, come along early for your dinner Wilf, we have not finished our breakfast's yet, Wilf looked at Ethel. "I thought I would give you a hand. It's hard work carrying all the water that you need, so I thought if I carried the water for the boiler, that's joined to the fire. I will also fill the troughs for, Buttercup and Alice."

"It would be a good help, by that's good of you Wilf. Declared Gran as Ethel is always busy."

Mean while at Eva's house, things were not running smooth, as Joe was referring to Prudence as the old dragon. He had said to Eva.

"She should go along there, and live with them bloody witches, meaning Prudence. Eva's nerves were jangling. Joe could be nasty and she could not see the situation getting any better. Eva looked up at Prudence, as she realised she was speaking to her.

Prudence was saying. "I think the twins and I will go along a bit earlier to your mam's then you and Joe can have a bit longer time on your own."

"You don't have to Prudence." She was still speaking, when Joe came into the room Eva felt embarrassed, as Joe ignored Prudence.

"Come on now Shirley, and Margaret, put your coats on, then we will go to your Gran's is that alright Eva?"

"Yes it is Prudence. And you should enjoy a walk to mam's as there is a bit of heat in the sun now."

As Prudence and the twins were walking up the path, on there way to Ethel's,

Joe walked over to the window and was watching them go he then turned to Eva and said." "look at that fat bugger; she is like a ship in full sail." it was the only thing he had said to Eva since he had got out of bed that morning."

As Prudence walked down the quiet road with the twins, she thought how lucky she was to live among the fields and trees, and the fresh smell of the countryside. Prudence and the twins knocked on Ethel's door and walked in. A delicious aroma came drifting to wards them.

Ethel was preparing dinner, what a lovely smell Ethel. "Well I have got liver and onions in the oven Prudence so come and sit down". The girls were asking if they could go and see Alice, and Buttercup, on their own.

"Yes answered Ethel, go through the garden and over the

stile and you will see Mr. Robinson, he has carried all the water for me this morning, while I gathered the eggs, and fed the pigs and Buttercup. He is still busy now as he is mucking them all out and putting clean straw down for Buttercup and Alice." As the girls were going out of the door

Prudence said. "I hope you don't mind me coming along so early, but I will give you a hand with the dinner."

Ethel shook her head, "there is no need, it's all under control .Wilf is doing the outside work for me."

Gran was not known for keeping her mouth shut. "I suppose you have come along here Prudence out of his bloody way, I know what he's like, and I still say Joe has a guilty conscience.

"Well funny you should say that Gran, he was leering at me in a funny way. But I told him straight, as soon as I got out of the taxi. I had heard of sex pests like him, and he could stop ogling my body."

Ethel said, "I am just going to see how Wilf is getting on, as she got over the stile she could see Wilf chatting to the girls, as he stroked Buttercup he was a nice man, if he wasn't so bloody randy. Ethel walked over to them to see if Wilf was managing. It was a nice dry day and the sun was shining Wilf told her,

"Every thing is done; you go and finish doing that dinner Ethel as I am ready for it, "Well I hope you like bread and butter pudding for after your dinner, as Ethel walked back in to the house she saw Eva, sitting with Gran, and Prudence, all three where in deep conversation. Ethel thought," just as well she had made plenty of dinner, as there was seven of them now to feed, just as well they had the big table that dominated the room. She had a feeling that in a short time it would be in use quite a lot.

Later after they had all eaten their dinners Wilf said, "I thoroughly enjoyed your cooking Ethel. I have not eaten any thing as good as that for a very long time."

"Prudence said you seem to have every thing running efficiently Ethel ".And before Ethel could answer her.

Gran said "I have thoroughly enjoyed my dinner, all our Ethel does is work, and some times, she is bone weary."

Wilf was thinking about the good dinner he had just eaten, he had also enjoyed doing the jobs for Ethel. It was better than sitting at home, he had no one to talk too, as he lived on his own on his own, and he did not find the work strenuous. There was a pause in the conversation, Wilf said," how about this Ethel? I "have plenty of time, and you are rushed off your feet and once you start that milk round, your going to need some help so why don't I come along every morning and help you with the animals? Then I could have my dinner with you as I have really enjoyed my dinner today."

"Well I will need someone. Ethel replied once I start the milk round Wilf, also I could do with a hand now, the only thing is! I have no money to pay you anything.

Wilf started to laugh, "Ethel all I want is my dinner, and if it's all right with you, I will come along in the morning." Wilf was just leaving as Grace arrived.

I have not called at a bad time have I Ethel? Grace asked as she saw Eva and another woman she did not know.

Oh it's alright Grace "Come on in this is Miss Breaker; she is staying at our Eva's. Prudence is one of the new school teachers who have come up ahead of the evacuees. She will be helping the billeting officer.

Grace said, "I will be there at the hall, when the children arrive, I offered to go along and help to serve drinks of milk, and probably dry lots of tears, I shouldn't say this to you really, Eva But your Joe has been saying a lot about these evacuees, how they will be ill mannered, scruffy, and verminous and he will not allow any of them to stay with you, he is not very patriotic. These children, are leaving there families behind and coming to a strange place, they have no idea as to where there destination is, and they are going to be stopping with people they have never met before.

Eva looked across at Grace, she had been sitting listening to what Grace was saying, and made up her mind, she would, take a couple of children in to live with her family. They would have company of there own age, with Margaret and Shirley, so it would help to settle them in. As far as Joe was concerned he had humiliated her in front of Prudence, and he was never in the house, and when he was he never spoke to no one. Besides she had Prudence, now to help her with the children.

When you know the arrival date Grace, let me know and I will make sure I 'm at the hall. And I will take two children, interrupted Eva .I don't think Joe will even notice, as he is never in.

Gran looked at Eva, "I don't like to see you looking unhappy Eva, but you will have a lot of heart ache to come yet with that bugger, he is on with something or someone, he's no bloody good, he's just like Jack, your father two bad buggers together."

Prudence said, "I know what it's like for people living in the cities, apart from getting bombed out of their homes, they are living in the toughest conditions, some children are literally starving. Mothers have to queue for the little bit of food they can buy, life is a lot easier in the country, and there is a lot more food to be had."

"Ethel said, as far as I know we are getting a couple of land girls, I have no idea thou when they are coming."

Eva said, "I am sure they will let you know mam a few days before they arrive". Then Eva turned and asked Prudence, "If she was ready to go home as they could all walk along together."

At the same time the twins were asking Ethel" if they could help her to feed the piglets."

CHAPTER 5

Prudence was not in a hurry to go home with Eva. The atmosphere at Eva's was terrible, if Joe was in. "If the girls would like to stop, and help their Gran to feed the pigs Prudence offered, and you don't mind Eva, I will stay here and bring them along after." So the twins went with Ethel to feed the pig and piglets,

Margaret and Shirley could hear them screaming, and grunting, as they climbed over the stile, Margaret asked Gran why they were making so much noise.

Ethel said, "piglets are always noisy, more so when they are hungry." As Ethel tipped the huge bucket of swill in to the trough, the piglets were clambering over each over in the rush for food. Ethel went out side the sty and brought some more food in for Alice, after they were all fed, Ethel left the twins playing with the piglets while she went to see to the hens, they were squawking while Ethel gathered the eggs.

The twins were laughing at the piglets as they were trying to bite their shoes they loved the little pink pigs. when Ethel had been gathering the eggs she had heard Buttercup bellowing, and making a lot of noise, she thought to her self, she would take the twins back round, then Prudence could take them home .The twins ran ahead of Ethel, they had so much energy. When they all went in to the cottage, Ethel said, "I will have to go back and see to Buttercup, she is bellowing."

Gran said, "I think she is due to calve very shortly."

Prudence said, we will go," I have enjoyed my stay along here today, but I think Ethel might have a busy night, so we will go home."

Gran told Prudence, "Come along any time you want, as she knew by what Prudence had said, and Eva seemed on edge. The arrangement to take Prudence in had turned in to a disaster."

As Prudence and the twins walked back along the quiet road, it was turning a bit chilly in this fresh country air. As they were walking towards the pub, they met Wilf going in to Tommy's for a pint. The twins ran over to him. He asked them if they had just come from Grans. "Yes they said Buttercup is not very well, she is bellowing, so Grans going back to the byre see to her."

Back at Rosebud cottage, Gran and Ethel were talking; Gran said "you might have a long night with Buttercup our Ethel. But there's one good thing she has calved before. It would have been bloody awful if it had been her first calf, as there might have been complications .if you help me around to the byre, I will stop in there with you tonight, rather then you being on your own." "No Gran, after I help you to bed, I will take the paraffin lamp and go back round, I am not having you sitting in a draughty byre all night with your arthritis."When Ethel got back to the byre, Buttercup was standing chewing her cud; her jaws were moving very slowly as if she was thinking. Ethel went back out and brought an arm full of straw in and strews it on the floor so she could sit on it

With her back against the wall, apart from Buttercup bellowing now and again the only other noise was an owl hooting out side in the ash tree, Ethel felt it was an eerie sound tonight when she was on her own. Buttercup started to walk around. Ethel desperately needed someone with her as she knew nothing about calving a cow .She had popped back in to the house, and banked the fire down for the night, as she did not know how long it would take Buttercup to give birth. So in the morning the fire would only need the poker in to stir it back in to life,

Along at the shoulder of mutton Wilf was just starting on his second pint, he did not go to the pub much, and when he did he never had more then two pints, he had been in deep thought tonight. He was contemplating going along to see Ethel, in case the cow was calving, if any thing went wrong? Ethel would be at a disadvantage, she had never had a cow calve before. He liked to have a real banter with Ethel, if she had not been married to that no good husband of hers, he would have asked Ethel out. He envied Jack having Ethel; she was so much like his late wife, as far as being thrifty. Aye he thought to his self. If his late wife and baby had lived the bairn would have been about Eva's age. Oh he'd had enough morbid thoughts for tonight. He would walk along and see if Ethel needed a hand. He finished his pint and thought she might just like a bit of company.

Ethel was sitting with her head in her hands. She was worried, alone, and desperately needed help, with a cow calving and not knowing any thing about it. As Buttercup paused in her bellowing Ethel thought she heard some thing out side.

Just then the door opened and Wilf walked in. Ethel was so pleased to see him. "What are you doing here Wilf? I didn't expect to see you tonight, but I am so pleased you have come." Well Ethel "I saw your Granddaughters earlier on with Prudence, and I thought you could do with some company. "

"It might be a long night Wilf." "That's all right Ethel, I have nothing spoiling." "I 'm just going to go round to check on Gran, I helped her into bed before I came back to see to Buttercup."

As Ethel went in to the house Gran shouted down. "Has anything happened yet?" "No Gran it has not." Wilf has come along. "So I am not on my own so try and go to sleep as there is no point in us all being awake all night."

Back in the byre Wilf had made his self comfortable. When Ethel walked in he said "what about a bit roll in the hay? You might enjoy it." "It happens to be straw, Ethel laughed that we are sitting on Wilf." "Well we will roll in that then, if you want." Then he started to laugh. "Come on Ethel don't look so worried."Ethel walked over and sat down next to Wilf she had wanted company, and Wilf was here. She did feel happier; as it happened they sat and talked most of the night. Ethel really liked being with Wilf, he was the opposite of Jack. At four o clock in the morning, Ethel got her much wanted calf. It was a beautiful brown and white hither, she stackered about a bit, then went straight to Buttercups udders.

Ethel and Wilf watched for a while, then when they were satisfied all was well, they came out of the byre, leaving Buttercup to suckle her daughter. Ethel thought she would never forget Buttercup licking, and murmuring, to her new born daughter.

Wilf always made Ethel laugh. As they walked back to the house together, Wilf said. "We can always say, we have spent the night together, as they stumbled stiffly in to the house. It had been an uncomfortable night sitting on the straw in the byre. Ethel was glad she had banked down the fire, as soon as she put the poker in; it burst in to flames. Both Ethel and Wilf were grateful for the heat off the fire. As she hung the big black kettle over it she thought they might both feel a lot better after a cup of tea, then it would be time to start work again. But before she did that, she would get Gran up and make sure they all had a good breakfast.

Gran looked across at Ethel and Wilf, they both looked bleary eyed, but at least he had been here for Ethel, and they had managed to deliver a healthy calf safely. Wilf was a good worker. Gran could see by his work callused hands, as he ate his breakfast. Gran wished that Ethel had a decent Man, instead of that poor excuse that she was married too; it was a long time, since she had seen him, or his money.

On his way home to get Changed, Wilf met Eva, coming the other way, as she hurried along the road, she told Wilf. "She was going to see what was happening at her mam's with Buttercup?" Oh Wilf said. "I have spent all night with your mam. Eva started to blush, Oh bloody hell. Wilf said. I mean I have been there all night helping with Buttercup, she had her calf."

Eva realising now, that there was no hurry as all was well, at her mam's, said "I will go home, and make the twins some breakfast. Prudence said she would do it if I'd had to go to mam's. We will all come along later and see the calf."

Eva was wondering were Joe was, she had not heard him come in last night, or go out this morning. When she arrived home the twins were dressed, and ready. Prudence was making their breakfast. She looked round as Eva walked in, then said. "It didn't take you long to go to your mam's" Eva explained how she had met Wilf. So I thought we would all go along together." Prudence was smiling at Eva, as she said. "You don't mind me tagging on do you?" "Course not Prudence, then she said to the twin's .As soon as you have eaten your breakfasts you can get your coats on."As they were all making their way towards Ethel's, they met a young pregnant woman walking up the road, Eva said, "that's strange, I know every one in this village but I don't know her. When they arrived at Ethel's the girls couldn't wait to see the calf. "Could, we give it a name Gran?" "Course you can. What do you want to call her?" they both said daisy,

Mean while the young pregnant woman was at the pub, asking Tommy where Joe Anderson lived? Lizzie on hearing Tommy talking walked to the door, as Barbara walked away.

Lizzie looked at Tommy with a smug look on her face. "What did I tell you, on the night of the meeting?"Tommy had to admit she had been right, but he thought he would play safe, so he kept his head down and said nothing.

Barbara tried Joes house on finding no one in she set off down the road again. As she was walking she met Ethel, and the twins, coming back to the house.

Barbara called to Ethel. Could you help me? I am looking for Joe Anderson, or Eva." Ethel said. "Eva's here, so come on in."

Ethel could feel trouble brewing. Wilf was sitting in the chair yawning with a cup of tea in his hand and Gran was busy talking to him, Eva, and Prudence.

All went quiet when Ethel, Barbara, and the twins, walked in. Ethel said. "Here's someone to see you Eva. As Eva looked up at Barbara, she said. "Do I know you from some where? Are you sure it's me you want to see?"

"Well I am looking for Joe Anderson. Barbara replied. I have been to the house and he is not in, so I thought I would leave a message with his sister Eva.

Gran looked ready to explode. "This is not his sister, the dirty bugger; she shouted I can see why you are trying to track him down now, by the size of your belly. Eva here is his bloody wife." The colour drained from both their faces. Eva sat down with a thud and started to cry. Ethel offered Barbara a chair, as she looked fit to drop.

Prudence looked at Wilf and asked him? Did you say you were going to feed the piglets, and Alice? Because the twins and me will come and help you." This was family matters and Prudence felt embarrassed for Eva .Gran was shouting. "Let that bugger come any where near me ,and I will cave his head in, with this bloody poker, he needs castrating then he won't bother any one else." Gran said to Barbara "It's no good sniveling here; you've had your pleasure now you have to face the consequence." Gran was blunt and heartless if any one hurt her or anyone of her family. "So you've had a sit down, you best be on your way now." Gran was saying. Ethel was bent down with her arms around Eva; Ethel thought she looked ill after the devastating news. Ethel said. "The lass has a long walk back." Gran sharply replied. "It will do her good, as she is no better then she should be. Eva asked Ethel

"Will you keep the twins, I want to go home on my own, as I am putting all his clothes outside for him, and he can bugger off."Ethel thought "she had better set too, and make some dinner for them all, it had been along night, and it seemed as if it would be along bloody day."After they had eaten their dinners Ethel had coaxed Eva to stop and have some food, then after a while

Eva went home, and dragged the battered suitcase, out of the cupboard, she stuffed his clothes in it then threw it out of the door. Two hours later as Eva was sweeping the steps, Joe arrived.

"Gran had been seen him heading home, as she had her rocking chair turned towards the window. "There's that bloody get just walked past shouted Gran. I think someone should go to our Eva's in case he is nasty to her."

"It's alright Gran. I'm going," Prudence jumped up to go the same time as Ethel." No you stay here Ethel I will go". And with that prudence was gone hurrying along the road. As Prudence puffed her way up the road.

Joe was furious when he realised that Eva would not let him back into the house and had told him to go to Barbara's. He smacked Eva across the face then got hold of her arms and shook her that much her teeth chattered. She felt her self feeling sick and dizzy then all of a sudden he shouted out and dropped her. As Joe staggered, holding his head, and trying to stop his nose bleeding. Prudence went over to Eva and said.

"He will not hurt you again, I have wanted to hit that bugger since I came here, now I have she said triumphantly."

Joe picked up his battered suitcase and headed for Tommy's, he would go and lodge in the pub for to night, then he would go tomorrow and join the army, he was determined to go now. As Joe walked in the pub Lizzie was waiting for him. "

"You are not staying here you devious bugger, before you ask, so sling your hook." "Could I just stop tonight Joe asked?" Lizzie gave a humourless laugh.

"I would not help you if you paid me. Go to one of your whores. Eva is a lovely lass better off with out you."

Gran started to laugh when she saw Joe walking back down the road, with his battered suitcase in one hand and a handkerchief in the other, over his nose trying to stem the blood.

Ethel knowing that Joe had gone decided to take the girls home, to save Prudence or Eva, having to walk back down for them. Ethel walked on very slowly as the twins skipped on ahead, Ethel's legs felt as heavy as lead ,when she arrived at Eva 's "she told her she wouldn't stop, she felt if she sat down she wouldn't be able to get up again. Ethel was pleased, that Prudence was there with Eva just in case that bugger, decided to come back. .Ethel said. "I will see you tomorrow", as she'd had 'a very exhausting day, one that she wouldn't like to repeat."

CHAPTER 6

Joe had stumbled away down the road, feeling very light headed, his nose was still bleeding continuously, but he didn't want to linger as he didn't want to meet Barbara, or any of the others .

Eva had been a bitch, he thought. "But she was worse now, that she had that bloody woman. He would go to the railway station, where he worked, and sleep in a side carriage, there was nothing else he could do, needs must."

As Ethel opened her eyes next morning, it was to the sound of the rain, and wind rattling the windows. Her first thought was of Eva, she hoped she would be trouble free, now that Joe had gone. She climbed out of bed thinking, Wilf would be here before she had time to turn round. Wilf came along every morning and did all the heavy work, he was a good man, and she knew that now. "He had strong brawny arms, and lifted heavy things for Ethel effortlessly". He was going to draw some milk off Buttercup this morning, she had too much milk for one calf, and if it was not drawn off she could get mastitis."

Ethel had just got the fire burning brightly, and the big black kettle hanging above it, when she heard Wilf coming to the door whistling. Ethel said. "You sound happy"

"I am hoping that you will have a bit roll in the straw with me that would put a smile on your face."

"Bye but you are a randy bugger Wilf. I don't know when you are joking."

"Oh Ethel lass, I'm not joking", "come on in Wilf and sit down, until I make some breakfast." "I 'm enjoying this meal Ethel, its lovely having company, instead of been on my own."

"What's in that parcel? You have there Wilf asked Ethel?" Well it's for you Ethel, all of us really, as he handed it to Ethel, it was so heavy, she nearly dropped it. Ethel was shocked when she opened it, to reveal, a full side of ham, and bacon. Wilf had started speaking again, and said. "Cliff gave it to me when he had his pig killed." "But I can't take this off you Wilf." "Oh yes you can, I have all my food here, so pass it back to me Ethel, and I will hang it on the hooks ,in the scullery ceiling." Wilf was hanging it up as Ethel was helping Gran through the scullery, to her favourite rocking chair in the kitchen.

Gran said to Wilf. "You are a bloody good fellow, and that meat will come in very handy."Gran had accepted Wilf being there all the time with out hesitation; she was rapidly taking a liking for Wilf. He had made Ethel's life a lot easier, also Eva would be along later with prudence. Gran had said that Prudence had saved Eva from a good hiding, and when they visited now Wilf had not to walk out, as he was accepted like family. They had finished their breakfast and Ethel went in to the scullery for the washing up bowl, which she placed on the kitchen table, she then lifted the lid on the boiler, which was joined to the fire and took out a jug full of hot water to wash the breakfast dishes. "Well I have supped my mug of tea Ethel lass, so I'm going to make a start in the byre." "Right thanks' Wilf, I will be round shortly". "There' s no hurry Ethel here' s Grace coming , you might as well have a bit chin wag with her."

As Wilf walked out he passed Grace on her way in, and as he was going over the stile Eva, prudence, and the twins arrived. The twins Margaret, and Shirley, saw uncle Wilf, as that is what they are calling him now, and ran to him, he stopped when he heard them, and   took them with him, they loved seeing the animals, more so now they had Daisy.

Gran loved Eva and she idolised the twins, but she also enjoyed seeing Prudence. As Prudence was out spoken like her.

After Grace had been introduced to Prudence, Grace said. "I thought I would come and see you Ethel, as I had a visit from the WVS billeting officer yesterday. Next week is going to be very busy. The land girls are coming, and some of them will need billets, as a lot of farmers haven't the room for them to stay". "We will take a couple wont we Gran?" Ethel thought it might be easier, sorting the girls out for the land army, then the children when they come. Grace was telling them that. "a billeting officer ,was saying she was at a centre last week, when the evacuees arrived by train, some of them remained unclaimed, so they had to go round the village, asking people who had never come along, to see if they would take a child? Some children where ragged, and dressed in thread bare clothes, some were filthy and their hair was full of nits" .The billeting officer was appaled, by the state of them. Grace was saying ,"you have to feel sorry for the scruffy ones, as no one will take them into their homes, and it's not the children's fault .Grace said when the mothers come to visit I have heard it said, some of them are slovenly, and people are not compelled to offer them a home. I am ashamed to say, a lot of people in our village don't want them." Ethel shook her head and said. "If I go up there, and see a child with nowhere to go, I will bring it home." "Yes I agree." Gran said.

Prudence had been sitting listening, and she said. "I've been corresponding with some of the teachers, who had the first lot of children to take, into the countryside, and the biggest problems, that the foster mothers found was the bed wetting."

"Well that would be a big problem for our Ethel," Gran said. "She has a lot of water to carry as you know, Mind you Wilf has made her life a lot easier, and happier he does most of the hard work ,but I wouldn't like to see, our Ethel having to do the washing every day."

Prudence was saying to Grace. "It hadn't been easy finding those children some where to stay, as people accepted them grudgingly. And a lot of the children did not know their destination. After a long journey a lot of them were exhausted, and frightened, it did seem as though, the biggest, and strongest, were picked first. The farmers wanted the biggest and strongest boys, to work on the farms. They were after getting cheap labour. And some bairns were not very well fed, but the foster mothers got an allowance for having them there."

While the rest of them, were sitting talking, Ethel had been to see how Wilf was getting on, milking Buttercup, Ethel would of liked to start making butter again, but Wilf said, "you cant use the milk, until it turns white, and it will take a few weeks as it's always thick yellow, almost like syrup, after they have had a calf." Ethel was pleased she had Wilf, as there was such a lot she did not know. Wilf said. "Look lass I've got a lot done here, so you can take them eggs in with you, and I will carry on here, or you will never get that bread made." Back in the house Ethel got out a huge bowl she was going to start making the bread before she cooked dinner Ethel bought her flour in eight stone sacks and five pound bag's of yeast . She was now, making sixteen loaves of bread a week. Eva the twins and Prudence were always at Ethel's the same as Wilf; he had a good appetite like Gran. They all put there rations together and managed well. Ethel placed the huge bowl on the hearth and thought it can rise till I make some dinner, as she had kneaded it earlier, and then she would put it in the oven and bake it.

Wilf said to Prudence "Ethel makes delicious bread."

Prudence replied," I wish I could cook as good."

Ethel turned and said to grace." Have you a bit of net curtain I could have?" "Well I have Ethel, but it isn't good enough for your front windows, explained Grace." "

"Oh I don't want it for my front windows exclaimed Ethel. "I want it to put around those sides of ham, and bacon, that Wilf brought along, I am trying to keep the flies off." Just then Grace stood up.

"I will have to be going Ethel and I will drop that net off for you in the next couple of days, as you will be busy getting ready for your land girls." The next day Ethel, was busy doing a huge bake, as she always had plenty of flour and fruit , Wilf was busy with the animals, as Ethel had been out earlier in the morning helping him .Eva was along at Ethel's, she was busy upstairs making the beds for when the land girls arrived. Gran was sitting in her chair watching the twins larking about.

Mean while two young women in London were packing there clothes ready to catch the early train the following morning. They were the two land girls, who were coming to stay with Ethel, for the duration.

One of the girls was, Jennie Brown she did not know what to expect, but she thought it would be better then staying here with a mother, who was at the pub every night, and she brought men home. Jennie's mother didn't want her to go as she always spent Jennie's money. There was never anything left, to eat for Jennie when she got home from work at night, her mother never bothered, about her, so Jennie thought" I'm away in the morning and I 'm never coming back." Next morning as Jennie made her way to the station, fear, and trepidation, was building up inside her, she was thinking, if she'd had a mum the same as her friends, she would have been up out of bed, to make her some breakfast, and wave her off. Jennie was sad, her mother had never even said goodbye, as she was still in bed, with the bloke she brought back from the pub with her last night. As Jennie arrived at the station she had not realised how many people were on the move, there was every kind of uniform. Jennie saw there was enough room on a bench, in the waiting room to sit down, the conversation ground to a halt as Jennie entered, a peroxide blonde girl with a cigarette in her hand, started chatting again. Then she included Jennie.

"Where are you off to then? And which service have you signed up for? I'm going on to a farm, I have joined the land army, and I am going up in to the dales, I'm supposed to be going to live with a Mrs. Ethel Harrison."

"Oh Jennie felt relief flow through her, at least she wasn't going to be on her own. Jennie asked are you going to the same place as me. As I am land army as well, but I haven't got a clue about farming."

"Neither have I, but we will find out together, I am hoping to get my self a good looking husband, by the way I am Linda Smith I have been working in munitions, how about you?

"Oh I have been working in a pickle factory I was sick of it, my home life as well, so I wanted a change". Linda said, "Here's our train I'm excited, I can't wait.

Jennie remarked, "It will take us all day to get there, and I'm a bit nervous, but I'm looking forward to it."

"Linda Smith said, "you will be alright, we have each other." The girls got on the train after humping their heavy bags; they contained their land army uniform. Linda asked Jennie. What did your family think about you when you put your uniform on?"

"Well there's only me and me mum answered Jennie, as Dad is away at sea, he dose not come home very often, as him and mum argue all the time."

"Blimey it must be strange, just the two of you in a bloody house, Linda was shocked .There is eight of us, mum always said, she wished she'd kept her bloody legs crossed. I've never had a bed to my self, this will be the first time, at home two of my sisters and me shared a double bed, I was always in the middle, and it was great in winter, when I was small as it was the warmest place. Our Jane was married last year, and when she moved out, our Emma and I got a bit more room. Dad said it doesn't feel as if she has moved out, as she is always at our house, and she just lives down the road. She has one little boy, and another on the way, she was up the duff when she got married. Dad said it's still flaming bedlam at our house. He is a docker; he and mum go down the pub on a Saturday night for a knee's up."

Jennie said, "It must be nice to have a big family, I had no one to show my uniform too."

"Oh I put mine on as soon as I got it, Linda laughingly told Jennie, and my bloody lot was roaring with laughter, when they saw me. Mind the uniforms are not very flattering, but mine does not look quite as bad, as it did, one of my brothers girlfriends, did a few alterations for me, but them green pullovers are awful, the wool scratched my skin, and those corduroy breeches will be bloody hot in summer."

"Well I don't like them fawn aertex shirts replied Jennie, and I think it's bloody daft having to wear a tie, and them over coats are too bloody heavy to work in. And some thing else Linda, that woman that delivered my things said if we live a long way from the farm, we might have to have bicycles .How the hell are we going to peddle them? In these bloody rigid land army boots, because the bloody things will never have any give in them."

The train was filling up fast with soldiers, Airman, and all sorts of nationalities. One of the lads offered them a cigarette, Linda took one, go on Jennie don't pretend you don't smoke. "Aye go on then. only I have some fish paste sandwiches in me bag, the old woman that lives next door handed me them this morning, I thought it was kind of her, as she knows what me mums like that, there would be nothing in our house to eat, when we get to the dales, I am sending her my address, then if Dad comes home, she will give it to him, then he will know where I'm at."

"Back at Rose cottage after they had all eaten their dinners, Eva and Prudence said, "we'll wash up, as Wilf is taking you for a walk." Ethel looked at Gran to ask if she knew any thing about it. Gran said don't stand there looking gormless "Ethel' Gran interrupted. Prudence is stopping, to talk to me, as Wilf wants, you to go with him, he has bought some thing for you, and he thought it would be nice to go and collect it together."

As Ethel and Wilf set off down the road, "Ethel thought what the hell am I getting, the last time I got a present, it was Alice." Wilf chatted away to Ethel as they approached Bluebell wood he took hold of her hand, to help her over the stile. "Come over to this seat Ethel, there is quite a lot I want to talk to you about. First of all, old Sid will be selling off them milking cows shortly and you want the milk business. You are going to have to get the cows very shortly, also every time a cow has a calf the udder gets bigger, so you will get more milk off Buttercup." "What are you trying to say Wilf, as I can't do any thing yet, as I am stuck in limbo, I have not got any money to buy the cows yet? But I could make money off the milk round." "If you hear me out Ethel, we work well together me and you, so I thought I would buy the cows off Sid, and we will go in to the business together, then we will both make money, as you have all the facilities, all we need is a bit more land, as Sid's is joined to yours, so I thought he might let us rent it, as he will not need it when he has no cows. Anyway let's walk now, to where we are going and you have a think about it Ethel, and let me know your answer." "Are we coming back this way Wilf?" "No Ethel you will soon find out why. They were getting nearer to Mrs. Hopes cottage where she kept hens, geese, ducks, and turkeys.

Mrs. Hope was standing at the window and saw them coming, at the same time as the gander he started to go towards them, hissing, and trying to peck at both, Wilf and Ethel. Mrs. Hope came hurrying out rubbing her hands on her apron; she called to them, "What a lovely day isn't it?" as she put her hands up, to shield her eyes from the sun. "So you have come to collect them have you?" Wilf said, "I have brought Ethel, to collect them herself, just then a goose walked round the side of the cottage, followed by six little goslings. "Here is your present's Ethel, walking towards you"."Wilf grinned. Ethel was over whelmed with her present, she said, "I don't know any thing about geese." "I do though Wilf said, and besides you didn't know any thing about cows, and pigs, not long since." Wilf asked Mrs. Hope for a box to put the goslings in, as it was a bit too far for them to waddle. Mrs. Hope brought out a box with a few holes in. "There you are she said, but I wouldn't like to be the one to be carrying that box, where that ganders at." Ethel asked the woman, "why she was getting rid of the geese?" Mrs. Hope replied, "I would rather concentrate on the hens, and turkeys, besides I am sick of that bloody gander, chasing, and hissing, at me and he peck's if I don't have the sweeping brush handy, to fend him off, and if I got rid of him I would not have any more goslings, but pity help who ever is going to carry that box, because he is the father of them goslings." Wilf picked up the box and started back across the field, with the goose, and gander, following close behind. After they had walked awhile, the goslings began to chirp, the gander on hearing them, promptly opened his beak, and gave Wilf such a nip he nearly dropped the box. But not content with that, the goslings carried on chirping, so the gander started throwing his self at Wilf, and hissing at him. Wilf said to Ethel. "I am putting this box down, those flaming goslings can waddle after us, and I bet my backside it black and blue in the morning." Ethel was laughing at Wilf but at the same time she was thinking that, she would have to keep a sweeping brush handy, because if that bloody gander went for her, she would give it a bat on its head with the brush."As they were heading home "Ethel told Wilf she had thought about his proposition, and thought it would be a good idea." Ethel agreed to Wilf buying the cows, as he told her. "We could milk them together Ethel, then I would push the hand barrow with the churns in, and you could serve it out when the people came to their door steps to buy the milk."Wilf was saying, you are a grand lass Ethel, if you didn't have a husband I would of asked you to marry me, I envy Jack." Ethel said. My answer would have been yes, but it could never be, as Jack is still out there roaming around, mores the pity, "I have enjoyed our look out together Wilf and the goslings are lovely, but we have all the feeding, and milking, to see too, when we get back. And I have a meal to cook."

Ethel was pleasantly surprised when she walked in to the house as Prudence had made the tea, all Wilf and Ethel had to do was sit down and eat it. Gran was sitting enjoying her tea, she asked about the geese. Ethel said, "So you knew about it then?"

Oh yes Gran said. "I agreed with Wilf, you need a bit of happiness some time Ethel, Mind you them ganders, are better then bloody guard dogs." Ethel noticed there had been a lot of food made, as there was still a lot left on the table. Ethel asked "who is all the food for." Gran said, "Those land girls are on their way, they should be here shortly "

"Oh bloody hell Ethel cried out, I have been out gallivanting and forgot all about them."

Wilf said. Come and eat your tea, you are entitled to a look out some time."As he and Gran relished every bite.

CHAPTER 7

At the station when the girls were beginning to think they were never going to get there, they stepped down on to the platform from the train .They were bewildered, there were no houses, or shops, "By this is bloody desolate, Linda decided as they humped their belongings along the road."

"I wonder how far it is. Jennie wondered, as we have travelled all bloody day, and it looks as if we might be walking all bloody night and I could do with a nice hot bath Linda, but it might look badly if we ask on our first night."

"I don't care what they think Jennie, as I'm used to queuing for food and thing's at home, and I don't mind taking my turn here, as long as I can have a nice hot bath tonight.

"I wonder what that woman will be like Jennie. And I wonder if she will be posh?"

"Which woman are you talking about now Linda?"

"Well Ethel you daft a 'porth, the woman we are going to live with. What have you stopped walking for now Jennie?"

"Well I am getting bloody big blisters on me heels; I wish I had put some flat shoes on."

"Well we will have to keep going, or it will be dark, it's bad enough on this bloody lonely road, and it's still light." Just then Linda saw someone walking towards them. "Look Jennie there's a bloke coming; I'm going to ask him, how much further we have to walk to the village."

As Peter approached them, the girls put there belongings down on the road. Linda asked him, how much further they would have to walk to the village."

"Oh only a couple of miles now Peter answered, two young lasses like you will manage that no bother."

Linda said, "I don't bloody think so, I'm bloody knackered now."

Peter replied, "you will soon get used to it, when you have lived in the country for a while, where are you going to be living?" Oh we are going to be living with Mrs. Ethel Harrison, what's your name? I'm Peter."

"Well I'm Linda, and me mate here is Jennie. Do you live in the village? And is there a pub?

"Yes to both but I live a bit out of the village. Do you girls go to the pub? As country woman don't?"

"Well we aren't country lasses, and yes we go to the pub, Linda promptly replied."

"Right I will be off then, see you around, peter was in a hurry, after he had walked away, he couldn't help wondering, what Mrs. Brown would make of them two."

When the girls finally arrived, Linda said, "I hardly have strength to knock on the door. Just then the door opened, and Ethel said. "I'm Mrs. Ethel Harrison you two must be the land girls, come on in". As Ethel ushered them in Gran turned in her chair and saw two worn out, and weary young woman .Ethel thought, "just as well all her company had gone home, it would give them all a chance, to get to know each other, and the girls to settle in."

"Well I am Linda, and this is Jennie," Sit down and have a cup of tea Ethel suggested, as you both look, as if you could do with a cup, and I will put some food out for you. Would you like to take your things up stairs? As they were getting up to do as Ethel asked, they handed her their ration books. Linda asked? If she could have a bath after they had eaten.

"Gran looked annoyed, and said. "Ethel will not want to start carrying water tonight, and what am I supposed to do ,while you are in the tin bath, in front of me bloody fire." Linda looked shocked, and said

"I thought I could have a bath in the bathroom."

Gran said, "What are you bloody talking about, we don't have a bathroom, and the lavs, at the bottom of the garden."

Jennie and Linda couldn't believe it. Jennie said

"What do you do through the night, when it's dark",

"Well we go down the garden, Ethel was saying, as she ladled them some rabbit stew out .Come on Ethel was saying, have some food, there is some jam roly poly with custard to follow". As Ethel put the plates on the table, Linda, and Jennie, both sat down, and picked up their forks. "This smells lovely Linda, said as she sniffed at her dinner, as she sat down. We are both starving aren't we Jennie."

"Well there are plenty of vegetables in it Ethel told them, and I got the rabbits given." Linda asked Ethel. What is the proper name of this stew? Before she had time to tell her, Gran said "it's bloody rabbit, what the hell do you think it is?" Jennie had just stabbed a piece of meat, and was going to put it in her mouth, but after what Gran had said, she threw down the fork, with the meat still on it, and started to get up off the chair shouting. "I can't eat little furry animals". Jennie was upset, and Gran had never heard any thing as daft. "Linda got up too, I would rather starve Linda retorted.

"Gran said "well if you are going to be like that, you will just have to starve"

Ethel didn't know why they were making such a fuss, "she had been brought up on rabbits and was still eating them.

Both girls needed the toilet, so they went together, as they were walking down the garden path an owl hooted. Jennie was so shocked she screamed, and grabbed hold of Linda. "We are going to be bloody nervous wrecks, by the time we leave here shuddered Jennie what a daunting prospect living here in the sticks, no shops, cinemas, fish shops, or buses and no bloody bathroom."

Linda sharply replied. "We might have been better off facing the bombs, then stopping here Mind you that old woman, looks as hard as nails."

"Aye you are right Linda, she seems to be a bloody old battleaxe".

"Should we go back in Jennie and ask if we can have the pudding, because I'm starving."

"Yes I am as well Linda." Ethel had already served the pudding as she knew they would be hungry, after they had finished eating it was beginning to get dark. Linda asked, Ethel "what time the bloke came to put the street lights on?"

Gran said, "what bloody street lights, we don't have any."

Ethel asked them, "If they knew who's farm they were going to be working on." "Yes

Answered Jennie he is called Michael Robson." Ethel hesitated, and then said, he isn't as bad as his wife, but he is bad enough."

"What's she like?" Linda wanted to know, as she took a cigarette out of the packet, and offered them to every one. Jennie took one, and Gran said. Do your Mothers know that you smoke? They both said, "Our mothers smoke as well." Gran thought I have never met any thing like these buggers before.

"Ethel had been thinking about the girls going to work for Michael Robson, people thought the Robson's weren't a very good family, but Ethel supposed, they would have to wait and see, if the girls were going to be working for them." So Ethel told the girl's what she knew about them.

"Michaels wife is called Sarah, she is a narrow faced woman, with cold grey eyes, and as thin as a rake , I don't think, she has ever smiled in her bloody life, but we will have to wait ,and see ,what you girls think about them ."Gran had been listening to what Ethel had said; she seemed to think about it for a while then, told the girls "time will tell."

Ethel had to smile as she thought about Wilf; he was always telling her he would like, to put a smile on her face, some day. "She thought some day she might relent and let him she realised her mind had wandered, when every one was looking at her. So she asked? "Are you two girls having an early night, as you seem to have had along miserable day?"

"Well we were going to the pub Linda replied."

Ethel was flabbergasted, "two young girls can't go to the pub surely?"

Gran thought, these two buggers were going to take some watching, "I can see it now, them local lads that had failed, their medicals, would not be bloody safe, where these bloody lasses were at."

"I don't know about you Linda, Jennie tiredly said, "but after our invigorating walk, I'm going to have an early night I'm knackered."

Gran said, "You'll get a shock when you start your farm work, but you'll get hardened to it, hard work never hurt nobody, and you will, be healthy working outside in all that fresh air, and you'll just have to get on with it."

Next morning Ethel was up early, the birds had wakened her up, with their morning chorus. This time of the year, the blackbirds some times sang, at four o clock in the morning, or before. The weak sun was streaming in through the window, Ethel thought, "I will get up now and get the fire place black leaded before I get Gran up. As Ethel was lighting the fire,

Wilf arrived, as he walked in, Ethel said "you are getting earlier Wilf ," "Well I like to get up and about on a bright summer morning, so I thought I would come along and keep you company, I had an idea you would be up. What are your lodgers like then? Do you think they will manage farm work?"

"Well they are going to be working for Michael Robson, and that miserable wife of his. Ethel had hoped that Linda, and Jennie, would have been sent some where decent."

Wilf said, "Poor buggers, going to work for them", Ethel said, "but at least they will be working in the fresh air, I would not like to live in a city Wilf."

"No you are right there Ethel, as I walked along this morning, I saw the swallows, and house martins, they are back again, so spring has arrived, mind you it's hot through a day."

"Well it is May Wilf." "Aye I noticed Ethel that the hawthorn hedges are turning to a nice fresh green."

"Aye Ethel remarked, "I was just saying to Gran, I don't care much for them when they, are a dull grey depressing winter colour, Hears a mug of tea Wilf, we might as well, have one in peace, before I get Gran up, and God knows what time them girls will get up, as they were tired last night, after travelling all day, then they walked from the station last night."

"Well you are kept going all day Ethel, Wilf reminded her, and you just get on with it. They will have to waken them selves up, if they are going to be doing farm work."

"While I get Gran up Wilf, will you cut me some slices off that side of bacon, that you brought along the other day as it will go down nice with some fresh egg's." As Ethel was heading towards the stairs for Gran, Wilf called after her. "Don't forget that tasty bread, that you make, I have never eaten as much bread as I do now." When Gran was seated in her chair she asked Ethel," what she intended doing about them lazy buggers upstairs, Gran said it's not normal lying in bloody bed, Half of the bloody day will be gone by the time they get up."

"Well I will make our breakfast Gran Ethel replied as I expect you and Wilf will be ready for it, and I will do theirs when they get up."

Gran said, "if they can't be bothered to get up, and have some breakfast same time as us, the buggers can do with out, I don't know who will get the biggest shock, when they start work on that farm, them, or Michael Robson, as I think he will have his work cut out, with them two."

It was half past ten when Jennie opened her eyes, she looked over at Linda in the other bed, and whispered are you awake yet?

Linda opened her eyes, and yawned, "What time is it? She asked as I have been awake all night. When I was at home, I some times used to wish that I could have a bed to myself, and now that I have, I don't like it, could I share with you tonight? I didn't like all those noises in the night."

"Yes course you can come in with me Jennie smiled."Oh but I would love a hot bath Linda moaned, but first I think we should get up, and go downstairs, and see what kind of a meal Ethel has made for us today." As they both walked, into the kitchen, Gran turned around and looked at them,

"What bloody time do you call this? you will have to feed yourselves ,as my Ethel is busy outside, she hasn't got time to sit waiting, of you two getting out of bed. So make yourselves a pot of tea, and I will have one as well. Ethel has left you some bacon to fry. Do you know how?"

Are you going to see Michael Robson today? Gran asked them, as he will want you to start as soon as possible."

Jennie answered, "Yes we thought we might go this afternoon, how far is it?" Gran said, "Oh it's not far, only a couple of miles. Their daughter and son-in-law lives with them, she's like her mother, frosty faced, they reckon Peter, the son –in –law is a canny lad, he has a limp, he was helping her father a couple of years since, to milk the cows, and one slipped on him, and broke his leg in two places, he's limped ever since .Here's our Ethel and Wilf coming in now."

After Ethel had introduced Wilf, she said, "we timed this right Wilf, we are getting a cup of tea made for us."

Jennie was sweating, as she leaned over the pan, to fry the bacon on the fire, she asked Ethel, "and how do you cook in the summer?"

Oh Ethel answered, "we always use the fire, for cooking, as the oven is joined to it, and so is the boiler, it's the only method, we have."

colour was flooding Jennies, face she wouldn't like to cook like this again, at home, they had a cooker, while she was thinking about home, she was starting to wonder ,if she had done the right thing ,joining the land army",

"Are you listening Jennie? to what Mrs. Harrison is saying, enquired Linda." "Well first of all call me Ethel, and after you have eaten, them bacon sandwiches, you can both come out, and meet Buttercup, and Alice." As they all trudged over the stile, they saw Buttercup in the field. Ethel said,

"Come on then, say hello to Buttercup, and that's her daughter Daisy."

Linda had never seen a cow beforehand, she couldn't believe how big they were, and to think, she would have to milk them, she hesitated before putting out her hand to stroke Buttercup.

Ethel grinned at her, and said, "You will get used to them, but if I was you I would go and see Michael Robson, this afternoon."

Before the girls set off, Ethel said. "I will set to, and make some dinner," Ethel talked as she worked, and the land girls, started to feel more settled, as they were about to sit around the table.

Gran said, "you lasses should think yourselves lucky, that my, Ethel, makes good meals, you might not be so lucky with grub at Robson's, and we don't, cater for pokey folk, so don't try to wheedle your way around it, Gran was still talking as she pointed the knife at them, because as long as you live here You will eat the same as us." The girls had to admit that, "while they had eaten huge sandwiches for breakfast, they were ready for dinner."

Just then, Eva ,Prudence, and the twins arrived, but Ethel had made plenty of dinner for all of them, while Gran introduced every one, Ethel dished the dinner out, so the land girls had a huge meal of mince, and onions, potatoes, and plenty vegetables. Ethel had also made a huge bowl of rice pudding, with plenty of milk on it, the land girls said, "We feel too full to walk, but before we go we'll do the washing up for you Ethel."

"Gran had a feeling that things were going to work out right."

Jennie said," this is rather nice isn't it Linda, walking in this sunshine I had never heard of bird song till I came here."

Linda said, "I wonder if you will be feeling the same in winter? When we are trudging back in snow, and being frozen, after a long day?" Jennie looked at Linda and asked her, are you having second thought now? Because if you are, you had better tell me before we go and see MR Robson.

Ethel had pointed the way to the farm for the land girls, and as they knocked on the farmhouse door, the bloke they had met, when they had been walking from the station, came walking around the corner, and he said,

"I'm Peter and we meet again, it's nice to see you, and have you settled in alright?"

Just as his wife Hannah was opening the door, she scowled at Peter and the girls and then, asked, "How the hell do you lot know one another? Then she said as if she had just remembered, you two must be the land girls, you had better come in and see mam, and dad, her mother was ironing, with the heavy flat iron, she had to keep putting it on to the fire, to heat, as she put one on to heat, she took the other one off, as she worked with the two irons.

Mrs. Robson and her daughter, looked very much alike, both skinny, and narrow faced ,just as Ethel's Gran, had described them, and she had also been right when she had said they were a couple of miserable buggers.

Mr. Robson was a man of not many words, he just told them, "they had to be there, in the morning for six o clock milking." when they came back out side, Linda said.

"I fancy that Peter."Jennie said by what you have told me you've had a lot of fella's."

"Yes I have Linda replied, and I bet I have him as well, before we are there three weeks." they were both gigging, as they left the farm.

Jennie looked at Linda, and asked her, "If she would like to go to the pub tonight."

"Yes I would Linda replied, and see what the fella's are like up here." so after tea, they carried a big bowl of water upstairs, to get washed,

Gran was watching them take the water out of the boiler she said, "After you two use the water out of the boiler, you can get a bucket, and go to the well, and always put, back the same amount of water, in to the boiler, as you have used, as our Ethel, has all that water to carry."

As they were ready to go out, Ethel asked them where they were going. Linda said, "We are going to the pub." Gran thought it was outrageous.

"You young girls can't go sitting in a pub; you will get a bad name."

Jennie said, "We always went, when we lived at home, and I'm not going to stop now, just because we are living in the country." As Linda and Jennie walked in to the pub every thing went quiet as they went to the bar.

Tommy asked them?"What can I get for you two young ladies?"

Linda said, "Two glasses of cider please." Then they turned around with their drinks in their hands and sat down among the men.

Lizzie Tommy's wife had been watching, she said to Tommy. Bold as brass them two."

Tommy said, "don't start Lizzie, they seem canny lasses, and their money is as good as any body else's, and besides there, will be nothing for them to do on a night at Ethel's." By closing time, the girls were beginning to feel very jovial, quite a few of the men had bought them some drinks, so as they made their way back, to Ethel's, they both agreed ,"it may be wasn't such a bad place after all."

At five o clock the next morning, Ethel was knocking on the girls bedroom door, Jennie awoke first, she trying to work out where she was at, and her head was throbbing. Just then,

Ethel walked in to the room, as Linda was starting to sit up she was looking terrible.

"I see you had a good night then, I thought I had better come and wake you, come on down stairs, and have a cup of tea."

Linda asked Ethel, "Why are you up so early?"

Ethel said, "Oh I like to be upon a fine morning, I don't know what you girls are going to do about your dinners today?"

Linda said, "I think we are having it at the farm, Well I hope you are right or you'll have a hungry day, any way you have got a lovely morning for a walk, I like being up early, when the sun is starting to shine, and the birds ,are singing."

As the girls trudged down the road to Robson's farm, with their land army clothes on, "Jennie said do you miss all your family Linda?

"No not as much, as I thought I would, and besides I've got you now, haven't I? And don't forget there will be holidays, when we will see them."

"Well you are lucky Linda, I haven't got a family."

"That's o k Jennie, you can share mine, so come on hurry up or we will be late to see Mr. Frosty face."

As they got near to the farm gate, Michael Robson was waiting with his dog Floss.

"We are not late are we asked Linda? "No I just thought, I would meet you here, save you walking down to the farm, to walk back up again, to go and get the cows in for milking, you two can go and get them in your selves in the morning, just stand here and shout Floss, and she will come with you, as she knows when to go and bring, the cows in for milking. Where have you left your bates at?"

Jennie spoke up "sorry Mr. Robson what is bait".

Well it's your dinner's lass, Oh dear have you not brought any thing? I don't think my wife is going to like that, she will not want to feed you two, if you work hard this morning, I might ask her if you can have a pot of tea each, and a slice of jam and bread, but don't let it happen again," then he walked on ahead with Floss to round the cows up; Linda started to giggle, "bloody old skinflint."

Jennie was a bit nervous as the cows were amber ling along towards her, their udders swinging from side to side, as they all went in to different stalls, to be milked. MR Robson passed them a three legged milking stool each, a wet cloth, and a steel pail, now he said, "go to a cow each, and sit down, and wash their udders first, gently like."

Just then Peter came limping in to the byre he was only a few years older then Jennie, or so she thought, he asked her "do you know how to milk a cow? Have you milked one before?"

Linda looked across at Peter, and said "will you show me what to do as well, as I have never done any milking before." Peter sat on the milking stool with the pail between his knees; he started to milk the cow, as Linda listened to the sound, of the milk hitting the pail. She wondered, if she would ever be able to do it as quick as Peter, he looked up at Linda and said come on then Linda, let's see you get this cow milked, it will not learn you, me doing it. Come on then, gently pull, and squeeze, don't let the cow know that you are frightened, because they can be awkward, and hold their milk."

next he moved on to help Jennie, as he could see, that his Father –in-law was not going to bother, to help the lass, by they were a miserable lot these Robson's, including his bloody wife, he had only married her, because she was bloody pregnant, then she had a miscarriage, if he had only let a bit of time pass, that would of happened, before he got stuck with her, and he wouldn't of landed his self in this bloody mess."

Jennie was wondering why he wasn't answering her, so she touched his arm, "Sorry he said, I was miles, he thought to his self, I wish I bloody was."

After milking was finished MR Robson went in for his

90

breakfast, Peter said to the girls, "I will try and bring you some thing out, as you must be hungry."

After he walked away Jennie, asked Linda, "what are the chances of us getting some breakfast?" Linda said,

"I think we will get bugger all, but they might give us a bit of dinner."

In the house Peter, was asking MRS Robson, if the girls might have their meals with them to day? As they had forgotten to bring their bate, so they would have no food to day."

Peter's wife Hannah, who was the double of her mother, a right scrawny miserable cow, "said if they go hungry today, it might remind them to bring some food in future."

CHAPTER 8

Michael Robson was sitting saying nothing, over wise they might decide not to make him any dinner today, but then he thought, "them girls will take no hurt today, they finish at six tonight, and after they have walked the two mile or so home, they will be ready for their tea." The girls were sitting out side on the wall, swinging their legs, as the house door opened, and Peter came out with two cups of tea, and two biscuits hidden in his pockets, he said, "sorry you have to wait out here, but this isn't my house.

"That's all right Linda replied, thanks for this hope it dose not get you in to trouble." after breakfast Mr. Robson came back out side, and said, right you girls I have a job for you, it hasn't been done properly for a while, you can both work together, as I want them barns over there white washing, but first you will have to brush the walls, and ceiling, to get rid of the cobwebs."

As the morning wore on, the girls felt as if they had never been as filthy in their lives, Linda said, "I don't know about you but I'm going to stop and have a cigarette,"

"Yes I am as well replied Jennie."

"I think Mr. Robson's in the house Linda retorted,"

I'm not bothered where he's at Jennie said crossly, he has given us all the filthy jobs, and anyway its dinner time shortly, so we might be allowed a break, even if we get nothing to eat,"

"Yes Linda said but he did say, he might be able to get his wife to give us some bread, and jam, and a cup of tea would be nice, I'm fair parched. Have you thought Jennie we should try and get a bike?

"just then Mr. Robson or old Robson as the girls called him came round to them, and said "If you both go and sit on that wall near the house the wife will bring you some thing out to eat." Jennie and Linda badly wanted a cup of tea as their mouths were dry, after brushing down cobweb's and all the dust, flying around. As they sat on the wall waiting, the farmer's wife stepped out with a plate, with two very thin slices of bread, and jam, on. Linda said to Jennie, "blimey I think she has cut this bread with a bloody razor blade, it's so thin." after they had eaten the measly slice each, the house door opened again, and old Robson's daughter came out carrying the tea pot, the girls were pleased to see it, until they saw her go to the corner, not far from where the girl's were sitting, and promptly tip it down the drain. Linda said, "The spiteful cow."

Hannah quickly spun around and said, "You have had one cup each to day, think your selves lucky you got that." then she walked back into the house.

Linda said, "Come on Jennie, let's go to the horse trough, and get a drink of water." Later when they had finished the milking, and were making their way home, they were both so hungry, and weary. Linda asked Jennie, "If she was missing the city,"

Jennie said, "just now I'm missing the bloody buses."

"Listen Jennie, there was excitement in Linda's voice, "I can hear a clip clopping noise, I think there is a horse some where". There it is shouted Jennie look just down the road; he has a cart load of oats, and things to sell,"

"Linda said, "do you think it could be that Harold, that Ethel was talking about?" they carried on walking until the horse caught up with them; And then he stopped; An old bloke a bit scruffy, with a cap, on shouted down to the girls;

"Where are you two going to then? And dressed up like men, with bloody shirt and ties on? Never seen the likes of it before"

Jennie said, "We are in the land army, and are working on Mr. Robson's farm."

"Oh so you girls are not living there then replied Harold." "No we are not Linda sharply replied, we would be bloody starved to death in a week. We are staying with Mrs. Harrison."

"Oh Ethel I know Ethel very well, I'm going there with a few of these rolled oats, and these small potatoes, and turnips for her pigs, I had a few jobs to see too, up here, so I thought I would drop these off for Ethel. If you lasses jump on, I will take you to Ethel's."

As they climbed up Linda said, "what a relief I'm bloody knackered, as the horse and cart drew up at Ethel's she opened the door, I've brought you a couple of hungry tired lasses, Harold told her, they have been telling me, that they have only had a thin slice of bread each all day."

"So them Robson's have got no better then" Ethel answered. When they went in to the house Gran was waiting to hear how they had managed. After they had told her about Hannah tipping the tea out, Gran said,

"I have heard she is a nasty little bitch." Linda said, "I don't know how Peter puts up with her."

Gran was sitting listening to Linda. Then she said to the girls, "you seem quite taken with Peter, I hope you won't be doing any thing daft, because he might be lusting after you now, but he will be like all men if your belly started getting bigger, he would leave you to sort it out yourself."

The girls sat down at the table waiting for Ethel to start dishing the tea out. Ethel said she would as soon as Wilf came in, "she asked them if they liked jacket potatoes, but she knew what her answer would be, as the girls were famished." Linda said, "We will eat anything Ethel;"

Gran said, "it hasn't taken you two long to learn the hard way, the girls finished their tea before anyone else. Gran said, by you have made short work of that tonight, I think it's done you two good being starved today."

"Aye we have been sweating as well today in them buildings, I am not wearing a jumper, tomorrow or a tie, are you Jennie?"

"No I'm not, but just now ,I am going to wash up for Ethel, then I am going to get washed, and changed, do you fancy going along to the pub tonight, only I promised that lad a game of darts."

Wilf said, "You might meet some of your lot along there tonight, as I was talking to someone today, and they said, a whole lot of the land army came this morning."

Gran said, "Well if they are anything like these two, Tommy will have a good trade." As it turned out a lot of the girls were at the pub.

Tommy said to Lizzie, "Just look at that, who would have thought it, more lasses in then men."

Linda said to Jennie when they were in the pub, "Don't you think Ethel's Gran isn't quite as bad with us as she was?"

"No I don't think she is Linda why?"

"Because I'm going to buy her a bottle of stout, and see what she say's."

"Go on then Linda, and I'll get one for Ethel Jennie said." when the pub closed Jennie, and Linda, stumbled along home together. All was quiet as they made their way to bed, they had a lot to drink, but things were getting better, they were all going dancing, on Saturday night. But first they had the Robson's to face in the morning.

Next morning Ethel went to wake the girls again, "she laughingly told them, she would throw a pail of water, over them next time she had to wake them up. When the girls came downstairs, Ethel had their breakfast ready, and sandwiches, made for them to take for their dinners. As they were leaving, Linda said,

"There is a bottle of stout there for you, and Mrs. Brown, My Gran always liked stout, so we thought you and Gran might." As the girls were walking down the road, Linda said,

"we might have to get a bike, some of them lasses last night, said they had bikes it would be easier, and quicker, then walking," "Jennie Do you think Floss will come to us, when we shout of her to come and get the cows in?"

"I bloody hope so Linda, as I don't know how, we will round them up with out a bloody dog, and that will be a good start for today."

"Yes Jennie but it will be a better day then it was yesterday as Ethel's made us some sandwiches, and put some cakes, in for us."

As Linda and Jennie were getting the cows in, Gran was getting up;

Wilf said, "Do you not fancy having a lie in, now and again Gran?"

"No I don't Wilf, at my time of life, I mightn't have long left, and I'm not going to waste it lying in bed, and besides you only stiffen up lying in bed. Now is my breakfast ready yet?"

Linda and Jennie had the cows chained up in the byre, when Peter walked in,

"Well you lasses have been quick this morning."

"Oh we are quick learners us, two answered Linda, with a grin as she gave Jennie a dig in the ribs,"

Peter said, "what way are you quick learners," the girls looked at each other and starting laughing, Linda asked him? "Are you lusting after us?"

He said, "I could be, as he winked at Jennie."

Just then old Robson came in and went over to the girls, and said,

"You were in good time this morning; I hope it stays that way." Then he walked away. As the girls stuck their tongues out after him, and got on with the milking.

When Peter and his father-in-law went in for their breakfast, the girls sat on the wall having a smoke, Linda said, "do you think we'll get a cup of tea today, as we have, brought our own food, and we work bloody hard",

But just before Peter came out, Hannah came out again, with the tea pot and poured the rest of the tea out with a sneer on her face. Shortly after she went back in, Peter came out; he banged the door so hard it shook on its hinges.

When he looked at the girls he grinned, his good humour restored, "Come on girls lets get away from this bloody house."

Peter went for the wheel barrow, as the girls got the shovels, and brush, ready to start and muck the byres out, every time they filled the barrow, they had to trundle it to a muck heap, and empty it. After a few trips to the heap, the girl's arms and legs started aching, and the hot, early, summer sun, was burning down on them. after that was done, they had to go across the yard with another barrow, and bring back some rolled oats ,and hay, to go in the mangers, for the cows to eat, as they are getting milked Peter explained, "it's a treat for them, and it keeps them occupied."

.Back at Rose Bud cottage, Wilf was saying to Ethel, "why don't we walk over to Sid's place? And see about getting them cows, because as long as he has them, he's doing the milk round, and getting the money."

"Can Shirley, and I, come with you and Gran, uncle Wilf?"

"Course you can Margaret, as I can see your Mam, and Prudence ,would like a bit chat to your Great Gran.

"Well you have made me feel bloody old now, Gran shouted at Wilf. Shirley and Margaret just call me Gran, same as Ethel". Wilf started laughing I will remember next time Gran"

"Aye well you had bloody better, and while we are chatting, Gran said, I will drink that bottle of stout, if you wouldn't mind taking the top off for me will you please Wilf?"

As Ethel, Wilf, and the twins, left Ethel's house, Gran asked Eva, if that bugger, as Gran called Joe, Eva's husband, had put her down for an allowance, out of his army pay."

"Yes he has Gran, answered Eva, as I didn't think he would have done."

"Well if he hadn't, you could have still got it, as you are still his wife and entitled to an allowance stated Gran."

As the little party were walking down the lane. Wilf said, "Come on we'll go through blue-bell wood, as your Gran loves blue-bells. Do you want to pick some for her?

"Come on Ethel; hurry up old girl we'll sit on the seat as we had better make the best of this. If we get the cows tomorrow, we will be busy, but we will be making money, and best of all we will be together."

As they were going through the farm gate, Ethel said, "I hope we can see Sid, with out going into the house, because Nora seems to be getting worse, every time I see her."

Sid was in the house, and he saw them coming through the window, so he went to the door and called to them to come in."

Nora was sitting in the same place, as she was last time Ethel had seen her. "With her prematurely grey hair, and illness, she looked a lot older then she was, and she did have a cheerless life with Sid Ethel thought."

"Nora was sitting looking at Ethel, and thought she looked very happy, she had an idea, it might have a lot to do with Wilf, and he seemed a happy man, with Ethel, and Eva's two bairns."

"Are you not going to sit down Ethel? I never see any body. Have you heard anything about your land girls yet?

"Yes we have had them, for a couple of days now Nora, answered Ethel."

"Well listen Ethel, Nora leaned forward so she could whisper, we don't need help on the farm now ,as you are buying the milk cows, and they will be gone tomorrow, but we have plenty of room in the house, so if you know of any one, wanting some where to stay, we could take a few land girl's in. Sid does not want too, but it would be extra money and company for me."

Wilf paid for the twenty cows, and they all had a calf, which were coming with them. Ethel asked Wilf, "How will we get them all home?"

He said, "All the cows will follow each other, and the calves will follow the cows." Wilf always made things sound so simple, she thought, as he got hold of her hand and set off home. "I didn't do too bad off Sid Wilf was saying. I got £2 luck money back."

Well I have, enjoyed our walk out to day Wilf."

"Well I hope you enjoy it tomorrow as well Ethel, Wilf laughed, as you will have to come with me, to bring them cows back."

They arrived back at Ethel's to find Prudence, making the tea. "I hope you don't mind, me cooking the tea? But I feel like family, and thought you might like a break from it, and beside's you are always cooking meals for us."

The land girls had their jumpers tied, around their waists, as they walked back to Ethel's. Jennie's brown hair was a cascade, of curls, to her shoulders, but her neck was wet with sweat.

"I'm thinking of getting my hair bobbed uttered Jennie, just like your's Linda, it would be, easier to wash, and look after."

"If I had hair like yours Jennie, I would have it long, it looks lovely."

Linda seemed to give it some thought, and then said, "Perhaps I will, leave my hair for a while as it does seem a shame to cut it."

As Linda and Jennie were walking back down the road, Linda, was saying to Jennie, "you know them girls, I used to work with, if they could see me now, milking a cow they wouldn't believe it, just last week I had never seen a bloody cow, I have even surprised myself, how quick I have taken to it"

"I wonder if Ethel, and her Gran, has drunk their stout yet. Jennie wondered."

Linda exclaimed, "I bet Gran has, I think the way to her heart, is through her stomach, but we are nearly there, so we will soon find out."

As soon as Linda, and Jennie, walked into the house, Gran

smiled at them, and said, "I enjoyed, that bottle of stout, so much and I have been thinking, we all live here together, so why don't you call me Gran?"

Wilf said, "You girls look worn out, but you'll get used to it."

Linda asked Wilf, "How do we go about getting a bike? As we can't afford a new one, and we thought, it would be a lot easier, then walking, to Mr. Robson's."

Wilf scratched his head, and thought. "Well I have a bike, in my shed at home, it's an old bone shaker though, and I know the old man along from me, has one, he has never ridden it for years, and he is too bloody old now, but I will see what I can do for you."

Ethel asked them how they would peddle a bike with them rigid boot's on?"

Linda answered cheekily, "we have no bloody idea yet Ethel, and we will have to get a bike a piece first."

Gran seemed in deep thought, and then she asked them? "If they were going out tonight, as she told them, you can only burn the candle at both ends, when you are young, so you might as well enjoy your selves while you can."

Linda looked at Jennie, and they both laughed, and thought that bottle of stout has changed her tune.

Prudence said, "I drink brown ale, so I have been popping along to Tommy's, before opening time, for a bottle, as I did not like to walk in the pub, when it's full." Ethel said "Linda told us that last night, there was more land army, girls in then men didn't she Gran?"Prudence said "oh I might call in after and buy a bottle, would you like a stout Gran?"

"Well I won't say no, as I enjoyed that one today, our Ethel hasn't drank hers yet."

As the land girls walked, into the pub, they saw Peter standing at the bar; he asked them what they would like to drink? "Cider please, they both said together."

Peter bought them a drink each and as he went to put his arm around Linda she twisted out of his reach, but she was still smiling at him. Peter was drinking heavily, and every time, he bought a drink, he bought the girls one. Jennie whispered, to Linda,

"I wonder what he thinks he's going to get in return."

Linda said, "the state he will be in, at closing time it will all be in his mind." which set Jennie off giggling again, and she said"

"I bet frosty face, won't be very pleased when she see's the state of him tonight."Linda replied drunkenly, "I think he is drowning his sorrows."

Next morning found Ethel waking the girls again, they looked ill, but as Ethel told them, "they would feel better, when they were out in the fresh air."

Linda said, "I will not be going out tonight." "No I won't either say Jennie.

"When do you think your mam will write back to you Linda?" "I don't know Jennie even my sister's haven't bothered."

"I 'm dreading seeing Peter, and old Robson, this morning are you Linda?"

"Well its got nothing to do, with us ,we didn't tell Peter to get drunk, and its still got nothing to do with us Jennie, if he drink's at the same pub as us."

Ethel was sitting having a cup of tea, while Jennie, and Linda, were having their breakfast's, Ethel liked these two lasses, they were settling in well.

Linda turned to Ethel, and asked, "Are you and Wilf getting the cows today? As we will help, you all we can tonight, wont we Jennie?"

Ethel said, "tomorrow Wilf and me, will be busy, as we start the milk round, and our Eva, and Prudence, will be at the school, as the evacuees, will be here , I expect the poor little thing's will be upset, to leave their mother's. Oh come on you lasses, we are sitting ,talking, and time is ticking on, get your sandwiches, and get down that road, or you will be late",

As Ethel expected, Wilf walked in, as the girls walked out, she said to him, "people will be starting, to think you live here, as you are never away."

"If I lived here, you wouldn't be in that bed on your own, he laughed, as he gave Ethel, a playful slap, on the backside."

Ethel started to laugh, "I'm not in bed, on my own now, as I sleep with Gran, and talking of Gran, I will go, and help ,her up out of bed then after, we get the work done we can go for the cow's."

As Eva, Prudence, and the twins, walked to Ethel's, Prudence was saying, "I am pleased, there is no school dinners, in these small villages, as I have had some appaling food, at some schools."

"What will you be doing with your time Eva ?as the twins will soon be back at school, I know you help your mum a lot, but I was thinking, about the hall up the road, that has been turned, into a convalescent home, for the wounded soldiers, some of them, have lost their sight, and the staff would like people to go in, and write letters home for them, or just to visit them, some of them never have any visitors ,don't you think? It's worth thinking about Eva."

"Yes I will give it, some thought, after Prudence, but tomorrow we will probably have some evacuees. We had better hurry Prudence, Eva hadn't realised the time, and she had promised to sit with Gran, while her mam, and Wilf, went for the cows."

"Are you ready yet Ethel? As now that Eva and Prudence are here they can see to things, it's time we were on our way, to get them cows."

"Yes I'm coming now Wilf, Ethel, was beginning to feel harassed, I have never had so many walks out, as I've had lately, people will be thinking, and, that I'm turning lazy."

"Nothing of the sort our Ethel ,it will do you good, and you never know these's, two lasses might give you a hand with the tea." if you mean me and Prudence, Gran, Eva laughed we can always rustle some thing together," Gran thought Eva was looking a lot happier now that Joe had buggered off.

As Wilf, and Ethel, were walking down the road, Wilf looked at Ethel and said "by you are very quiet this afternoon, what's the matter with you?"

"Well it's just like this Wilf, up here in the country, you wouldn't think there was a war on, we don't have to get out of bed through a night ,and sit in a air raid shelter, and as for food shortages, I have never had as much stuff, with all of you eating at my house, and giving me all the coupons, and besides, we are so self sufficient ,we have plenty fresh eggs, and milk, them poor folk in the towns and cities are eating dried eggs. So really we are having a good war, while people are getting killed and injured every day."

"As far as I see it, Wilf was losing his temper, as he was frustrated, as he loved Ethel, the only dark cloud on the horizon, is your bloody Jack, you never hear from him, and you never get any money off him, as far as I'm concerned, he's standing in the way of our bloody happiness, he has never appreciated you Ethel."

"Well we are here now Wilf, we will talk about Jack after, and see what we can do, just look at all them cow's, and calves in that field."

"Aye and they are all ours Ethel."

I am pleased they are Jersey's Wilf, just like Buttercup, they are so placid." as they reached the gate Sid was there to meet them.

CHAPTER 9

"By it's an unhappy day for me today, Sid grumbled, having to get rid of my milking cow's, and I know they will be well looked after, and I've been thinking, seen as you are taking the calves as well, I will walk back with you, and my dog will keep rounding them up, if any of them happen to stray."

"Well if you come back with us Sid, you will have to come in and say hello to Gran, Ethel told him, and have a cup of tea."

"Aye I will have a look in and see her Sid said, I like a bit banter with Gran, as Ethel looked round the kitchen, she couldn't help thinking, how well off she was compared ,with a lot of people, "there was Eva, and Prudence ,starting the dinner, the twins were playing happily, Gran, Wilf ,and Sid, sitting chatting, and enjoying a cup of tea, even Sid's dog, was getting on alright with Jess Gran's dog as they were both laid asleep, side, by side."

When Ethel and Wilf went to milk the cows, they had already walked into the byre ahead of them and were stood chewing the rolled oats, that Ethel had put in the manger for them, they didn't seem to notice they had a new home, the only one to take notice was Buttercup, who looked at them, just as much as, what are them lot doing in here, I was looking forward to a bit of peace tonight, don't they know I have Daisy to look after all day.

Ethel thought just as well, they were all turned out now, after milking, at least there was not a lot of mucking out to do, by the time Ethel, and Wilf, had finally finished the farm work, and Ethel had gathered a huge bowl of eggs, as the chicks were at an age now where they were laying eggs. The land girls were approaching; they started to hurry to catch up to Ethel and Wilf.

Linda said, "guess what Peter did last night, he only slept in the barn, old Robson wasn't speaking to him today, as they walked in the house, Eva, and Prudence, had set their plates of dinner on the table.

104

Gran looked up and asked what have I missed? Who isn't Michael Robson speaking to?

"Linda said nothing gets past you does it Gran?"

"No I don't miss nothing, Linda and that Peters, one for the girls, so you lasses watch out, when you are in them barns ,if I was you, I would keep that pitch fork handy, he would move fast out of your way if he had that stuck in his arse."

As they were all eating their teas Ethel said, "You wont be here tomorrow teatime will you Eva? As you will possibly have your evacuees. I might have a look up tomorrow, if Wilf and I have time we will go together."

"Ethel I will come with you Wilf replied."

"When you go home Eva ,Ethel decided, I will give you two big plate pies, to take with you ,they are mince and onion, they will help with the meal tomorrow night ,if you have the evacuees."

"Oh I love your pies mam they are delicious I wish I could bake as well as you."

Gran looked across at Eva, "have you never heard, practice makes perfect, if you never try, you never learn, so I suggest, you buy some flour, and lard, and start and make some pastry, there is plenty bottled fruit, if you want to make sweet pies, if you are getting some evacuees tomorrow? You will all have to eat as cheap as possible, but it will have to be filling."

"Prudence has been telling me, Gran, how some of them children haven't been getting fed properly."

"You will have to give them plenty nourishing food then Eva, Gran said.

Jennie said," just as well the Robson's don't want any evacuees; they would be worse off there, then what there are now."

Gran asked, "If Peters wife was still emptying the teapot in front of them?"

"Yes she is, answered Linda, but we are not bothered, as

Ethel fills us a bottle of tea every morning now, so we drink that cold."

After tea was eaten, and the washing up done, every one sat around talking, the girls took the dish, and two pails of hot water upstairs, they would have an all over wash, then do each others hair, in front of the old mirror that was spotted with age, then they were ready for a night along at Tommy's pub, it was better now that Lizzie had excepted them.

Next morning every one seemed to have risen early, the twins were excited may be they would have some children to play with before the day was out. "Eva was wondering how she would manage someone else's children." Prudence was hoping Grace wouldn't be late, as her and Prudence were going to be helping the billeting officer." along the road at Rosebud cottage, even Gran was up, before Linda and Jennie set off for Robson's farm. Wilf was sitting drinking his first cup of tea of the day with Gran. Ethel was saying to Gran

"We are going to milk the cows, then deliver the milk, then we will all have our breakfast when we get back."

As Wilf trundled the barrow along the road, Ethel was walking by his side she thought, "We make a good pair me and Wilf, he is like me he isn't frightened of hard work, and Gran always said, if you don't put anything in to this life you don't get anything out." Ethel felt as if she was getting some thing out of this life now that she had Wilf. He had now stopped walking as Ethel was day dreaming.

"Come on Ethel knock on the door or we will be here all day." it was a good arrangement Wilf pushed the barrow and Ethel, ladled the milk out in to what ever bowl or jug, and was brought to the door. Ethel had a pint, and a Jill, measure made of tin; it hung over the rail of the churns, by its long handle. After they had arrived home, Ethel couldn't believe the amount of milk they had sold, they had a good standing order, at the convalescent home, she had sold all, the spare eggs that, she had taken with her. Back home, as Ethel cooked the breakfast Wilf ,went to check on   Alice, who was expecting piglets again, he would feed the hens, and geese ,while he was out. Wilf thought "that bloody Gander, has come to peck at me again," as it came waddling, over on its webbed feet, the bloody gander chased every body; the only one he seemed to like was Ethel.

Wilf made a hasty retreat back into the house, have you been running Wilf? Gran asked as Wilf hurried in.

"As a matter of fact Gran, that Gander chased me over the stile again."

"Aye I told you lad, when you brought it, they were as good as a guard dog, and it seems to like our Ethel though."

"Aye well she can feed it in future then, answered Wilf."

After breakfast Wilf thought "he would try, and cobble, the bikes together for the lasses, as he had plenty of time, before he went up to the school with Ethel. Linda, and Jennie, seemed to be happy at Ethel's he was thinking, mind Ethel fed every one well and she was very easy to get along with."

The afternoon soon came around, there seemed to be a few people standing around the school, as Wilf, and Ethel, arrived, the billeting officer was standing just inside the door, the children eventually arrived late. Ethel was standing with Wilf, Prudence ,and Eva, The children had gas masks, they also had labels tied to their coats, some of the better dressed had small cases ,the dirty verminous ones, had brown paper parcels, some of the younger smaller children were getting fractious, some were in deep discomfort, as they had wet them selves. Ethel's kind heart went out to the children, as people were walking up, and down, looking at them, as if they were buying animals. Ethel noticed that the better dressed children were starting to leave with their new foster mothers. Eva pointed over to where two small girls, were standing on their own, their arms around each other, they looked very frightened, as Eva made her way over to them, the oldest girl looked up, at Eva as two huge tears rolled down, her not very clean face.

Eva asked them, "Would you like to come and live with me? As I have two little girls and you look about the same age." The older one of the two said,

"we are not being parted, mum said we have to stop together, she put a protecting arm around her smaller sister," Eva noticed their clothes were threadbare, the older girl said, "we are stopping together, so don't try taking my little sister." Eva asked them? "How old they were, the older said I am six, and my sister's four, and she has wet her knickers."

Eva asked them, "What they were called? The older, of the two said,

"I'm Violet and my little sister is Rose."

"Well should we go to my house Eva asked them? as I have made some lemonade, and you can meet my two little girls, they are Shirley, and Margaret, as Eva walked down the road, holding on to Violet, and Rose's, hand she was thinking the first job, would be a bath, and some nit cream, as she could see the nits moving in their hair, at least Shirley, and Margaret's, clothes would fit these two little girls, with there paper parcels."

After Eva had left, nearly every one else had gone apart from two small boys sitting in the corner.

Prudence said, "it looks as though no one wants them, it's always the same, the best dressed and the very clean ones always go first."

Ethel asked the billeting officer, what would happen to them boys?

The billeting officer said, "It won't be the first time that I've had to take the children around the village, knocking on doors asking people to take them in."

Ethel said, "I can't see them little boys, with nowhere to go, I will take them, only God knows where, I will get the time to see to them."

Wilf put his hand, on Ethel's shoulder and whispered, "Don't worry Ethel, I will help you all I can"

So Wilf and Ethel made their way over to the boys, Ethel looked at the oldest boy and asked? "What do they call you then?

"I'm Frank Mrs., and this is my brother Colin, he's seven, and I'm nine. Are we going with you and your husband?"

"No this is Wilf, answered Ethel, a good friend of mine; he will be uncle Wilf to you two."

"Oh that's alright said Colin, with a grin, I've had more uncles, then any one I know, Gran goes to the pub, and brings a bloke back ,and if he stays longer then two days we have to call him uncle."

"Do you live with your Gran asked Wilf?

"Yes we did, explained Frank, because mam pissed off with a bloke, and dad had gone off before that, so we had to live with Gran, she said we had not to go back to her. As why should she be stuck with us? As they were walking down the road, Frank looked around and said,

"It's going to be bloody boring here, there are hardly any houses."

Wilf looked at Ethel," just as much as, we've got two wild buggers here."

"We are here now" Ethel said as she opened the door, and walked in to the house, the boys followed with Wilf walking up the rear.

As they walked in Frank said, "Who the hell's that old biddy sat in that chair?"

Outrage flared through Gran, and she glowered at him, at the same time picking up her stick, and swinging it threatenly at frank;

"Well you cheeky young bugger, you had better get yourself squared up, or I will hit you with this bloody stick, and you will be going back to where you came from ,and I am Mrs. Brown to you, and don't forget it, other wise I will remind you with this bloody stick."

"Ethel they will need a bath, Gran shouted, as they can't

go to bed like that, they bloody stink, and they both have snotty noses."

Ethel asked them, "If they were hungry? and they both said "yes "; So Ethel ladled some stew, in to a bowl each, for them out of the big black pan, that sat on the side of the fire .As Ethel handed it to them, they asked what it was? As they had never had stew before, but once they had tasted it, they weren't long in eating it.

"These boys have been neglected, Ethel was heard telling Wilf, after the boys were bathed, and in bed, they seemed to have lived on chips, and jellied eel's."

Prudence said, "It's a revelation, what them boys have lived on, but there will be a lot of children like them, but they will be alright here though, as they will have stability."

Ethel was going to let them sleep, in the pullout bed, in the sideboard, but Linda, and Jennie, said, "Frank and Colin could sleep in their room, as there was a double bed spare", as the girls slept together. Ethel felt that the boys had been strangers to washing, as they were not happy, about getting a bath tonight. Wilf said,

"He would hold them down, in that bath tonight if he had too." The youngest boys eyes had widened in terror, Ethel thought, she had given them a good feed before going to bed, as they were skin and bone, but some good nourishing food would soon fill them out.

Along at Eva's house, tears had been rolling down Roses face, she was tired and hungry, after she was fed and bathed, Eva tucked her up in bed, and it wasn't long before she was asleep, with her thumb in her mouth. Prudence, and Eva, sat down with a cup of tea, after the twins, and Violet, went to bed. Eva said,

"I suppose it will take time for the children to settle in, I wonder how Mam is managing them two boys." Prudence said,

"Gran, Wilf, and the land girls, are there so she will get help with them, and the school starts back in two days, so they will all have a routine." Along at Rosebud cottage, Ethel was telling Gran,

"That in the morning, she would let the boys have a lie in, and she would get the farm work done, and the milk delivered, before she woke them for breakfast." Next morning dawned lovely and warm, the sun was just starting to rise, and the birds were singing in the trees.

As Wilf pushed the heavy barrow with all the milk churns in, It was heavy work, having the milk round, and it was a long walk on a morning, but it meant Ethel, and Wilf, could spend some time together, on their own. after all the milk was delivered, and they were back at home, Ethel had helped Gran out of bed and in to her rocking chair, then she took down the big black frying pan that hung over the fire, and started frying the bacon, later she heard the patter of small feet on the lino upstairs, then both boys walked in to the kitchen.

Ethel said, "You are having egg, and bacon, for your breakfasts."

Frank said, "My Gran always said, she couldn't get eggs for love or money." Gran growled at Frank,

"You just behave yourself, as you are in clover here, and I won't put up with your bloody cheek." Just then Wilf walked in, with a large bowl of eggs, so they all sat down to eat their breakfasts. Colin asked "which shop he had got the eggs from." Wilf said,

"Well they have come off the hens." Colin said, "When we used to get them, we got them from a shop."

"After breakfast, you can both come with me, Wilf told them, and see the hens, geese, cows, and the pigs and then auntie Ethel can get her bread made, and no doubt Prudence, Eva, and the four children, will be along later.

"It might do the bairns well, to get together Ethel, Wilf, said as he was going out of the door."

CHAPTER 10

Along at Eva's, she had dressed Violet, and rose, in some of Margaret, and Shirley's clothes, it had taken ages last night, to apply the lotion, to kill the nits in Violet ,and roses head, then Eva, had sat and combed them out with a nit comb that Prudence had been and bought for her. The little evacuees had slept soundly, but this morning their bed had been wet. Prudence had changed the beds for Eva, and they were gong to buy something to put over the mattress, before it got wet and stained. Eva was starting to wonder if she had done the right thing, taking these two little girls in to her home, she had to admit, they were bonny children now, with their light brown hair and freckles, Eva didn't know that they had freckles, until they had a hot bath, and a good scrub last night, Violet, and Rose, had not brought a change of clothes with them, the clothes they had on, were rags. Eva wondered how their mother could have sent them away, in the state they were in. Eva had wrote a postcard out with their address on it, and had added that the little girls would be well looked after, surely their mother would want to know, where they were staying, She would post it on the way to mam's, and see what was happening to those two boys.

Mean while Wilf was taking them to the henhouse ,It was a large wooden shed now, as Wilf had got some wood and extended it, just before he, and Ethel, had bought the extra hens. The boys started to hurry towards the henhouse door, and before Wilf, had time to stop them, they had bounded in, causing the hens to flap, and squawk, then they started to fly off their perches ,Wilf got hold of the door, and held it wide open, to let the hens out, after the hens were out, Wilf said,

"Let that be a lesson to you, if you ever do that again, you will feel the back of my hand, I know you don't know anything about country ways, but you can slow your selves down, or go back in the house, and where have you put that bowl Colin? Because we collect the eggs in that," Colin asked Wilf where the eggs came from.

Wilf said, "Where the hell do you think? Well out of the bloody hens,"

Colin said, "I'm not eating them, I want mine from a shop."

Ethel had been very busy, she had got all the bread made, and she had made a huge, dish of shepherds pie, and a lot of vegetables for dinner, followed by apple pie and custard. Frank and Colin ate it, as if it were their last meal, Frank said, "this is nice could I have some more?

Ethel said, "Yes course you can." Then Frank asked? What is it; we used to go to the chippy at Gran's."

After dinner Eva, and Prudence, walked along to Ethel's, with the four girls, Eva was going to stay a while with her mother, and Prudence, asked the boys, if they would like to go for a walk, with her and the girls, then they would get to know there way about, After Prudence had taken all six of them, Ethel, asked Eva,

"How, are you coping?" Eva was telling her mother Ethel, about the bed wetting.

Ethel said, "Grace has some clothes for me, that will fit the boys, as they only have what they stand up in, you should ask her for a rubber sheet, as I know she has some, with her being a nurse."

Well I noticed Graces bike, was in mam, when I came along Eva said, I will pop and ask her now, or I will end up wanting a new mattress."

Along at Robson's farm, they had got the fields cut, the girls were turning it with a rake, the midday sun was burning down on them, as they had their shirt sleeves rolled up ,also their trouser legs were rolled up to their knees. Although they had their heavy regulation shoes on, they were better then the rigid boots. Both Linda, and Jennie, were both as brown as a berry, they were both fit, and healthy, as well with all this out door work. Wilf had been as good as his word, and fixed them up with a bike each.

Peter was working in the field, so were the two old men, as all the younger men were in the forces. Linda was going home this Friday, she would be back on Monday, as she was going to visit her family, and see her new niece, Jennie would not be sitting in, as Robert Lee, was home on leave, and he had popped along to see Ethel, and Gran, after he had been introduced to the land girls he had asked Jennie out. Linda, and Jennie, were both looking forward to the weekend, for different reasons, the girls arms, and necks, were aching, they both thought it was bad when they were learning to milk the cows, they thought nothing of it now, although the cows ,were uneasy this morning, as it was hot, and they were swishing their tails ,as the flies were everywhere ,and the sweat was running off the girls, but they would enjoy tonight, as they were going down the river for a swim, they had promised Frank, and Colin, that they would take them as well.

Next morning Ethel, and Wilf, did the milk round, then Ethel started doing the breakfast, then she would have take the boys to school, she thought thank God for Grace, or the boys would have had no decent school clothes. As they were all sitting down to breakfast, Frank said,

I don't think I will go to school today, my Gran always said, she wasn't bothered, if we went or we didn't." Ethel said,

"As long as you live here, you will go to school, or you will be sorry, do you understand?

The boys realised, they would have to do as they were told, as long as they lived with Ethel, but both boys agreed, it was better then living with their Gran, as they were always hungry, and when she brought men back through a day, they had to go out side, they didn't mind when it was dry, as they played on the old bomb sites, but when it rained ,and it was cold ,they tried to huddle up some where to keep warm, the boys knew that Ethel had sent their Gran a card telling her their new address, but Gran had not answered. Frank knew she wouldn't, he didn't know where they would go, when Ethel got sick of them, but he did know that he would not be parted from his younger brother, well! may be school wouldn't be so bad here, as they only had to go half days, so they would only be there till dinnertime, then the local children would go for the afternoon lessons. As the boys walked up to school on there first day with Ethel, Frank thought what a difference, a few days had made, he always had to look after his self, and his younger brother, as long as he could remember, Ethel had been the first one, to show any kindness to them, so today when he finished school, he would ask uncle Wilf? If he could help, may be put the rolled oats, and hay, in to the mangers, it would save Auntie Ethel a job.

They were at school now, auntie Ethel, was talking to Eva, her daughter, and then she turned to the boys, and asked them if they could walk back on their own? And to come straight home at dinner time"

Frank said, "yes hadn't he and his brother ,run the streets at night, in London on their own, Gran didn't know, and didn't care, as she went to the pub, every night, but the boys used to hear her, and some bloke come in on a night, as Gran used to giggle, when she was drunk, it was the same every night, the bed springs used to squeal, and Gran used to make funny noises, like groaning as if she was in pain, but then, she would giggle. Frank used to tell Colin, to try and get to sleep, before she came in. Gran's friend lived next door, Dorothy, they called her, she used to make the blokes give her money, before they went home with her, she used to tell Gran to stop giving it away, and charge the buggers for it. Frank used to listen to them, but he never did find out what Gran was giving away."

As Ethel walked back into the house, she said to Gran.

"Just you me, and Wilf, for a cup of tea this morning, I

saw our Eva taking Violet and Rose to school this morning, then at dinner time, she will have to take Margaret, and Shirley, and bring Violet, and Rose, back home, so I don't think she will be along today, I will just pop and see Wilf, and tell him to come for a cup of tea, and he will likely want a scone with jam on."

"As Ethel was talking to Wilf, in the field, and telling him she had made a cup of tea, Eva and the twins had come along and were in the house, when Ethel, and Wilf, walked back inside, Ethel could see by Eva's face, that some thing wasn't right." Hello darlings, "Ethel greeted the twins, I didn't think I would have seen you lot again this morning, then Ethel, saw Gran, with a letter in her hand."

I've had a letter off Joe, mam ,Eva wistfully told Ethel, and he is wanting to talk to me, about some thing, he is wanting me to meet him at the station, and he said, not to take the twins, do you think he's sorry for what he's done to me ,and the twins?"

Gran said, "If you don't meet the bugger, Eva you will never find out what he wants' but why should you have to go to the station? its him that's after some thing so tell him, to come to you, as what ever it is, it will be for his own ends, and some thing else Eva, he's never bothered before, so don't you go home, and cry over him as he wont be crying over you, he will wheedle his way in, as he's after some thing, so don't be shocked by what ever he suggests. I don't trust that bugger, I never have and I never will."

Ethel said, "what ever day he is coming, I will walk the kids to school for you."

"Right thanks mam, Eva was relieved, I will go and make some dinner as Prudence will be in for hers shortly, she is bringing Violet, and Rose, back for me so we will all have our dinners together, before I take the twins to school."

Ethel thought she would give the boys a treat, they had never even heard of dumplings, let alone eaten them, so she would do them with mince, and plenty potatoes, and vegetables and, Gran wanted rice pudding for after's.

As the boys walked in, their mouths started to water, as they smelt the dinner cooking. Ethel was smiling, and asking them if they had enjoyed their morning? Colin went over to Ethel, and put his arms around her waist, and his head against her body, he said,

"I love you Auntie Ethel and I want to stop here for ever."Ethel swallowed hard as her eyes filled up."

However down at Robson's farm, the girls were still not getting a cup of tea, when Hannah had poured the rest of the tea down the drain, she had looked over at them and scowled, then she had tossed her head, and gone in the house, as Linda and Jennie, drank their cold tea from a bottle. It was very hot, and they had started to turn another field this afternoon, Peter was cutting the long grass, on the bank side beside the hedge, with his scythe.

Linda said to Jennie, "Just think tomorrow, I will be on that train, going home to see mam, dad, and my family."

Jennie said, "they will see a big difference in you, as you have a good suntan, and you have filled out, mind there's no wonder, with all Ethel's dinners." Later as the girls got in from work, Wilf asked,

"How Linda was going to get to the station?" Linda said, "I suppose I will have to walk."

Wilf said, "There is no need to do that, just ride your bike down, and tell Alan at the station, that Wilf would like him to look after your bike, till you get back, as he is a friend of mine."

Next day sitting on the train heading home, excitement was building up in Linda; it had been a while now, since she had last seen her family, although she was enjoying working on the land, she liked Ethel, even Gran, was alright now, that they had all got to know each other. As the train got nearer its destination, more and more of the armed forces, were filling the train, the soldiers, who were sitting next to Linda, were including her in their conversations, and sharing their cigarettes. As the train pulled in to the station, Linda felt she knew every thing about them; she even had a date arranged with one of them. Later as she was looking out of the bus window, heading home on the last lap of her journey, she couldn't believe the bomb damage. The damaged streets were still standing, with houses missing, it looked like a big wide mouth with teeth missing, every thing looked grubby, as she got near to her stop, she got up, and lifted her case down from the rack, and then she walked down the bus. once on the footpath if she hadn't of known better, she would of sworn that it wasn't her street, it looked so different, people pushing barrows, witch had all their possession's in, and looking so down at heel, she made her way home, when she got there, she pulled the key through the letter box, that was hanging on a string behind the door. As she went in she shouted mum, but there was no answer, so she put down her case, and went further down the street, to her sisters' house. When Jane, saw Linda, she said,

"I can't believe how much you have changed, you're a sight for sore eyes, and what a beautiful sun tan."

Linda said, "Can I see my new niece? I feel like a stranger here now Jane and so much seems to have changed."

"Yes I suppose it has said Jane as looked puzzled, and she is three month old now, she is in the pram over there. Keith has been home, she explained to Linda, and I think I have fallen for another one."

"Oh bloody hell Jane, Linda exploded, you are going to have a house full if you carry on at this rate, anyway where the other one at? My bonny little nephew."

"Oh he's having his afternoon nap Linda."

Jane do you know where mums at? As I would have thought, she would have been at home."

"People are not at home most of the time now Linda, Jane told her, as we spend a lot of time queuing for food."

"Well I have brought you and mum some eggs and butter, Linda told her as she rummaged in her bag."

"Oh that's lovely, Jane replied, I do appreciate it, as I don't remember the last time we had an egg. Linda, mum will be in later, as she is working in the ammunition factory. Emma, and Jean, are there as well."

Two hours soon went over, as Linda told Jane all about the Robson's farm, and Gran, Wilf, Prudence, and Eva. Jane couldn't believe the eggs butter and milk that Linda got or all the food that was available. Linda couldn't help herself for comparing, the concrete back yard, and bombed damaged houses, to the tranquil countryside, and as Linda walked backed home, she was starting to feel as if she didn't belong here, as she walked back into her parents house, her two sisters were just going to sit down for their teas, Linda 's mum had put a bit of tea out for Linda, as she had seen the case, as soon as Linda's mum saw her, she held out her arms and Linda went in to them, they all agreed that Linda, was looking fit, and well .Her mother said,

"No wonder the food she is getting, but I still, wouldn't like to live in the country."

Linda asked, "If she was still sleeping, where she was before she went away, as she was beginning to feel as if she didn't belong here anymore."

Linda's mother looked at her, sisters and said,

"You have no idea have you? It isn't very often we go to bed, as the sirens go then, we go down the shelter."

Linda found out just how bad it was as she was sitting in the shelter later with her family, with the ack ack guns shooting back, at the low flying planes, and the ground shaking, as the bombs dropped. Linda asked them how they managed to live like this."

Linda's sister Emma, said, "You get used to it, I would rather be here, then stuck in the country, don't you get bored in the sticks Linda?"

Her mother spoke up and said,

"I don't know what made her go to live in the country, none of us are country people, I've never even seen a cow, and I never want too."

Well Linda said, "I didn't know what to expect, when I first left home, I had never seen a cow, but now, I just get them in on a morning, chain them up, and milk them, the same at night, they get milked twice a day, I would hate to be still stuck in a factory, are you liking it mum?"

"well its hard work Linda, more so when there is food to queue for, and a lot of the nights, we try and get some sleep in the shelters, but I go out most nights now, as I have a lot of mates, I work with, but when I come back in, I have to come back in to the bloody shelter, and every morning when I walk out of here, I just hope that the house is still standing."

"Well I'm going out tomorrow night, on my way down I met a sailor, he was coming back off leave, and I'm meeting him tomorrow night. I forgot to tell you I've got a bike,

Emma said, "Do you know how to ride it?"

course I do Emma ,I ride it to work, and I also rode it to the station, and left it there when I came here, and I will pick it up on the way back ,its easier then walking." they all started laughing at Linda,

Emma said, I couldn't imagine you, on a bike with bloke's clothes on as well." Linda answered,

As it happens Emma, it is the land army uniform, and you wouldn't believe the amount of the girls, that have left the cities to join us on the land." Just then there was a tremendous bang, Linda was beginning to wish she hadn't bothered coming home to visit, when her father put his head inside the shelter door, as he was on fire watch duty, he said

"There is a big fire and, the docks have been hit, and the gas and water pipes are punctured around here." Linda's mum said

"There goes any chance of a cup of tea, in the morning or a wash, she looked across at Linda, and said, "Now you can see for yourself, just what we have to live through, while you are enjoying yourself in the bloody countryside."

CHAPTER 11

The next morning as they all went back in to the house, everything was covered in soot, Mrs. Smith, Linda's mum said,

"I don't know where to start; she said unhappily, as there is no water, and if there was, there is nothing to heat it on. Linda run down to our Jane's, and make sure her and the babies are alright, as they are usually in the shelter with us."

When Linda arrived there, she found her sister's house covered in soot, the children were crying, and her sister was in a right fluster.

"let us get the children dressed Jane, Linda told her, then you will have to come back to mam's ,then our Emma, can go to the mobile canteen, and get us all a welcome cup of tea, as I know I could do with one ,couldn't you Jane? And don't you think you should move to the country side? It would be safer, and better, then this for you and the babies."

"No bloody fears Linda, I'm stopping here, I don't like bloody animals, and there is no bloody chip shops, no hair dressers, no I will chance my luck with every body else, she smirked as she said, we are not all bloody farmers."

It was a long day for Linda, the blast had shaken the houses in the street, and the surrounding streets and it had broken ornaments, cups, plates, and her mum's one and only mirror, there was debris under foot, Linda went out side, to see if all the houses in the street were still standing, she noticed the bedroom curtains, blowing in the windowless frames, it was so sad, as the curtains were shredded. mum had stopped off work, and she was crying now, Linda, and Emma, were trying to brush the soot up,but it was all over the room, as there was not a pane of glass left in the house, it was clogging every one snose, and throat,every one was coughing , it had blown, over every thing in the room, the glass had blown out of the windows, dad had gone to find some wood, to board it up, and Jane was sitting in the soot covered chair, with both babies crying on her knee, what a depressing situation they were all in.

Linda started to wish again, that she hadn't come, she thought roll on morning, and I'll be on that bloody train, just as well she had tonight to look forward too ,or else she might of tried to get back to Ethel's sooner, she was going to meet the sailor tonight, that she had met on the train, as long as the soot hadn't got inside her case, and on to her clean clothes, as God only knows, where she would be able to get a wash, as the soot was ingrained on her hands, by tea time the punctured pipe had been mended, but the gas was still off ,so it was a matter of a wash with a kettle full of hot water, Linda had helped all day, to try and get rid of the soot, she could even taste it, the babies had cried all day, Jane was in a foul mood . Linda was pleased, when it was time to escape to the pictures, she just hoped the sailor would turn up, but she had made her mind up, if he didn't ,she would go and watch it on her own, as she was in no hurry to go back there, as when she had left, mum had taken her temper out on dad, and he had done all he could today, it seemed as if every ones nerves were on edge." as she stood waiting out side the pictures house, she looked around her at all the bomb damage, it was depressing, luckily she didn't have long to wait till Paul turned up, once inside they sat, and talked till the film started, it hadn't been on long, when the bombs started to drop, a message came up on the screen, saying, "them people wishing to leave could do so now", they were telling people, what was happening out side, but them that wanted to could stop in, and watch the film could do so.

Linda thought, "the whole city must be getting bombarded tonight, by the noise it was making ,her and Paul decided to stay where they were, as there was no where else to go,at least it was warm, and she was in no hurry to go home, to sit in that damp shelter, she thought, even the animals on the farm, had better accommodation, before she left the city to live in the country, the sound of the sirens, with there chilling warnings, used to make her stomach churn, wailing Minnie, as every one used to call it, and she still felt uncomfortable, sitting in that claustrophobic shelter."

Linda had been lost in thought, the film had ended, and Paul was starting to get off his seat,

"Are you ready Linda he asked? as I'll walk you home, then I 'll have to get off down the docks, as my ship leaves at midnight," as they were making there way out, the noise of the throbbing engines, and of the ack ack guns, made it feel eerie, and the search lights, kept lighting up the street, as shrapnel was showering down everywhere, Linda said,

"I think the whole world has gone crazy, and I'm frightened, I hope you will be alright on that ship in the docks."

"I will see you home first, promise me you'll write to me Linda, as he said goodbye, at the top of the street, and they swapped addresses.

Linda then ran to the dreaded shelter, Mam, dad, and sisters Emma, Jean, Jane, and Jane's baby, and her little boy, who had plague the life out of every body all day, were all squashed in to the shelter. As Linda sat down, they all shoved along a bit, to make room for her. Mr. Smith. Linda's father, unscrewed the top of the thermos flask, and offered Linda a cup of tea, he asked,

"Would you like some thing to eat, as I have made some fish paste sandwiches, why have you had a smile on your face Linda? What's so bloody funny?"

"Oh I was just thinking Dad, I don't like fish paste, but I didn't like rabbit, when I went to Ethel's, well I tell a lie, it tasted alright, it just put me off with it being a little furry bunny rabbit." they all looked as if they could be sick,

Jane said, "to think you were telling me, to come and live in the country, no thanks Linda, I will stay here, and hope like every body else." it was along uncomfortable night, sitting on a hard wooden bench, with the droning of the planes over head, and the ground shaking, as a bomb was dropped near by,the noise off the guns was deathening, as they fired back at the retreating planes,Linda noticed that Jane was sitting wringing her hands to stop them from shaking, and every one was bleary eyed the next morning, as they made their way out of the shelter to see if the house was still standing as Linda emerged from the shelter she looked up at the sky which was a very bright red off the fires that were still burning.

Mam, Emma, Jean and Dad, to go to work with out a nights sleep, Jane to go home with two children, and she was certain, another one was on the way, Linda was looking forward, to boarding the train back to Ethel's, she was setting off early so she could get back, before it got dark, and there was nothing, for her here, she had said her goodbye's to every one ,but as she was closing the front door behind her, Jane came hurrying towards her, with a huge black pram, and both snotty, nosed and none ,too clean children, inside. She came puffing along as she said,

"I thought we could walk along together, to the station, as no bugger else has bothered, about seeing you off."

Linda could feel the tears, sliding down her cheeks, as she hugged Jane, "thank you Jane, I was beginning to think, I was on my own and nobody cared."

"Well you have been lucky Linda, Jane told her, theses last two nights to see mam, as now that she is working, she is out now most nights, with her new found friends." As they walked along the sun was scorching down,

Linda told Jane her sister, that "they would be busy, at Robson farm, where I work, they will be turning hay."

Jane looked at Linda,

"You really do like it don't you? Jane could hardly believe, that her sister enjoyed it so much," Linda didn't have to think twice, yes I really do like every thing about it, and now I have home, I know I made the right decision." After a long thought Jane said,

"well I don't blame you getting away from here, but I wouldn't like to live in the country, some times I think I made a mistake getting married ,the babies are coming far too quickly, and I am not, getting any sleep on a night, having to sit in the shelter, I am spending my days queuing for food ,the other day I was walking past the butchers, and someone told me after I had stopped to ask, that there was sausage to be had, so I joined the queue and stood for an hour, and when it was my turn, he had sold out of it, I could of cried, it was so frustrating, I had two baby's crying in the big heavy pram, and nothing for their dinners." Linda looked at Jane, pushing the big heavy pram, it was only six month since she had seen her, but it felt like years, and Jane had prematurely aged.

"Here we are at the station, Jane said with relief, we will get a sit down, just as well you didn't need to come here at night, as it's packed with people, all bringing their bedding, and flask's, and they sleep here, because it's safer than stopping in their houses." They had been sitting awhile, and then the babies had woken up, and started to cry. Just then an announcement came over the tannoy, telling every one that the train would be two hours late. Jane jumped up,

"That's it then kid Jane hurriedly said, I can't hang around that long these two will want some thing to eat," Linda said,

"I will walk back down the road with you, and then I will turn off."Jane said,

"Why where are you going?"

"well you know about Jennie, who I work with on the farm Linda explained we both live with Ethel, she has left her address, with the little old woman that used to live next door to her, and her mam, then if her dad comes home on leave, she will give it to him, so I thought I would call and see Mrs. Roberts, that's what you call the old lady, if she is still there. After they had walked awhile Jane said,

"This is it kid, look after yourself and keep in touch", they stood with their arms around each other, Linda said,

"If I'd had stayed here, I would of helped you Jane, but I can't, I don't like it."

"I understand kid, Jane said, as Linda stood and nodded; now I'm going ta ra then."

Linda stood and watched, her sister walk away, with tears glistening in her eye's, everything seemed to have changed, as she made her way to the old woman's house, she had to walk past Jennie's old home, she noticed no one was living there, as she knocked on Mrs. Roberts door, it took a while for her to open it, Linda could hear her feet, shuffling towards the door, in her slippers, she was a small woman, as she opened the door she looked up at Linda and said,

"If you are another one looking for her next door, as she has been with your fella, you are out of luck, she has gone and good riddance."

"No I'm Linda, Jennie's friend, I thought I would call and see, if you knew her dads address yet?"

"Well why didn't you say so, the old woman said come on in", Linda thought you didn't give me chance, well sit yourself down Mrs. Robert's said as she pointed to a chair, there's plenty tea left in the pot, I always make a big pot of tea, in case any one calls, no one ever does, but it saves me having to make another one, as I live on my own , my husband died a few years back, and I lost my two sons, in the last lot, so there's only me ,I miss Jennie, as I have no one to pass the time of day with ,now she's gone." Linda felt sorry for her, there seemed to be such a lot of misery about,

"But you will meet people, Linda said, down at the shelter on a night, are they not a friendly lot?

"Oh I don't go there! said Mrs. Robert's looking surprised, at my age, I think if I'm going to go, I'm not going in an uncomfortable shelter, no, I've made my mind up, I will go in comfort, so while all them folk's are squashed in the shelters, I'm tucked up in bed. How is Jennie getting on? she's such a nice girl, her mother was a proper floozy I never had time for her, well her dads never turned up yet, but when he does I will pass her address on, are you working with Jennie? I'm seventy six years old, and I have never seen a cow, don't want to neither, couldn't be doing with that, no you wouldn't catch me in the country, I'm told as how they have funny ways, but tell Jennie, when she wants to come back for a visit, she can stay with me." As Linda got up to go, Mrs. Roberts said,

"Oh your not going yet, are you? Well it's been nice talking to you, call again when ever you want."

As Linda walked back down the street towards the station, she thought what a lovely, lonely old woman, Mrs. Roberts was, she had talked to Linda, for one hour with out stopping for breath, but Linda thought, it could be six months before she saw another soul, to talk to or visit her. The train finally arrived, every one was packed in like sardines, it was red hot, and Smokey, Linda's eyes were sore, every one was smoking, there was every nationality on this train in uniform, Canadians, Americans, and Poles, Jennie was offered a few knees to sit on, but she declined, and sat on her small case instead, along with a lot more, Linda couldn't help but feel she had changed a lot ,once on she was happy here, it was her home, now she couldn't wait to get away, she felt as if she didn't belong here on the dirty streets, everybody was queuing for food, she hadn't realised, just how much she took eggs, and milk, for granted now, and Ethel always had a good table full of food. Linda sat and gathered her thought's, and wished she was home, as that was how she thought of Ethel's now, just before she had set off, Wilf had been sharpening the scythes up to start to cut the fields, some blokes from along the village, would help him cut it, but she thought her and Jennie would help, to turn it, she knew how to do it now, as she was doing it at Robson's farm. At the next station, someone got off, so Linda grabbed the seat before someone got on, Linda was thinking, the last time I made this journey I was as green as grass about farming, and when me and Jennie had to go for the cows, to bring them in to milk, and they ambled along towards us we were terrified. But Linda thought, not as much as that bloody great stallion, Jennie and me knew the stallion man was coming, as Mr. Robson wanted brambles to have a foal, she is a lovely chest nut mare, and when the horse wagon drew up, and Mr. Carson walked him down the ramp, we had never seen a horse as big. Mr. Carson had hold of him by his bridle, in his out stretched hand, as the horse was so huge, he walked it in to the yard ,Jennie and me had gone behind the byre door, to watch the great big horse, he had a strange look in his eyes, and he was impatiently sniffing the air, his nostrils were flared, as he tossed up his mane, then he threw up his head and made deep rumbling whinny noises, as his eyes were blazing, he started pawing the ground, he was bucking ,and shying, as he beat his hooves on the yard, then he curled his lip back to reveal yellow teeth, then Mr. Robson, brought bramble outside, and when she saw him, she started doing a little dance, it took MR Robson all his time to hold her, then the big stallion, rippled his muscles ,and climbed on to brambles back. Jennie shouted look at the size of that Willie, Peter had moved along nearer to them and said, "If you girls come with me I'll show you a bigger one." Jennie had said no thanks, we have just seen one on that horse, and I bet you couldn't match that one. Linda felt as if she had travelled all day, she had been lost in thought, and now it was nearly six o clock, the train chugged in to the last station, Linda was nearly home, she opened the carriage door, and stepped out on to the platform, and the first person she saw was Alan, he asked?

"What has taken you so long, and have you enjoyed it?

First of all Alan, I felt the odd one out, I have never been to bed since I left here and I have spent my nights sitting in a bloody shelter, then the train I was going to get was two hours late, but thanks for looking after the bike, it'll be a while before I go back there." then she thought to her self if ever, but then she supposed she would have to if she wanted to see her family, as she knew they would never come up here to see her, as she biked up the road, she saw Jennie coming out of the farm gate, Jennie asked her if she had just got back? Linda said,

"you have no idea, what a time I've had, then she went on to tell Jennie, all about it, then she broke it to her about her mother, but the old lady is still going to give your address to your dad, if he shows up."

As they walked in to Ethel's, Wilf, Ethel, Gran, and the two boys, were sitting round the table, Ethel said,

"Come on you two, we were only giving you five minutes, and then we would have started with out you. Frank, and Colin, has been busy today, they went to school this morning, and then they have been turning hay, this afternoon with uncle Wilf."

Colin said, "We have been drinking milk all afternoon, Colin, and I, we got it from a cow, At home we got it from a bottle, Ethel had put them a huge dinner out, and she said to the boys,

"if you eat it all up, there is apple pie, and clotted cream, for after's," Linda thought, if Jane could see this food, she would realise she would be better off in the country ,Ethel was saying,

"Eva, and Prudence, is coming along tonight, to help turn the hay, so I will be doing the milking."

Linda said, "I will help you to do the milking, then I will help turn the hay." Gran said,"

"seen as you girls, Prudence, and Eva, are all going to be working, as you know I can't help, but I am going to do my share, in a different way, she looked at frank, and Colin, and said, you two can go along to Tommy's for me, and I will buy all the workers a drink."

Wilf said,

"There is no need Gran, I don't like to think of a woman buying me drink, and besides you haven't got a lot of money," she said,

"There is every need Wilf, would you like brow ale, same as Prudence, and all us girls, will have stout, Oh, I forgot Linda ,and Jennie, like Cider, so I will give you boys some money, and you can come straight back, and have some lemonade."

Later as Linda sat, with her head against the cows belly, filling the pail with milk, she felt as if she had come home tonight, she would be in a warm, comfortable, bed beside Jennie, and no bloody bombs going off, At nine o clock that night all the grass that was down, and had been turned, one field was ready to put in to small pikes, they all trudged back, in to Ethel's to enjoy a glass of what ever Gran had bought them, Ethel had set the table, with sandwiches, and cakes ,and milk for the children ,as they had drank the lemonade earlier.

Prudence asked Linda, "If she'd had a good journey,"

"No I didn't, it was crowded and tedious, and it will be along time before I go back again." "How did you get on with Robert? She asked Jennie.

"Oh Linda I enjoyed it, we went to the pictures, then he was telling me about his new posting, he took me along to have a cup of tea with his mam yesterday morning."Gran said,

"If you have a good bloke hang on to him, as I have always liked Robert, he is reliable, that reminds me, what time is that bugger coming tomorrow Eva?

"He's coming about one o clock Gran, I don't know why he wants to see me, as he hasn't bothered before."

"Well what ever it is Eva, he dose not mind, putting his self out for his own ends."

As Linda put her head on the pillow that night she was a sleep, Jennie had never seen any one go off as quick, but Jennie thought, if Linda had, two full nights with out sleep, and all the travelling, she would be worn out. Jennie laid awake thinking about her mam, wondering if she would ever see her again, Jennie thought she could at least sent her an address. The following morning as Linda, and Jennie, were bringing in the cows for milking, Mr. Robson was near the farm house, when he saw them getting near, he strode purposefully over to Linda,

"I see you are back with us then, I hope you wont go gallivanting off again, in the near future, as there is work to be done here,

Linda said, "I have nothing in mind, at the moment, but when I do I will let you know, as both Jennie, and me, are entitled to holidays." he turned on his heel his face as red, as beetroot, and stomped off, the girls started to giggle. As the land girls were herding the cows in for morning milking, Eva was sitting at home her mind was in turmoil, as she held the cup in her hand, she kept looking in to the brown sweet tea, as if her answer was in there she could not think straight. Violet, and Rose, were at school this morning, so when she picked them up, she would leave Margaret, and Shirley, at school and take Violet, and Rose, to her mam's ,Gran would keep a eye on them, if Ethel was busy, then when school finished, Prudence would go straight to mam's house, with Margaret, and Shirley as Joe, was coming this afternoon, Eva had done as Gran had said, "Its him that's after some thing, so let him come to you ,"but Eva kept thinking, what does he want, he has never bothered since he went away, and he never mentioned the twins, but then he never had bothered with them, If truth be told, he probably didn't know their birthdays, and the twins couldn't be missing him, as they never mentioned him, they seemed very happy lately, having Violet, and Rose, living with them. Eva couldn't help wondering ,what kind of a mother would let two little girls go to a stranger, and never enquire about them, it had been a very trying few weeks, what with the bed wetting, and nits, food had been a nightmare, as all they had been used to was chips, from the chip shop, they were pasty faced, little things when they first came here, she thought, but with plenty fresh air, and decent food inside of them, they were starting to fill out a little bit, Eva had given up looking for the postman, in the hope of getting a letter off their mother, The little girls had cried for the first few nights, for their mother, but they hadn't mentioned her now for a while ,Prudence's voice brought Eva back to the present.

"I thought I would find you sitting here moping over Joe, but I think, if you do as Gran says, you wont go far wrong."

"Do you think the same as Gran? Eva asked Prudence."

"What that he dose not intend living here again?"

"I don't know Eva, but as long as he is in the army, the railway authorities will they let you stay here? Hopefully, they will think that he is coming back to work for them, after the war, so it will allow us time, that's the trouble with these tied houses, and if he does not come back to you, we will need some where to live, but some thing will turn up Eva .Anyway you don't know, what he's after yet, Prudence took the cup out of Eva's hand, You've 'sat that long looking in to that cup that it has gone cold, I will make us a fresh pot, before the children get up.

CHAPTER 12

Mean while Joe, had just got out of bed, at the house that he shared with his pregnant girl friend, he had just started his leave last night, and he'd known he couldn't put it off much longer. He had to see Eva ,he knew by the letter she had sent, that she hadn't changed none, Joe was hoping that after such a long train journey, that she would of met him at the station, but oh no, he had to go to the house, three bloody miles he had to walk there, then three miles back, but if that was the only way he could see her, he would have it to do, he wouldn't be surprised, if that bloody old crow had told her to do that, but he would have to be pleasant to Eva, or she might refuse, then he would have had a wasted trip.

At Rosebud cottage, Ethel, and Wilf, had milked the cows, and delivered the milk, then as soon as they'd finished breakfast, Ethel had gone to feed all the pigs, and geese, the last to be fed was the hens, after Ethel had let them out, she gathered the eggs, Wilf was busy in the field turning the hay, and In the other field, where the pikes were standing, they would be made in to a stack tonight when every one would be here to help thought Ethel, As she went in to the out building to get the gripe so that she could lift the potatoes out of the garden, She thought by three months have gone quickly, since I planted these potatoes sets, I'd better fill a big bucket, as Eva, Prudence, and the children will be here as well for tea. As Ethel took the potatoes in to the house, to start and scrape them, Gran asked

"Have you brought the spring cabbage in? as you know it's me favourite cabbage, and I hope there is some left over, as I like it fried up, with the potatoes that's left over."

Ethel answered yes, "We have been lucky this year with the spring cabbage,

I just put the net over in time, to stop the wood pigeons, getting the young plants."

As Joe was getting nearer on the train, he was going over in his mind what he would say to Eva, he had never been stuck for words before, but he had a bad feeling he might be today, such a lot depended on the out come, and Joe thought it was time his luck changed, and he was bloody sick, of being stuck in this bloody compartment, there wasn't room to move ,the bloke next to him ,kept shoving his elbows in his ribs, the bloke had tried a few times to strike up a conversation with Joe. Now he was blowing smoke in his bloody face, Joe could feel the sweat running off his forehead and in to his eyes, it was running down his face as well, he could taste the bloody salt, his clothes were sticking to him, he could fancy a pint when he got off the train, better not, he thought about it, then he thought he had better keep a clear head. The train had stopped now; he wondered what had happened, as they were running late as it was. The bloke next to Joe was talking to him again, he was saying,

"I don't know why we have stopped do you? We might have broken down. Joe felt he'd had enough, for one day; he looked at the bloke and said,

"How the hell do I know? I'm on the bloody train same as you, and try and sit still, you keep shoving your elbows in my ribs, I will be bloody black and blue, and by the time I get off this train."Joe didn't realise, he was raising his voice, and every thing went quiet in the compartment, someone shouted over,

"There is a war on you knows, and you're not the only bugger that's quashed, but you are the only bugger that is making a fuss, "Joe was beginning to wish he hadn't come, but he knew he didn't have a choice. He was getting shoved and jostled along, now every one was shuffling again, someone must of thought that there was a tiny space, to squeeze a bloody big arse in, to it, he couldn't move along any more or he would be out of the bloody door, he was well, and truly stuck now, if he needed to blow his nose, he wouldn't be able to reach his bloody hankie. As the train finally pulled in to the station, Joe had to wait till some folk on the seat moved, so he could get up, as he opened the carriage door, his legs were so stiff, he tripped on the station platform, only just managing not to fall, now he thought I have a bloody three mile walk.

As Joe walked up the road, he was thinking this is the last time I will be coming up here, bloody back of beyond, he was now approaching Ethel's, there was Wilf turning the hay, but who the hell was them bloody kids? Joe was pleased, Wilf hadn't seen him, he preferred it that way, he didn't want anything to do with them buggers, no doubt that old crow, would be sitting in her rocking chair, watching out of the bloody window, it's a wonder the bloody old witch wasn't sending smoke signals to Eva, to let her know that he was on his way.

Eva kept walking to the window, if Joe was going to ask her? To move away from here, she didn't know what she would say, she didn't want too, but he was her husband, maybe she should give him a chance, and try and make this marriage work. Gran always said, "if Joe fell in shit, he would come out smelling of roses." And Gran did say, "He was coming today for his own ends."Eva was beginning to think he wasn't coming, when she caught sight of him coming up the road, Eva was feeling nervous, as it was a while since she had seen him, she felt like a young girl on her first date again.

Then he was there, walking in to the room as if he had never been away, and slumped down in to the chair,

"I've had one hell of a journey and a three mile walk, muttered Joe.

Eva thought, same selfish old Joe, "all self never asked after the twins, or how Eva was managing, Eva looked down at Joe, and asked to what I owe this visit? Although Joe had gone over his story a lot of times, he didn't know where to start.

"I want a divorce" he blurted out Eva was flabbergasted, she just stood rooted to the spot.

"Well I don't know what to say, this is a bolt out of the

blue, why now? Don't you care about the twins? Do you not think about my feelings?" She answered her own questions, "Well you have always, thought about your bloody self, Well I'm telling you now, you are going to keep paying for the twins, you are not getting away that easy, Why are you so desperate?"

Well if you sit down Eva, I will, tell you and besides, I'm getting a bloody crick in me neck looking up at you, as Eva stood menacingly over him.

"Well I have met someone else."

"Well she's bloody welcome to you, so you might as well go."

"Yes I will be pleased to be shot of you, and them bloody twin's Joe shouted as you never were any good, and you'll never alter."

"Shut the door on the way out," Eva shouted at Joe, as she threw the poker at him.

Joe was pleased, he'd got that over, by she was getting more like that bloody old Gran every day, and she had, just missed him with that poker.

After a while Eva made her way along to Ethel's, she had very mixed feeling's and she didn't feel very well, she thought it could be shock, after what she had just been told.

As she walked in to her Mam's, there was only mam, and Gran, in the house.

"Well are you going to give us the bad news or the good news first? Asked Gran

.Eva said, "It depends what you call good and bad Gran, He only came to day to ask for a divorce."

"Well I told you, to prepare yourself for a shock Eva, and if you think about it Eva, giving him a divorce, means you will be well rid of the bugger, you are still young, so you have chance to meet someone else, who's decent, you will feel better when you have eaten your tea, I always think its better to face problems, on a full stomach. We are having new potatoes, out of the garden, with some bacon, and egg's." As they all sat down to tea,

Linda said, "I really didn't realise how much I'd started taking this food for granted, until I went back home to see my family, you wouldn't believe, the shortages, and you can't get any food at all, without your ration card." Linda could see Gran's jaw's moving, as she was listening to what was being said around her. Then Gran said, "Don't forget to pour some of that fat, out of the pan over my potatoes our Ethel, I couldn't be doing with them shortages" Gran said, as she shoved another potato into her open mouth.

"Aye pour some fat on mine, as well Ethel please Wilf asked? As he said, you can't beet these new potatoes, straight out of the garden, as he patted his stomach, and smiled at Ethel."

Prudence said, "I've never had food as fresh until I came here, and I think I am putting weight on, but I can't resist Ethel's cooking."

Ethel said, "After we have all enjoyed our tea, we have them haycocks to gather in, and make a stack tonight",

Jennie said, "There is another two people coming to help as well tonight." Ethel looked up, and asked." "Who are they Jennie?"

"Well they are friends of mine, and Linda's, Jennie answered Ethel, they are land girls, just like us, they said they would rather work here, on a night, then stop on that farm ,where they were sent, where old John's at, he walks about with his button's open, and his private bits hanging out, he had an armful of hay thee other day, and asked Susan to put her hand in his trouser pocket, to get his pocket knife out, and the dirty old get, only had a bloody great hole in his pocket."

Linda said, "He is bloody disgusting, and he is sitting in that church, on a Sunday like a proper gentleman."

It wasn't long before Susan, and Mable, arrived Ethel said, "It's good of you to come and help us,"

Susan said, "its good to be out of the house, so if we hadn't come here, we would of gone to the pub ,to be out of his way, mind you it was worse still when his two sons were on leave, they used to try our bedroom doors on a night, but we used to wedge it shut."

Gran said, "It sounds as if him, and his sons, are sex mad, it's a pity they couldn't get some pills, or some thing to calm them down a bit."

Ethel asked, "Susan, and Mabel, what it was like working for him?"

Susan replied, "he tried to get hold of my bottom last week, so I picked the hay fork up and chased him with it, then I threatened to tell Mrs. Rain, but all she thinks about, is how to cut our food down a bit more."

Ethel, asked her? "Do you keep hold of your own ration books?"

MRs Rain has them, answered Susan,

"she demanded them as soon as we moved in, we didn't mind handing them over, it's just not right, her hanging on to them, as she doesn't feed us, I have been going out with brad he is a G I Susan explained, to Linda, and Jennie, we are going dancing this weekend, and they are sending some transport to pick us up, are you two coming? Linda looked at Jennie,

"Yes we might as well Jennie chuckled; it will be a look out."

Linda said, "I can't wait,"

Susan started to tell everyone, how "a lot of American solders, like going to ordinary family homes, on a Sunday afternoon, or Saturday, depending when they are off camp, and they bring loads of food." Gran had been listening, and she couldn't resist asking, what kind of food?

"Well one of my friends, Susan told Gran, invited about six American soldiers to her Mam and Dads house, and they brought, American style doughnuts, real huge oranges, big tins of corned beef, coffee, and a big bag of sugar, they bring allsorts of things." Gran's mouth was watering as Susan said, "I would never invite them to the Rains house, and as soon as Mabel and I find a fresh billet we are out of there."

"Have you got room for two lodgers, MRS Harrison? Susan asked cheekily, as Linda, and Jennie, are happy here."

"I'm sorry girls, Ethel told them, it pained her to turn them down as they seemed good lasses, but we are full up, I have a spare bed in the sideboard, but I will have to use that, when my husband comes back, at the moment I sleep with Gran." Wilf just felt jealously rush through him, when he thought about Jack, coming back to sleep with Ethel, he loved Ethel, and some day he would have a commitment off her, and he would wait, how ever long it took, and he knew Ethel cared for him.

Gran was sitting in deep thought, thinking about the food the GIs brought with them, and the girls seemed alright, and they were friends of Linda's, and Jennies, Gran said,

"There is a spare double bed in our room Ethel,"

"Yes I know Gran, but theses two young girls would not want to share a bedroom with us,"

"Susan, and Mable, both said together, we would Mrs Harrison, we promise we will be very quiet on a morning, so we don't waken you up."

Oh Ethel said, "you wont wake me, I will be up before you, as Wilf and me have twenty one cows to milk, and then we have to deliver it, Ethel made a decision, come back here tomorrow after work, and bring you clothes, and ration book, with you, I Suppose an extra two to cook for, wont make a lot of difference, all I seem to do is cook food, for more, and more people, Ethel asked them? Have you eaten any tea tonight?"

No she doesn't give us a lot remarked Mabel,"

Ethel was annoyed, that rain woman had the girl's ration books and was not feeding them, and well I will make sure you are fed, before you leave here tonight."

Next morning as the sun was rising, and it was looking to be another hot day, Wilf said,

"I tell you what Ethel, as they were sitting having a cup of tea, them four land girls are bloody good workers, I will have to get that field ready for turning tonight, and you are getting another two lasses, are you happy about that Ethel?"

"Well we will all have to muddle through together Wilf, with all of us now, when Eva ,Prudence, and the four girls come for a meal, we will have to have two sittings,"

"Them lads have changed a lot haven't they Ethel? And they have settled in alright, but I suppose its surprising how a few good meals, have swayed them."

"They have changed though Wilf, I don't know the last time I fed the hens, and gathered the eggs, they fill the mangers, and do allsorts of jobs, and I never have to ask them, I bet their Gran would get a shock, if she saw how much they have grown since they came here."

"Do you know Ethel, Wilf replied, "I have a feeling that them lads ,will never see her again, I think she would be pleased to be shot of them, It's a shame as they have turned in to nice lads."

"So after the war when all the kids go home they will have nowhere to go will they Wilf?"

"No they won't Ethel, but I can't see you kicking them out."

The next night Eva, prudence, and the four girls came for tea, so they could meet Susan, and Mable, Ethel had spent all afternoon cooking, but it was worth it to her, to see every one enjoying the huge dinner, that she had cooked,

"But they were full to bursting, as Susan, and Mable, said after they had eaten a big portion of plumb pie, and custard,"

Wilf joked to Ethel, "I hope you haven't over fed them he laughed as they have that hay to turn."

Linda said, "before we go to turn that hay, we where

wondering, if you would like to go the dance on Saturday night with us Eva?"

"Oh I couldn't, I'm married, and I have four girls to look after, and what would people say?" Gran spoke,

"First of all Eva, you are married in name only, and not for long,"

As far as the girls are concerned, Prudence said, "I'm not going any where on Saturday night,and I think it would do you good Eva, to go out for a change,"

Gran said, "enjoy yourself Eva, while you are still young, as Joe will not be given you a second thought, now that you have agreed to give him a divorce

Eva's eyes were shining, and her face was flushed, she said,

"I think I will come with you girls then, because I'm going to be old before me time, sitting in that bloody house day and night, but now I will wash all theses pots for mam." Prudence said,

"I will dryas there is a lot of washing up to do, Prudence turned round and looked, then she said, "By its gone quiet in here, all the kids have gone a well."

Gran said, Violet, and Rose, have filled out, since they came to you Eva and they seem happy enough, have they stopped wetting the bed?

"Oh yes Gran, Eva replied, "they are alright now, that they have some food and stability, I feel awful though some times, in stead of them calling me auntie Eva, they call me mam, like Margaret, and Shirley, I don't know what I would say, if their mother turned up, and they called me mam in front of her."

"Well she hasn't bothered up to now Eva," Ethel said, as she walked through the door, and just caught the end of the conversation."

"But its Violets birthday, in a fortnight's time Eva wailed, you'd think that she wouldn't forget that, but we will have to wait and see, and now Mam, I'm going to get the girls, and take them home to bed."

Prudence asked Eva, "Do you mind if I stop awhile and talk to Gran?"

"No Not at all Prudence, Eva replied, as mam will soon be starting to make every one a snack soon, for they will be hungry, after they have turned the hay."

"Will you bring Frank, and Colin, back with you, when you go for the girls   Eva? Ethel shouted after her, as she went out of the door, "then they can have a wash before going to bed" but Eva didn't hear the rest of the conversation, as she was half way across the field by then.

Saturday night arrived,and the four land girls who lived at Ethel's, were giggling, trying to paint a seam on each others legs, as they had no nylons, so they would have to make the best of it, and pretend they had. A straight line drawn down the back of the leg, looked the part, until it started to rain, but it was the best they could manage, or as Linda said," Until we meet the GI's." Eva was upstairs with the girls, joining in the hilarity, and sharing, each others make up, and clothes.

Frank asked "why do woman take so long to get ready Uncle Wilf, and share clothes?" I don't understand woman uncle Wilf."

"I don't either Frank,"Wilf said, as he shook his head, "If I live to be a hundred I will never understand them." just then the transport drew up, and Wilf could see it was full of girls, then the land girls, and Eva, ran down stairs, and wilf said,

"it's just like a bloody stampede, and laughed," Eva couldn't remember the last time, she'd enjoyed herself so much, she'd danced every dance, and she was never short of partners, they had done all the regular dances ,then the GIs were throwing them over their shoulders, jitterbugging, they called it, the girls were really enjoying themselves, Jennie noticed that Linda was sticking to the same lad, then she disappeared out side with him,and when Linda came back in, she was rearranging her clothes. Jennie knew what Linda had been doing, but it was nothing to do with her,she didn't realise she had been standing, watching for Linda ,when another GI came up to her, and said, "you can't stand there, when there is some dancing to be done," So Jennie found herself doing the hokey-cokey. There was more food then Jennie had ever seen, she had really enjoyed herself but she didn't want to get involved with any bloke, as she really liked Robert Lee, and they had agreed to write to each other. After the girls were dropped off and they were getting ready to go to bed, Jennie said,

"How could you Linda? You only met him tonight,

"Oh but I'm in love Jennie, and his name is Dale, and besides it was just a quickie against the wall",

"You'll look sick, if you get pregnant Linda, because I dread to think what Gran, and Ethel, would say,"

"Don't be daft Jennie, said Linda, who was getting irritated, you can't get pregnant, when you do it standing up, I should know, I've lost count of the blokes I've had against the wall. Linda started to giggle, as she said, there was hardly any room against that wall tonight, as all the girls leaning against it, had their knickers around their ankles,"

Jennie started to laugh, "I don't know you dare Linda,"

"Oh I'm game for anything Jennie, but we'd better get some sleep, as it will soon be milking time,"

Eva was pleased, she had gone to the dance with the land girls, as she had enjoyed herself, and everyone was friendly, she had seen Linda, go out side with Dale, she remembered going outside, and doing the same with Joe, but look where that had got her. She really loved the twins, but her life was complicated now, as Gran would say, "she was neither fish nor fowl," She couldn't go out, as regular as the girls she'd been with tonight, would be going out, but she was too young, to sit in for the rest of her life, and if she did meet someone, what would they say when she told them she had twins? Joe had a single life now, he could do as he pleased, Gran was right, when she said, "he had always looked after his self," and Eva had another problem next week. It would be Violets birthday, and Eva, wondered would her mother, bother to come up? Or would she just send a card and a present? Or may be doing nothing? So Eva thought, it's going to be down to me a usual.

Linda knew, that it was Violets, birthday next Sunday, and Eva, didn't know what to do, as she didn't have a lot of money, Linda was worriedly telling Dale all about it, when she met him a few nights after the dance.

"Well that's easy fixed, laughed Dale, me, and some of my buddies, will come and give the kids a party,"

"But how will you manage that, Linda asked? As I hope you won't let the kids down,"

Would I do that to you Linda? Dale asked, as he cuddled up to her, and I also like kids."

"Well If your sure, you'll not let us down, Linda told him, you'd better come and meet Gran, and Ethel, then, as it's their house," so it was arranged that it would take place the following Sunday afternoon, every one was excited, and waiting, for the jeep to arrive. Eva had made the four little girls a new dress each, for the occasion, and she had told them, it was for all of their birthdays, so they were having one big party. The GIs were running backwards, and forwards, carrying food in to the house ,there was a big jelly, and ice cream, also cakes, and a big bag of doughnuts full of jam and cream, a big sack of sugar, and a big tin of corned beef, for Ethel and Gran, there was a huge box of chocolate's. The table was groaning, under the weight of all the food, Grans mouth was watering, Ethel was standing looking at all the food, she couldn't believe her eyes at the amount of food, that they had brought, there was chicken, beef, pork, and plenty to drink for the kids, they could have orange juice, or tomato juice, Gran not being one to miss a trick, asked what was in the other box? Dale said lucky strike, and camel fag's ma..Gran had never seen any thing like it, but she would be telling them lads, they could visit any time they wanted. After the party had got going, Brad said,

"Oh you have a piano can anybody plays it? Ethel said, "

None of us can, I sometimes wonder why I brought it home? I should have listened to our Eva."

"Brad asked do you mind if I do as I love playing pianos at party's,"

Ethel said, "not at all it'll be good to listen to some music coming out of it." Brad sat down and began to play, there was soon some foot tapping, as he played the popular songs of the day.

Gran saw Linda, leave with Dale, after a while they arrived back, and Gran noticed Linda looked pink cheeked, She also noticed Wilf never left Ethel's side, Gran thought it's a pity, Ethel never thought about getting a divorce like her daughter Eva, Gran was trying to think, what the big blokes name was, that was deep in conversation with Prudence. Gran noticed that when he went over to speak to Prudence, she kept patting her hair nervously, as if to make sure that it was looking alright, she needn't of worried, as there was not one hair that could escape out of that tight band, that she had secured tightly to her head, it was getting late when the party broke up.

Ethel thought Wilf, wasn't looking very happy, and when she asked him what was the matter?

He said haughtily,

"I suppose it was good of them to come for the children's party, but we could have had one with out them, they are all show, it's like people are saying. They are over paid, over sexed, and over here, I bet they couldn't get out of bed on a morning and milk cows, and do a milk round? No they are all show Ethel. I just hope, they don't turn your head, are you listening to me Ethel? You look miles away said a jealous Wilf."

"Oh I'm thinking about that 7lb tin of corned beef Wilf, said Ethel with a far away look in her eye, and I will make sure,that none of it gets wasted, and that 4stone bag of sugar, will do us nicely." After every one had gone, Ethel, and Gran, was sitting enjoying their coca as Linda came back in, after saying goodbye to Dale. Gran said,

"I saw you disappear earlier, and I know what you were on with, so don't try and contradict me, as I'm not daft, Linda, fumed Gran."

"Oh we were only leaning against the wall talking Gran, lied Linda."

"You could of leaned against the wall here, Linda and talked, or sat down, it would have been more comfortable, so don't tell me bloody lies, but think on, there is a lot of children running around, that wouldn't of been, if their mothers hadn't been up against a wall, and these GIs are here today, and gone tomorrow, and they are all sweet talkers, till they get in to your knickers."Linda said,

"Eh Gran, you shock me,"

Gran said, "I was young once, and you'll be bloody shocked if he leaves you something to remember him by."

"Jennie has gone up said Gran, as she leaned forward in her chair, to glance out of the window, but where's them other two lasses? Susan and Mabel,"

"Oh they are coming in shortly, said Linda, trying to pacify Gran, as she looked round, to see if, Susan and Mabel, were coming in yet, they are just saying goodnight, Linda muttered."

Gran said, "I hope they have the sense to say it with there knickers on, because I don't know, what you lasses are thinking about some times."

Next day, Prudence, surprised Eva, by saying "she was thinking about getting her hair bobbed, what do you think Eva? Do you think it would make me look a lot younger? Eva asked her, "Has it had any thing to do with that GI."

Prudence turned crimson, and before she had chance, to answered, Eva said,

"Yes I think it would suit you, and it would be easier to look after, so when are you seeing Billy again?

Prudence said sulkily" how did you know I was?"

"Well you looked very cosy together from where I was standing the other night, Eva replied."

"No it has nothing to do with Bill, I just thought I would have it done, I have never had it done in years."

Eva was thinking the party had gone well, and all the food ,Mam was going to make corned beef, onion, and potato pies, this week she knew Mam wouldn't waste nothing, Eva was beginning to wonder if Violet, and Roses, Mam was alright, Eva had written to her, but had got no reply, and she wondered about their dad,did he not want to see his children? or may be he was like Joe, and didn't care about them, the poor little things, had just been dumped, and forgotten about, now which mother could forget their child's birthday? Eva wondered.

CHAPTER 13

In London June Parker was sitting enjoying her drink, she had moved in to this club now, with her boyfriend a spiv, he could get every thing he needed off the black market, as he had minders looking out for him,June Parker, Violet, and Rose's mam was working for him, as a hostess, her job was keeping the punters happy, and making sure that they spent a lot of money, she had every thing she wanted, and she loved this life, as she was never stuck for nylons, or anything now,as she was when she was stuck with Mark, and two kids, she some times thought, about Violet, and Rose, but she could never have them back, he would never agree, to them coming here to this club,as he didn't have time for kids, and she definately wasn't giving this life up for them, she would go next week, and see them, and give that woman who ever she was, Marks address, then that was her finished with them, if Mark wanted them when he came back, after the war, or if he came back? he could have them, she had never felt very motherly towards them, they were a blooming nuisance, she would tell Ross, after they had closed the club tonight,and she would send that woman word, that she coming to see the kids.After the club had closed Ross looked at her and said.

"If you must go, and see them kids of yours, make it the last time, and don't ever think about bringing them here, or you will be out. I don't want kids I thought you didn't either."

"Well I don't, she said with sincerity, I'm going to see them, and leave Marks address for that woman they are billeted with."

There is a bloody post you know June, Ross shouted at her." June didn't want to upset Ross, as he could get nasty, and after all he was her meal ticket, she was starting to wonder, what she should do? As she crossed one nylon clad leg, over the other, and smoothed down her skirt, as she drank her gin and orange.

After Ross had ordered his men to lock up for him, he crossed over to June and put his hand up her skirt, and said,

"Come on; let's see if it is worth your while leaving here, for the sake of two snotty nosed kids."

June made her mind up, as she teetered up to bed, on her high heels.

Two days later, Eva got a short letter, telling her that if she wanted, to get in touch, with Violet, and Roses dad, she had enclosed his address, as she wanted nothing more to do with Violet, and Rose.

As the letter arrived at Eva's from June, Eva read it, then she past the letter to Prudence, who said,

"Those two little girls are better off with out her." Eva wasted no time in writing to Mark, and telling him all about the letter, she had received from his wife June, and telling him, he would be very welcome to come, and visit the girls, when he had some leave."

Mark was a very happy man, when he received Eva's letter, which she had sent to him. He badly wanted to see his two daughters, he hadn't known where to start and look for them. He knew him, and June, were finished, and she had gone off with a bloody spiv, well Mark thought, he would soon tire of her, but to leave the kids, and not even going to see what this Eva was like,she was a heartless bitch. Well he would go to Eva's, the following weekend,as he had some leave to come ,he would write back, and tell Eva, that he was coming, he would find somewhere to stop when he arrived there.

When Eva received his letter, she told Prudence, that Mark seemed relieved to know where his kids were, and he was coming through to see them the following weekend. Eva explained to Prudence,

"I'm not saying anything to the girls, incase he doesn't turn up, his wife has never bothered, so there is nothing to say that he won't."

As Mark sat on the train heading for a reunion with his adorable, little girls, he was wondering how much longer it would take him to get there, he was hoping they were well looked after, but the woman called Eva, who was looking after them, had taken the trouble to write to him, so maybe his children were, getting looked after. As Mark left the station, and started to walk up the road, a bloke with a motorbike and sidecar drew up and offered him a lift, Tommy dropped him at Eva's gate, Mark felt happier now, that he'd been told that the girls were well looked after, and according to the pleasant bloke on the motorbike, this Eva was a canny lass. As Eva watched Mark, making his way down the garden path, she went and opened the door, she noticed Mark had light brown hair, and a ready smile, he shook hands with Eva, and introduced himself.

"Come on in then Mark, said Eva, with a smile, I have the kettle boiling, I expect you will be ready for a cup of tea, and a bite to eat? I 'll just calls the girls in then, as they all play well together," Eva went to the back door, and called the girls in,

"Go inside all of you, she said, as there is a nice surprise for Violet, and Rose. They ran in, and as soon as they saw their dad, they started to walk slowly, almost shyly. Mark had got out of the chair, and opened his arms wide, the girls looked at each other, and then they both ran in to his arms. Eva went to scold the tea, she had to keep busy, or she would of cried, the afternoon was going so quick, and the girls were wanting Mark, to go along and see the animals, and both Gran's.

Mark asked Eva? "If she would walk along with them, as he said, I can't just walk in to Gran's house." So Mark, Eva, and four little girls, walked in to Ethel's, Gran was pleased, that Mark had turned up, as after the war the little girls would have had nobody, and he seemed a nice enough lad. Wilf, and Mark, hit it off straight away, he even chatted away to Gran, Ethel said, after they had all been to see the animals,

"now as you are all here you might as well stop for tea and

Prudence, will call here first, as she is bringing some paraffin for the lamps," Ethel was going to let the boys have their teas outside as they said, it was too warm inside and it would be like having a picnic, the boys were helping a lot now, which made it easier on Ethel, but she still had a lot to do, as she had all the extra people to cook for, and still had the milk round to do. Wilf and Ethel had told Frank, and Colin, that they only had to do the farm work, if they wanted too, as Ethel would never force them. Ethel was cooking chips, tonight with corned beef pie, and peas, the children had chips now as a treat, rather then living on them, as they used to do, and there was apple crumble and custard to follow. Mark thought that, he would never eat, the food, that Ethel had placed in front of him, but he managed,and enjoyed it Just as they had been sitting down to eat, Prudence had arrived. Ethel had already put some tea out for her, as she pulled out a chair from under the table; Eva noticed Prudence's hair,

"I do like your hair Prudence, Eva was shocked that Prudence had gone through with it, when she had first mentioned having it cut in to a bob, Eva thought she was just talking," Every one agreed it suited Prudence,and Gran thought, it gave her a softer look, it took some of the sternness off her face.

Mark was talking to everyone, as if he'd known them for years, Ethel asked him where he was staying tonight?

"Well I will have to find somewhere, Mark replied, as I haven't given it any thought, as my mind was on seeing my daughters."

Prudence said, "he could stay with us couldn't he Eva?

"Well he could, said Eva panicking, but what will people say?"

Gran said, "What can they say? It isn't as if you're there on your own".

Eva said," well that's settled then, you can stay with us."

Gran said, "It's a pity your wife couldn't of come, and enjoyed the children, but I'm pleased, that you have come."

Mark confessed, "I'm going to divorce her, as our life together is finished." little did he know, that June's life, would be finished tonight, as the club got a direct hit, and there was no survivors.

Next morning when Mark awoke, he had to think where he was, as he rubbed the sleep from his eyes, he had spent a comfortable night in the pull out bed, of Eva's sideboard, he liked Eva, she treated his kids the same as her own, June his wife, had never been maternal, she only thought of her self, at least he could go back to camp, knowing that his kids were safe, and well looked after, he had told Eva last night, that he had been sending money regular, to June for the kids, but from now on he would send it to Eva, after all it was Eva that had the kids, and June was keeping the money, and not sending it on to Eva. Mark thought that Joe, must be crackers going off with someone else, Mark had one more night, and then he would head off back to camp, Eva had just come downstairs, with all the girls following her, Marks little girls, went over to him, and asked him? If he would stop here and live with them? Violet said she liked being here with auntie Eva ,and auntie Prudence, and they liked going along to Gran 's ,as they had two Gran 's, and a uncle Wilf ,and they were telling Mark, how they went for walks, and saw all the animals. Mark knew he would go back to camp with an easy mind now, as they were getting good food .Eva was busy frying egg ,and bacon, for breakfast, and inviting Mark, to come and stay when ever he wanted. Mark said after breakfast,

"I thought about taking the girls along to your mams for a walk Eva and I've enjoyed talking to Wilf, so should we all go along together?"

"yes mam would like that replied Eva, she loves all the girls,lately mam has a full house, so she spends a lot of time cooking, as you know she has Colin, and Frank, the two evacuees, and the four land girls, she only had Linda ,and Jennie, then their friends needed some where to stay, so Susan, and

Mable, arrived Eva was telling Mark all about the party, for the children ,and how she'd had a night out, at the dance. Eva said it was the first night out I'd had in years."

Mark said, the next time I have some leave, I'll take you to the pictures, as you have been good, letting me stop here."

Eva said, "I will look forward to it, as I know; Prudence will look after the girls for us,"

You know Eva, "I was a country lad once, I was brought up in the country, and when I was twelve, my parents moved down south, I always intended coming back up here, but I met June, and there is no way she would of lived in the country, then I was called up to do my bit, but when this lot is over, I intend to settle in the country, with Violet, and Rose."

Eva said, "I could never live in a city, more so now with all the bombs dropping, and having to queue for food, she laughed as she said, living up here we hardly know there is a war on."

As the land girls made their way home,

Susan said, "I don't know about you three, but I'm knackered,

"Why asked Linda, what have you two been doing today?"

Susan said, "It was bad enough, when MR Rain had his sheep sheared, and we had to run around and catch them",

Mable said "we had to roll all the fleeces up, then we had to store them in the barn, till the bloke came to take them away, well he came today for them, and you know how hot it's been outside today, so imagine how hot it was for us in that bloody barn, having to carry all them fleeces out ,and they still have all the oil in them, so my hands were shining, and I was trying to milk the cows, and my hands were sliding off the cows udders.

Jennie said," the sheep would be pleased, to get shot of all their wool in this hot weather, I didn't realise they had such spindly legs."

"Oh we see a lot of sheep's legs said Mabel, as they always have muck round their backsides, and it sticks to the wool, so we have to clip it off with clippers."

Linda said, "On Monday MR Robson wants Jennie and me, to start hedging, but tonight and tomorrow night we'll be helping Wilf to stack all his hay."

Mable said, "Me, and Susan, will help, then we'll go along to the pub, as I think we will have deserved a drink."

Linda thought, what care free lives we live up here, compared to my family, and all those people that live in the city's, Linda had received a letter a couple of days ago, telling her that her brother David, who was in the army, had come home to introduce his new wife to every one. Linda felt as if she was getting further away from her family, as her brother Liam, had got married last month, and she'd never met his wife, if it wasn't for Jane, Linda would never know what was going on, Linda had wrote to her mum, a few times, but had never received a replie,when she had asked Jane about it ,Jane had replied, that mum had said, if Linda was daft enough, to go and live in back of beyond ,that was her look out, she had plenty to do going to work,and having to queue for food,there was house work, to be done, if you were lucky enough to have a bloody house, after them planes had been over, and then having to sit, in that bloody shelter, on a night, with out having to write bloody letters. Jane had said, "She felt worn out with it all, and it wouldn't be long before the new baby arrived." Linda wondered how the hell, would she fit three baby's into that old heavy black pram. Linda's mind had wandered, and she had been lost in thought, since they had mounted their bikes, and now they had reached Ethel's.

There was Wilf, leaning over the garden wall, talking to Jim he was an old man, but he enjoyed growing flowers, and as Wilf, always made sure, that Jim and his wife always had plenty of vegetables; the old man had started bringing flowers to Wilf, for Ethel. Wilf always used to refuse flowers, until now, as he always said "what good are flowers to me" but he knew Ethel loved them, Linda noticed that Wilf had a bunch of flowers ,and as Ethel was dishing the tea out, Wilf walked in with the flowers in his arms, and handed them to Ethel, she said,

"Oh Wilf, they are beautiful, I've never had any flowers given to me, before, you gave me some."

"Aye I know Ethel, Wilf said, and I've never had such good meals, till I started coming here, so I will put these flowers in a vase for you, till you finish dishing up, then we can all sit down and have our teas." Wilf asked, Ethel,

"Has Eva, Prudence, and the four children, been a long today?"

"No Ethel said as she shook her head, but I do know, that our Eva received a letter today, as I was talking to Sam, the postman, and he said, he had delivered a letter to our Eva's this morning, so if she calls tomorrow she'll tell us who it's from." later on in the night, as the girls were getting ready to go the pub, Eva, Prudence, and the four girls called at Ethel's.

Eva said, "We have been for a walk," and Prudence, said,
"I've been commiserating with Eva,"Gran said

"What the hell are you talking about Prudence? And what does that mean." "Well I have been feeling sympathy then,Prudence spluttered,just some times she really felt like telling Gran,what she thought about her, as she, Prudence, was the educated one, yet Gran could make her feel stupid, by not understanding, some of the words,Eva got a letter this morning from Mark."

Wilf said, "are you girls coming with me, to fasten the hens in,as Wilf thought there may be trouble ahead, as there was a force to be reckoned with, if Gran, and Prudence crossed swords, Frank, and Colin, are around there now,so hurry up girls." as the door closed, behind Wilf ,and the girls,

Eva said, "Marks wife is dead, you know the weekend,

that Mark, was here seeing Violet, and Rose, their mother, Marks wife, was in the club, with her boyfriend, and it got a direct hit."

Gran said, "I for one would lose no sleep over her, if she'd been here, where she should have been, seeing her little girls, she would still be alive."

Ethel asked Eva, how did Mark find out? It must have been a shock for him,

"when he went back to camp, mam, Eva was trying to explain, as tears were running down her cheeks, his commanding officer called him in, and told him that his wife's parents, had sent word, they knew she was living with another man, So Mark, is all, Violet, and Rose, have left, as her parents, don't want any thing to do with them."

Gran said, you'll not be saying anything to the children will you? Gran looked up at everyone , when she'd finished, dipping her biscuit, into her cup of tea, and with a toothless grin,as if she had just thought about it, she said "Every cloud has a silver lining, it'll save Mark divorcing her."

Eva said, "I'm not saying any thing to the children, any way it's not my place, and they never mention her, but I didn't think you would have been so heartless Gran."

"Well it's just like this our Eva, if she'd lived; those two little girls wouldn't have seen her, so it's not going to make a difference to them."

Just then Wilf brought the four girls back, and the four land girls finished doing each others hair, then went to the dance. As Eva, Prudence, and the four girls walked back along home, Prudence said, "

"The more I see of your Gran, the more I like her, she has a no nonsense outlook, on life, its just that she some times makes me feel a fool."

CHAPTER 14

The land girls were all enjoying their social life, the dances on a Saturday night, run by the Americans, were not to be missed, as far as the girls were concerned, even Prudence was going out regular with Bill, Eva noticed her taking care over her appearance, Eva had never known her, to wear makeup, and gone were the thick stockings, and sensible heavy shoes ,that she wore when she first arrived, Susan, and Mable, had settled in very well at Ethel's, the girls worked hard. But Gran said "they played hard as well." Jennie, and Linda, was still working for MR Rain, and he seemed, to find the worst jobs, for the girls, but they took it in their stride, Linda was saying to Jennie,

"We'd better get on, and sharpen theses scythes, so we can cut theses thistle's, roll on the weekend, then we can go dancing, as there is no eligible men around here."

Jennie said, "Oh I don't know about that, I found Robert round here."

Linda said, Oh I like playing the field,but I don't want to end up like our Jane, as soon as she has one kid, she is away again, I think I have told you Jennie, when I went home on a visit, our Jane, had aged ten years."

"Well at least you have been home, Jennie unhappily, told Linda, and I have no one to visit."

"Well it'll be a bloody long time, before I go again, Linda retorted."

MRs Roberts had been as good as her word,when she'd promised to help Jennie, so she had watched, every morning for the postman, incase there should be a letter from Jennies dad, then one morning as she watched for the postman, she saw a middle aged man, in army uniform ,making his way towards her, as he got closer she recognised him, as Jennies dad, he went over to Mrs Roberts, and asked her, if she knew where, his wife, and daughter, had gone? Mrs Roberts said,

"You had better come in lad, and besides, I have some tea in the pot, and I expect you could do with a cup? Jennies dad looked relived, when he found out that Jennie was alright, he said, "he knew there was some thing wrong, as he'd not heard from his wife, for a long time, but now I have Jennies address, I 'll catch the next train,"

Mrs Roberts said, "look lad, you've been travelling all last night, and all morning, so why don't you stay here tonight? And have a fresh start in the morning."

Norman Bowron said, "I couldn't put on you, Mrs Roberts."

"You wouldn't be putting on me lad, you would be a bit of company, so at night, while the bombs dropped, Mrs Roberts and Jennies, dad slept, uninterrupted till morning."

Next night as Jennie walked in to Ethel's after work, she got a shock to see her dad sitting talking to Gran, he looked up then went over to Jennie, and cuddled her, Jennie was so over come to see her Dad, that she had tears running down her cheeks,as she was saying,

"Oh Dad, I didn't know if I would ever see you again?"

Norman was invited to have tea with them all; he kept looking at Jennie, and saying how well she looked. Wilf asked Norman where he would be staying.

Norman said, "I have no idea Wilf," Jennie asked Ethel?

"Could Dad sleep, in the pull out bed in the sideboard please Ethel" Ethel thought about it then she said, "Well I don't see why not, it's only for a couple of nights."

Norman said, "I will be no trouble to you, and I'll help with the farm work." Wilf scowled at him, and spoke sharply to him,

"Ethel does not need another man, to help her she has me,then he looked at Norman and said, I would of thought,that you would of arranged,some accommodation, for yourself, when you arrived here,

158

Jennie said, "It's alright Wilf, I'll make sure that Dad, isn't under your feet, I will go in to work tomorrow, and tell MR Robson that Dads here, and ask him if I can have two days off?

Linda said, "you needn't bother, going in to ask him anything as you haven't taken your holidays yet, so when I go, in the morning, I will tell him, that you are not coming in for a couple of days, as your Dad is here."

As Linda cycled down the familiar road, she thought, old Robson wouldn't be very happy with her, once she told him about Jennie, but she deserved a holiday, and to spend a bit of time with her Dad, as God knows how long it would be before she would see him again. Linda thought there seemed to be a atmosphere, at Ethel's when Wilf, and Norman, were sitting together last night, but this morning when she had set off to work, there had only been Ethel, and Wilf, sitting by the fire, having a cup of tea before they started the milking, Susan and Mable had left for work before Linda. Ethel was wondering what Jennie would find to do today, with her dad as she had told Ethel; that he had always lived in the city.As Gran and Jennie were walking towards the kitchen, so that Gran could sit in her rocking chair, Norman woke up and rubbed his eyes, as he yawned, then stretched, he looked at his wristwatch, and thought it's only six o clock, its early yet ,but he presumed country folk, did rise early, he couldn't believe the silence outside, no sound of people walking, talking, and calling to each other, there was no buses, or horse drawn vehicles ,none of the noises,that he would associate with morning, as he sat up in bed he could hear bird song, and the cockerel was greeting the hens, to the start of a new day, he didn't think he could live with all this silence, but Jennie seemed to have taken to it, as he got out of bed he saw Wilf, going past the window pushing a barrow loaded with churns, Ethel was walking by his side, they must be going to deliver the milk, Norman thought, country people were well off, compared to the city folk, that was if you could stand the boring life, he couldn't believe how well the land girls had settled. As Norman made his way into the kitchen, he saw the big black kettle, that sang, and spluttered, on the fire that was burning brightly, for Ethel and Wilf's return,

"Come and sit down Dad, Jennie beckoned him, would you like some porridge? Gran likes hers, with plenty sugar, and creamy milk."

Norman said, "by but you eat well here Jennie."

Gran said "I like my grub as well, I always have," Jennie brewed the tea as Ethel, and Wilf, walked in. Gran said,

"Will you slice some of that side of bacon, Ethel please?"

"I will do it now Gran, Ethel replied, then I will fry it for breakfast." as Ethel set off through to the scullery,

Norman asked "couldn't I do it for you Ethel?" As Wilf was standing near Ethel, he impulsively put his arm around her, and said,

"No you will not, it's alright I will see to it, I usually do, we don't need your help." Wilf came back carrying a plate of sliced bacon, ready for Ethel to fry; he turned to Jennie, and said,

"Have you thought where you are going to take your Dad today Jennie? you could may be take him, for a long walk and show him around." As far as Wilf was concerned, as far away as possible from Ethel .Gran had watched Wilf for a while now, any one could see he loved Ethel, and Gran thought, they could have a good life together, if only something could be done about Jack. Gran had never believed In divorce, it wasn't the done thing in her day, but now, she was older, and she had time to sit and think, and watch what was happening, it seemed a pity to stop with someone for the look of it, look at poor Eva ,what a sod Joe was to her, but now there divorce was going through, mind it had helped Eva, having Prudence there for company and someone to confide in, even Shirley, and Margaret, were looking happier, as Joe had never bothered about them, also Eva wouldn't of been able, to take violet, and Rose, in if he had of been there, they were two nice bonny little girls, they all played and lived together happily. Gran gathered her thoughts, but soon stored them away, when she got the whiff of the bacon frying .Ethel knew there was some thing wrong with Wilf, he was usually pleasant with every one, even when all the land girls, and Frank, and Colin, were in, just then the boys came downstairs,

"We will just go and feed the hens, and gather the eggs, for you Auntie Ethel". "No have your breakfast first, Ethel told them, as it's nearly ready."

Norman said, "You have a lot to cook for, and look after Ethel, if you need any help, you only have to say."

"Oh she manages well enough, Wilf gruffly replied, and she always has me to help her." Ethel thought, Wilf is not going to be very tolerant towards Norman. Jennie said,

"After breakfast Dad, I 'll take you out, and show you around, then this afternoon, I will introduce you to Prudence,as she comes from the same city as us." Ethel said, "Prudence will probably come along today, with our Eva, as she is supposed to be coming, to help me make the butter.

CHAPTER 15

The pig breeding was growing fast, Ethel, and Wilf, had made money out of the pigs, more then Ethel could of imagined, but Wilf had a good business head on him, and they split everything, including the money between them. They'd had a pig butchered yesterday, so Ethel had plenty of pork, at teatime Norman couldn't believe, the meal that Ethel dished out for every one, the children all sat on the floor with their plates on their knees, as there was so many adults to feed, Norman had never seen Yorkshire puddings, rise as high as Ethel's, the potatoes, and vegetables, that Ethel had grown, were delicious, and the amount of meat, she had piled on his plate, would have fed a family in the city.

Wilf was pleased, to see that Norman was taking an interest in Prudence, he didn't dislike him as a bloke, as long as he didn't show an interest in Ethel.

Norman thought, no wonder them land girls including Jennie, looked so well with meals like this and country air, it was along time since he'd had a meal as good as this, mind you when he thought about it, he'd never had one as good, his wife wasn't a good cook, well she was good at anything really, apart from lying on her back, he should of never married her, he knew, she had been with numerous men, but the best thing, that came out of that marriage was Jennie, when he looked down at his plate, he'd been eating, as he'd been remembering, and now his plate was nearly empty. Ethel was handing him a big bowl of treacle sponge, and custard, he glanced across at Gran, who was shoving her dinner down her throat, as though her life depended on it, the old girl seemed to sit and eat all day.

Linda asked Jennie, "If she had enjoyed, showing her Dad around the village?"

"Oh yes I have, Jennie answered happily, and we had a lot of catching up to do."

Norman said, "I'm so pleased, that she left her forwarding address, with Mrs Roberts, or who knows, we might never have seen each other again."

Linda said, "I have had a hard day, cutting thistle's down in the pasture fields."

Norman raised his eye brows, and looked at Linda, "I thought a field was just a field."

Jennie said, "Oh dad you don't know anything about country life, do you? A pasture is a field, where the animals graze, and a hay field is left to grow, then its cut and the grass turn to hay, that feeds the animals in the winter."

Prudence laughed, and, "never mind Linda, it will keep your waist line trim, may be I should learn, how to use a scythe." Linda thought Prudence, had a lot softer side to her, when you got to know her, and she had lost the startled look with getting her hair bobbed, because when she had it pulled back, her eyebrows practically reached her hair.

Susan the other land girl had her hair tied back, and round her ponytail she had a ribbon, it kept her hair out of her way, when she was working, but when she went out she let it flow on to her shoulders, hers was not severe, as she had a fringe which came down to her eyebrows,Susan, and Mabel, worked on a different farm to Linda and Jennie, the four girls often said, it would have been good, if they had all worked on the same farm. Linda was telling Jennie,

"Tomorrow when you come back to work Jennie, we have to start hedging, in the bottom field."

Norman said "what ever's that?" everyone started to laugh,

Linda said, "Our arms will probably ache tomorrow night."

Jennie explained to her Dad, "its called a slasher and it has a long blade, and a wooden shaft, its about 3ft long, and we have to cut all the hedges, and all the bits we cut off go in to a pile, then we set fire to it, but he has a lot of hedging in that bottom field, he had a bloke there today, mending the dry stone wall."

Prudence asked Linda, "When will brambles have her foal?"

Jennie said, "Not for a while yet, it takes 11 to 12 months, and they come in to season as soon as they have their foal, so just think, a horse could have a foal every year."

Norman said, "You have a lot of knowledge about the country side Jennie, I'm impressed, then he asked, who is going to the pub with me tonight? Would you like to come along Ethel? Before she had time to reply,

Wilf said, "We have arranged, that I will go along to the pub, and get a couple of bottles of stout, for Ethel, and Gran, so we will stop here and have a drink."

Norman then turned and asked Prudence, if she would like to come along? She said,"Oh thank you, I would love too, and then she asked the girls, are you coming?"

"Yes answered Susan, but you two can go on ahead, until we all get washed and ready."

Norman and Prudence walked along to the pub arm, in arm, giggling as if they had known each other for years.

Gran said, "Bloody hell, Prudence is full of surprises, she doesn't let the grass grow under her feet, but I suppose at her age, she can't afford too."

Wilf said, "Me neither, what are you going to do about Jack?

Ethel said, "He has probably forgotten all about me now."But Ethel would never know how far wrong she was, as Jack her husband, was sitting in a pub, near the dock's, at Portsmouth thinking he might have to go and see Ethel, surely that old Gran would of died by now, Ethel was the only relation that she had, so she would leave, all she had to Ethel.

Jack had enjoyed all theses years living with Betty in

Portsmouth, he'd met her, when she was plying her trade,and as Jack was a good talker, it wasn't long before, he moved in to her flat with her, and lived on her earnings, but she looked haggard now, and didn't make the amount of money that Jack was used too, Jack knew he was ill, he'd caught a dose off Betty, along time since, but Jack knew it was a risk you took when you went with woman like Betty, she went with all the sailors, and he had lived with her along time now, although he spent his time, and her money in the pub. when he went back to the flat, and she had blokes in, he just went to bed, and when she was in bed making money, he just got in beside them, and went to sleep, as long as she made enough money to keep him in drink, she would be alright, But the first time, there was no money for him, she would get a bloody good hiding, Jack knew he would have to be looked after sooner then later, as his dick was so rotten with pox, it was a wonder it didn't drop off,and he couldn't see Betty looking after him. He would go to Ethel's, after all she was his wife, she had a right to look after him, then he remembered, he had a daughter, but he couldn't remember her name, He thought he would hang on here, as long as possible, then when he felt he didn't have long left, or that dirty cow, didn't make enough money he would go to Ethel's.

"I didn't know that we were going to have a bottle of stout tonight Wilf, Ethel looked hard, at wilf, as if she was looking for an explanation." But before Wilf could find the right words,

Gran said, "You'll be glad to see the back of Norman wont you Wilf? Well you have nothing to worry about, he's not after our Ethel, and he has his eye on Prudence."

Ethel's face was an expression of disbelief, is that why, you ignored him most of the time Wilf? Did you think he had taken a fancy to me?"

"Well it's like this Ethel, Wilf started to stutter, Norman lingered next to you tonight."

"Well he had to Wilf, Ethel was getting vexed, when we

are all in here, we have to stand close, as there is no bloody room."

"Yes I suppose you are right Gran said, as she thought about it, I'm pleased that's settled, now are we going to have a bottle of stout tonight or not?"

A long at the pub, the girls kept the other land girls company, while Norman and Prudence chatted away as if they had known each other along time, Norman asked, "Will you write to me Prudence? And I will come up here as much as possible to see you and Jennie."

"Yes I will Norman, Prudence said, smiling at him, and I will look forward to your visits."

Along at Eva's house, she'd got all the girls to bed, but she couldn't be bothered to wait up for Prudence, and as the wooden clock, chimed the hour on the mantelpiece, she went to bed. She was thinking, Prudence is a lot older then me, but her social life, is getting better by the day."

Next day as Jennie was back at work, after the cows had been milked, Linda and her, went in to the outbuilding's and collected their slasher's. it was a hot day and a warm breeze was blowing,as the girls worked they were sweating,as it was physical labour,cutting the hedges, they also had a fire burning behind them, to get rid of the hedging that they had cut off .

Linda said, "I don't think, I've ever been so hot in all of my bloody life, then she said, your Dad, and Prudence, looked cosy thee other night in the pub, I thought Prudence, was going out with Bill."

"Oh said Jennie, she told Dad, that Bill, was just an acquaintance."

"Well Linda laughed, I've heard it called all sorts, when you're seeing two fellers, but never an acquaintance, I thought Prudence seemed to think a bit about Bill though, don't you Jennie? Asked Linda

Gran was saying, "It wont last, Prudence will get her heart

broken, Gran has some funny notions though, doesn't she Linda?" "Well Jennie, I think, Bill is honest, and lonely, and I don't think, Prudence has ever had a social life, so good luck to her."

Back at Ethel's house, they were all sitting having tea, and Susan, asked Ethel, "is it alright? for some G Is, to come to the house, on Sunday for tea, as you know, that they will bring their own food, and plenty for all of us, and we are all going dancing again on Saturday night, aren't we girls, and besides, in three weeks time, some of them are getting shipped out."

Mable said it's alright, as they are bringing some more in."

On Saturday night, when the girls arrived at the dance, Prudence, and Bill, were already there, they were on the floor doing the tango, and later on when Mabel, went to get a drink, they were still dancing, they were doing the waltzes now, but as Susan giggled, as she said, "it would be no good them two jitter-bugging, as Bill would never be able to through Prudence over his shoulder."

Linda said, jealously, "look at him, dancing with Eva, he has his shirtsleeves rolled up, look at his tanned muscular arms, she manages to get all the good looking blokes."

Mabel said, "Eva wasn't coming out tonight, because Prudence is out, and she thought she would have nobody to look after the girls, but with Jennies dad, going back to his unit, the bed in the sideboard, at Ethel's is available, so the girls are staying there, Ethel has put two girls at the top of the bed, and two at the bottom, and Ethel enjoys having them to stay, and it gives Eva a social life."

Linda said, "I think they they will be a good help to Ethel tomorrow, as she has a lot of fruit to pick for jam, the boys Frank, and Colin, have picked all the gooseberry bush bare, but tomorrow Ethel wants, the strawberry, raspberry, and redcurrants, picking from her garden, also the blackberry's are all ripe, and ready for picking, she said, she would bottle the plumbs, and keep the apples, in straw, Ethel was gob smacked wasn't she Susan, when the GIs turned up, with a four stone bag of sugar."

Mabel couldn't believe the meals, that Ethel cooked for them, they had landed on their feet coming to live with Ethel, and no mistake, Mabel knew that, that there was another bag of sugar, coming tomorrow, as she had asked the GIs, to bring one, as she knew, Wilf, would be bringing all of the fruit, from of his own garden, he has already, brought an armful of rhubarb along this morning."

Ethel made her own chutney, as well as the jars of jam, and by they tasted lovely, she made enough to last, until the berry's were ready, to be picked the following year.

The dance hall was starting to liven up, every one was up dancing, the dances that the GIs put on, were not to be missed, as they provided food, and plenty of it. Tomorrow the GIs would come back along to Ethel's, loaded down with food, and Mable, couldn't help smiling to her self, as she thought about Gran, now! She liked her food.

As Ethel, and Wilf, sat either side of the fire, in the rocking chairs,they had the house to them selves, as Gran was in bed, they felt snug, and warm, as the rain out side, lashed against the glass in the windows. Wilf,looked over at Ethel,and asked her, "would you like to go to the pictures Ethel?,or I could take you dancing, if you wanted to go, only, I'm not much of a dancer, I feel as if I have two left feet."

"Well as you know Wilf, Ethel, tenderly,replied,I'm not one for gallivanting about, it's pleasant sitting here, quietly talking to you, as it's rare that we are able, to sit together just me and you."

Wilf had long since gone home, and Ethel, was tucked up in bed, before the girls all arrived back from the dance, they wouldn't be in bed long, before they all had to get up again, to go and get the cows in to milk, that's all they did on a Sunday, and later on in the day the GIs were coming.

Next morning after the land girls had gone to work ,Eva walked along to Ethel's, to collect the four little girls, she found they had all enjoyed a good breakfast, of egg and bacon, Wilf, had black pudding, with his egg, and bacon, and so had Gran, after breakfast, Margaret, Shirley, Violet, and Rose,had gone out, in to the garden, to help Ethel, pick the berrys ,when Eva mentioned,taking the girls home, they asked to stay with their Gran? Ethel, Eva, turned to Ethel, her mother, and said,

"I will take the girls home shortly, but we'll be back along later, with Prudence, as all the GIs seem, to be able, to bang out a tune on that old piano." It seemed to Eva ,such a long time ago, since her Mam, and her, were pushing the barrows up the road, and the bloke with the horse, and cart, delivered her and her mam some things, Eva thought at the time, that her Mam, was mad, getting a piano, but they'd had some lively nights with it. Eva was happy now Joe had gone, and Margaret, and Shirley, never mentioned him, they seemed a lot happier, if Joe was in the house, he was always complaining about the twins, and they were getting on very well now, with Violet, and Rose. Eva ,was thinking about Violet, and Roses, Dad Mark, he was sending, Eva money regularly for the two girls, and he always enclosed a letter enquiring about the girls, and not just his own, he always included Margaret, and Rose,and Eva always wrote back to him. Eva, never used to see the postman, but he called regular now, apart from Marks letters which she looked forward too, she'd received a lot of forms to sign, for the divorce, she had felt deflated, when Joe, had asked her for a divorce, she was wishing it was all over, and she didn't think she would ever see him again, and she didn't want to neither.

Ethel was asking Eva, "If she wanted to help pick the Berrys, or go in for a cup, or would she rather stand there daydreaming?"

"I was lost in thought Mam, but I will help you now, seen as you had all the girls last night for me."

"Oh they were no bother, Eva, but what do you think about Prudence and Bill," Ethel wanted to know

"Well as long as she is happy Mam, Eva answered, but Bill is American, so if they stop together, Prudence will be going to America after the war and I will miss her."

"Yes,Gran and me will as well,"answered Ethel in deep thought, as she liked Prudence, and didn't like the idea of her going away,but then she realised life goes on,and also , what time a day it was, she said to her self, "I'd better get on as well."

Susan and Mabel arrived back home from work, before Linda and Jennie.

Gran said, "You've finished in good time today, have you done all your work?"

As she ran her fingers through her dishevelled hair, Linda replied, "We have rushed about all morning so we could get ready before Dale and his friends arrive."

Bill had arrived earlier, on his own, in a jeep, and he went straight along for Prudence. He was telling her that he was one of the first soldiers that was getting moved on next week.He asked Prudence if she would write to him and the next time he had some leave, they could may be get married, but he would let Prudence make the arrangements.

Prudence was over the moon, "Are you asking me to marry you Bill? " She was jumping with joy."If so, of course I will."She couldn't wait, to tell every one, especially Gran."Then she realised and said, "But what about your family bill, surely they would want to see you getting married?" Bill replied,

They are in America ,you'll meet them after we are married, and we'll need, plenty of photos, as my Mum, and sisters, will want to see them, as I have wrote and told them all about you, and said I would like you to be my wife,so they will all be looking forward to meeting you."

When the GIs arrived, the land girls were all washed, and changed, and ready, for a good afternoon. Prudence only seemed to have eyes for Bill after she had made a grand entrance, and making sure, that everyone knew that she was marrying Bill.

The G.I's and land girls, were a lot younger then Ethel, so she filled Gran's, plate wilf's, and her own plate, full of food, and took it through to the kitchen, where she would stay with Gran, and Wilf ,as Ethel, walked into the kitchen,she said, "

Linda is not in there, with them, so I thought she must be in here."

Gran said, "Linda has never been in here, she will be outside canoodling, with a bloody soldier, and there's another bugger, that bloody Prudence, she's heading for a fall with Bill, she's hardly known him five minutes, and talking about getting married."

"I suppose people, are getting married quicker, now Gran, then before, Ethel tried to reason with Gran, with there being a war on, they are trying to find a bit of happiness, for a few days, incase their boyfriends don't make it back."

But Prudence is going around with her head in the clouds, Ethel but marks my words; she will come back to earth with a bump."

Prudence walked back in to the kitchen, and stood beside Gran and said, "I know you don't approve of me, and Bill, getting married as quick, as what we are, as her eyes narrowed at Gran, but we do love each other, and it will last."

Gran sniffed, and looked at Prudence, as if she was mad, and said, "Aye time will tell."After everyone had gone Gran said to Ethel,

"Those young lasses are getting very free with their favours, but I think there will be trouble ahead for a lot of them."

A week after Bill, and a lot more, including Mable's boyfriend, were moved, or shipped out as the GIs called it, a lot of girls from all over the country were upset, and all they would have, of their boyfriends ,were letters, apart from Mable, as her condition, would come to light in a few weeks time.

All Prudence could talk, and think, about was her wedding, Eva was making a new dress each for the girls, as she would have to run some thing up for her self as well, she had always been good at sewing, her most prized possession, was her treadle sewing machine, Mam, Gran, and Prudence, had plenty of coupons for a new rigout, Prudence had never bothered, buying many clothes before Bill came along. But now she was buying, some thing, or other, every week, she said she wanted to look good, for when she went to America, with her new husband, to meet her new in-laws, and she had lost a bit of weight lately.

The land girls were still working hard, just now they were planting potatoes sets, as Ethel, and Gran, both agreed, it was back breaking work, planting them, and then picking them in October, Gran, and Ethel, both said, "They had done plenty of that work in their time."

Susan was asking Ethel, How, old Sid's wife was keeping, and Ethel stood still for a minute,

"I don't really know, the last time I saw her was when me and Wilf, went for the cows, and she didn't look too good, why do you ask Susan? Have you heard some thing?"

No its just Mary, his daughter is always at the dances, and I thought she had to look after her mother."

Ethel said, she does, but I would think, Sid will have a lot of time on his hands now that he hasn't got the cows, and the lass deserve a look out, as it must be bloody miserable, for her sitting with them all the time."Mable had been sitting listening,

Well we've seen her walking up the road, as we've been going to work, haven't we Susan." Ethel said,

"I don't know what she's doing then, she must be on with some thing." Wilf had just walked in, and heard the conversation, so he said,

"If you are talking about Sid's daughter, last week when I was coming here Ethel, to milk, she was walking up the road, I meant to tell you about that Ethel, but I forgot." The girls took notice after that, and some times Mary was walking up the road, as they were biking down to work, Mable said,

"I think she must have a boyfriend hidden away." Susan said, "I wish I had a boyfriend."

A few weeks had passed, and as Linda, and Jennie, were approaching old Robson's farm gate, they heard shouting, then they saw two people rolling on the ground, pulling each others hair, and hitting each other, Peter was there, and so was old Robson, and then old Robson, went over to Peter, with his hand raised, ready to hit him, but Peter was a lot taller, so he just held old Robson at arms length.As the girls got nearer, Linda said,

"look Jennie, it's old Sid's daughter, Mary fighting with that bloody Hannah, as the girls got off their bikes, old Robson shouted across at them,

"I bet you two know all about this, well, there is no need to stand, and stare, go and bring them bloody cows in for milking."On their way back with the cows, they met Mary, walking towards them, her hair was dishevelled, and her clothes, were filthy after rolling about in the dusty yard, she looked up at Linda, and Jennie, and said with a laugh.

"It was good while it lasted; old Robson disturbed us this morning, as we were laid, just in side the stack. Well I will see you girls at the dance this weekend, but I'm going home to bed now, as I gave him a good roggering all night, so I am knackered now." As she went on her way, Linda said,

"Look here's Peter coming, he's carrying a case, and it looks as if he's homeless,"

Jennie said, "I thought Peter had a bad leg, as he limps,"

Linda just looked at Jennie, and said, "Well it wouldn't be his bloody leg he was using, and I bet we have a horrible day to day, as the Robson's, will take it out on us."

CHAPTER 16

Eva wasn't having a very good day either with Prudence, as she kept asking Eva, if she had seen the postman? As the wedding, was all arranged, and taking place in five weeks time. Eva felt as if she was living with a time bomb, Prudence, couldn't settle, and Eva, had a lot to think about herself, as she had been, sitting up at night sewing, and she was tired, she had to do it, at night as she didn't have time, through a day, and all the girls needed new dresses, she had Mam, and Gran's, to make yet, then she needed some thing to wear for her self, she was walking, to the school four times a day, she had to take Violet, and Rose, on a morning and then at dinner time, bring them home, and feed all four of them, then take the twins to school, and pick them up at teatime, and in between, she helped Mam to make the butter. Prudence always used to walk Violet, and Rose, back from school for her, but lately she always had some thing to do for herself. Eva had tried asking her, where her relations were going to be staying, when they came for the wedding. Prudence just replied,

"I don't know yet, with a flick of her hand, then she said to Eva, wont it be exciting going to America? I never thought I would be going to live in Texas, but you know Eva, we must keep in touch, we will write regular, and you can tell me all your news, I think I 'll get on all right, with Bills relations, he has told me all about them. The only thing is, they don't like writing letters, over wise I would have written to them all. But Bill said leave it for now, as it will not be long, until I meet them all. Then he said, we will, all be a big happy family."

Linda, and Susan, were not having a good day, old Robson, was saying,

"The local girls were turning out just like the land girls; they will sleep, with anybody." Linda said,

I'm not putting up with this."Jennie said,

"No and I'm not neither, so come on Linda, let's go across the yard, and tell him we are not, putting up with his slander." As they were walking across the yard, Hannah came out side, and when she saw Linda, and Jennie, she came towards them, her hands on her hips, and then she shouted,

"I suppose you two knew all about what was going on, with my husband, and that conniving little bitch?" Jennie said,

"No we didn't actually,but we are just on our way, to tell your Dad a point or two, he has no right to say what he has about us, and we are not putting up with it."

"Well Dad did say, Hannah replied haughtily, that you were a couple of little trollops." Jennie thought the hard slap, as Linda, hit Hannah's cheek, and would sting for quite a while. Hannah was not a small girl, but the hard smack made her stagger back, she started to run, holding her cheek, shouting Dad, Just then her Mother opened the door ,to shake her duster, hearing the commotion off Hannah, she came down the steps, "Just what do you think you have done to my Hannah?" Linda gave her a resentful luck, it had rankled the girls, old Robson saying they were trollops; well he could do the bloody work himself, because they were going to tell Ethel, and they weren't coming back.

Ethel's eyes were blazing fire, after the girls had told her, about Mary, and Peter,

"Well let them Robson's manage, the best way they can, Ethel said nastily, but I know, they will never manage, all the farm work, with you girls walking off, and Peter, going as well,but it serves them right. But you will, have to tell the land army lot, or they might know, now, as Robson has maybe told them, don't worry you are good workers, they will put you on another farm." just then Eva walked in,

"I've come to help you Mam, and I thought, I might get a break from Prudence." she stopped talking, as she realised Linda, and Jennie, were at home.

What are you girls doing home she asked? Are you on holiday? Linda and Jennie told her,

"We have had one of them days as well." So after they had told Eva, all about it. Jennie said

"I hope we can get another farm some where local, as we don't want to leave here."

Gran said, "It will not come to that, you'll see, things have a habit of working out, and it wasn't your faults."

Eva said, "Well I'm bloody sick, of hearing about her bloody wedding, I am sorry girls, for going on about it, when you two have a bigger problem, but I have to live with her, and that is all I hear off her."

Ethel said, "Well she is bound, to be excited, and she is going to live in another country, and its not long now, I expect she's nervous, and she doesn't seem to have, any relations to turn too."

Gran said, That's if she ever hears from him again, I'm telling you all now, as sure, as eggs are eggs, she will never see him again, all that cock, and bull, story about his family, not wanting to write Prudence a letter, mark my word's, he's hiding some thing, I can see that, and its Prudence, that's supposed to be educated." Ethel asked Eva, how she was getting on making the clothes.

"Oh I have a lot to do yet Mam, but I thought, I would come out, and leave Prudence on her own, as my head was spinning, she spends her time, watching for the postman." Gran asked Eva,

"Does Bill write her a lot of letters?"

"Well that's the problem Gran, Eva, signed he hasn't wrote for two weeks."

"Well I think he is getting cold feet, and she won't see him again."

"Don't say that Gran, or Prudence will be devastated."

"Aye she will be," Gran replied, "if he doesn't come back for the wedding."

"Oh Eva," Ethel said "while I think about it, have you got the material for my dress yet?"

"No I haven't got it yet Mam, but I'm getting it next week."

"Well I think, I will play safe,"Gran said, "and hang on for a while, then if this wedding doesn't come off , I haven't wasted my money on a dress that I will never wear."

As Eva had walked in, Wilf was on his way out, but just then, the door opened again, and Wilf came back in. gran asked him,

Have you forgotten some thing Wilf?"

"No, but I think, I've got theses lasses a job, he turned to Ethel, and said, you know David Emmerson, from low farm, he's only gone, and lamed, his back, and now he is laid up, and the other old feller that helps him is off bad, Margaret can't manage that farmon her own, and both their sons, are away in the army, I don't know how long, it will take her to get the milking done." Frank said

"Do you want me to go and see if I can help her Uncle Wilf?"

"Aye take the bike lads, Wilf told them, and help her to milk, and ask her, if she wants's two hard working lasses?" It was nearly three hours, before Frank arrived back, with the good news that, Mrs Emmerson, said, they could they go and see her tonight, as she could badly, do with them." "Her sister Gladys, was there tonight, but I helped her to milk, and then I took the cows back up the lane for her, she gave me a big piece of chocolate cake, and a glass of orange juice, he turned to Linda, and Jennie, and said,

"You will like Mrs Emerson, she was very nice to me." so after tea the girls set off on their bikes, down the narrow country lane, they had to cross a small narrow bridge, with a stream running under it, at the neighbouring farm, they found Mrs. Emmerson, walking towards them, in a pair of black wellingtons, swinging an empty bucket, she was smiling at them, as she offered her hand to shake.

"Well I'm pleased to see you two she said, so one of you is Linda, and the other one is Jennie, I have heard all about you from Frank, so come on in, we will sit around the fire, and talk,after the girls had told her how it came about, them needing a job so quick, she tilted her head, and laughed, about Peter, Hannah, and Mary, well I think they are all a queer lot, I don't know what Peter, was thinking about, getting his self mixed up with them Robson's, and I don't think that Mary is all there."

"Jennie told Margaret, that Gran has always said that."

"Yes replied Margaret, Sarah Brown, always speaks her mind and I respect her for it, and she did bring Ethel up. So tell me a bit about yourselves." Jennie told her all about finding her Dad again, and Linda said, "I think I'm losing my family, but me and Jennie, are both happy doing this work, and living in the country."

"Would you girls like another cup of tea, and a biscuit, Margaret asked Linda, and Jennie, as she got off the couch?"

"No thank you Margaret, Jennie, replied with a voice full of gratitude, we will get off home now, and we will see you at six in the morning, is that all right? Only that is the time that we started at Robson's."

Margaret said, as she shook her head as she was seeing the girls out, "It was nasty of her tipping the tea out, but I could believe it of her, Oh yes six will be fine, and you will be able to meet my husband, tomorrow if I can manage to help him downstairs."

When Linda, and Jennie, arrived home Gran said, "I can tell by your faces that you have both got a job, and I know you will be happy there, as Margaret, and David, are a very nice couple, they have a married daughter called Kate, and two sons, in the army Paul, and John, she also has two grandchildren."

When the girls arrived, there next morning, Margaret

waved at them through the window, then she walked to the door, as the girls, put their bikes up against the byre wall, the dog was already waiting, his tail wagging, he was in a hurry, to go and bring the cows down to milk.

Jennie, said,to Linda, "We will have to remember,that this is a different dog, with a different name, although collies, all look the same to me,so just as well, Margaret, told us last night, that this one is called Trixie,or we wouldn't of known, what to call her, when she was herding the cows in."

As Frank, and Colin, were having their breakfast, Frank, looked up at Ethel, and asked her, "if he should go to Mrs Emerson's farm, incase the girls couldn't manage?" Ethel, was standing behind Frank, and as she, walked round the table, to pick up the big brown teapot, that was sitting on the hearth, she ruffled his hair, and asked him,

"What have you got enticing, over at Emmerson's farm?" Colin, looked up at Ethel, and said,

"He likes Mrs Emerson's, chocolate cake," just before he got a kick on the shin's off Frank.

Theses summer days, were so hot ,and Margaret Emmerson, was a plump country woman, her floral pinny, was straining around her hips, but hot day, or not,she thought, it was her baking day, but first, she would have to make David, some breakfast. She thought she would, give Linda, and Jennie, some as well, as they were good workers, and she knew herself, you couldn't work on an empty stomach. also she didn't think, it would David, any good lying in bed, he had tossed and turned all night, so when she saw Linda, and Jennie, coming back down the lane, after taking the cows to the field, she took her hand out of her pinny pocket, and waved at them, to attract their attention, before shouting at them to come over,

Jennie said, "I wonder what she wants us for?"

Linda said, "Old Robson's, maybe told her not to employ us."

Jennie pursed her lips as if in deep thought, then she said, "No I don't think, Margaret, is that type of person, she will probably, want to tell us what she wants doing next."

Linda, looked across at Jennie and asked her good humouredly,

"Where do you think that, Peter would go too, Jennie? As I think he would be pleased to be away, from Robson's farm, I know he was a randy bugger, and he was to watch, but he made life easier for us." They were going through the little garden gate now, and Margaret, was standing at the door, with a big smile on her face.

"Good morning girls Margaret welcomed them, you are nice, and early, just as I knew you would be, I just said to David, last night, Linda, and Jennie, will be good girls, when Sarah Brown, has let them stay,and live with her, and Ethel, as she would not, put up with any shenanigans, Margaret was talking to the girls, as she was walking in to the big kitchen, come on in girls, she said ,and have a cup of tea,then would you help me down the stairs with David? I think he would be better, propped up in a chair, rather then lying in bed, besides it will save me having to run, up and down stairs after him."

David didn't take a lot of helping out of bed, it was surprising how strong the girls were now, with doing all the heavy work, on Robson's farm, they didn't realise, how big a bloke David was, until they had helped him out of bed, he was very tall, and very round just like a barrel, he had a florid face, and a hearty laugh.When he saw the girls coming towards his bed, he said,

"What a way, to meet two bonny lasses, has to help me get out of bed." After Linda, and Jennie, had staggered downstairs with him, it was a relief to help him into a chair, which creaked under his weight, he turned to the girls, and said, sit your selves down, and take the weight off your feet, as I know ,my wife is making us all a cup of tea." Margaret said,

"Aye they can have a bacon sandwich as well, as there is a lot of work to get through out there." David was asking them about Robson's farm, in between mouthful of breakfast, and then he said to the girls,

"I was just going to start hedging, when I lamed me back." Linda said,

"That's alright MR Emmerson, as we are old hands at it now aren't we Jennie?" As the girls went to fetch the slasher, to start work, Margaret said,

"If our Judith hadn't just had Roy, she would have come and given us a hand, Brian,our Juith's husband, said as soon, as he finishes at the quarry on a night, he will come, and help if we needed him." As the girls were working, the blazing hot sun shone down on them, their hair was plastered to their heads with sweat.

Jennie said," I can taste the salt, as the sweat is running down my face and into my mouth."

They knocked off at twelve o clock, and made their way back to the farm, as Margaret, had told them too, she also said,

"I don't hold with this Mr, and Mrs, as you know my names Margaret, and my husband is David, as it sounds a lot friendlier." As the girls walked in to Margaret's kitchen it was hot, and stifling as there was heat coming off the cooking, and also the fire, it was like Grans, and Ethel's, kitchen, as the fire heated the oven, and the water. Margaret had set the table, and she said to them,

"Come on in lasses, and sit down, I'm just going to serve the dinner out, the girls watched her open the oven door, and take a piping hot pie, out of the oven, there you are, she said, you can't get fresher, then that corned beef and potato pie, with peas, and gravy, as it's my baking day today." the girls already knew that, by the delicious smell. Also they could see the huge dish on the hearth with the dough rising in it.

"Our Frank enjoyed your chocolate cake the other night

Margaret, Linda, was telling her, between mouthful of dinner. Ethel was saying if she could get hold of some icing sugar, she would make chocolate cakes like yours, but we haven't been able too yet, and if we did it would have to go to Prudence's, wedding cake, that Ethel has made for her."

Margaret said, I have some big bags of icing sugar, but I haven't got a lot of ordinary, sugar left,but you are welcome to take a couple of big bags of icing sugar to Ethel."

"Right thank you we will, and we'll bring you a four stone bag of sugar."As Linda knew, that she could get some more off the GIs. Margaret 's face lit up, as she said," Oh that will be grand." As they were eating their dinners, Margaret was asking them about them selves.

Linda said, "my sister Jane, has had another baby, and two of my brothers have been married, and I've never met their wives, I feel as if I don't belong to my family any more, I've only been home to visit them once, and I was never in bed, from leaving here, as the sirens were screaming, as they were having nightly raids."

David, and Margaret, were pleased for Jennie, when she explained about leaving her address with Mrs Roberts, and through doing that, she was reunited with her father. The girls noticed how David, was tucking in to his dinner, with relish, Jennie, and Linda, both thought, he was just like Gran, as nothing put her off her food. After dinner the girls went back outside to finish the hedging, Margaret never saw them no more, until they were walking over the little bridge, to fetch the cows in for milking, the girls were both complaining to each other, about the pain in their shoulders,as it was hard work hedging, but they had got a lot done today, they could have done with out, having to burn it today, as they were sweating ,from the heat off the sun.As both girls, were sitting on a three legged milking stool, each with a pail between their knees, they kept getting a swish across the head, off the cows tail as the flies were crawling all over them. Linda felt sorry for the cows, as they stood in the milking shed, with their big brown sad eyes. The girls were so hot, they could feel their clothes clagging to them, just as they were letting the cows back out, to take them back to the field, Margaret, stepped in.

"I am sorry lasses, Margaret, was hurriedly saying, to Linda, and Jennie, I was going to give you a hand to milk, but I have left it too late, as soon as you have taken the cows back, get off home, as you have both had a hard day, I'm pleased you helped David, back upstairs for me, before you started milking, because I would never have managed. What are we going to do about this sugar? Margaret, asked the girls, as you will never manage it home, on your bikes?"

Jennie, had been wondering, as well, what to do about the sugar, then she said

"Frank, and Colin, can bring the sugar, for you tomorrow, on their little trailer, and take the icing sugar back the same way, for Ethel."

"Over tea, the girls had such a lot to tell, Ethel, Gran, Wilf, Mabel, and Susan, Ethel, was tickled pink, with the thought, of so much icing sugar, that she had coming. Gran was busy eating, but she was listening all the same. Wilf was pleased like the rest of them, that Linda, and Jennie, had got a good place. "Prudence will be pleased to have her cake iced," Frank voiced, what every one else was thinking, Colin, was looking forward to seeing Mrs Emerson, again tomorrow, and taking her some sugar, as she made lovely chocolate cakes, Frank, and Colin, thought, she might be so pleased with the sugar tomorrow, that she might offer them a bit more .But it was auntie Ethel's, baking day, tomorrow, and auntie Ethel, had promised them some cakes, now as she was getting some icing sugar, and they knew Auntie Ethel, never broke a promise. Linda was fascinated, watching Gran, finish her tea, as Gran's head had come up for the first time, since she had sat down for tea, and then her hand reached over, for another thick slice of bread, then she started, mopping her gravy up with it, and shoving it in her mouth, as if her life depended on it By it didn't take Gran, long to shift a plate of food.

Wilf said, "I'm pleased Margaret, and David, is happy with you two lasses, as they are a nice couple."

Gran said, "Robson's, loss, has been Emmerson's gain." Gran noticed how quiet, Mabel was, as she was, sitting saying nothing. But Gran knew, what was wrong with her, as she had seen Mabel, running down to the lav, on a morning, she had heard her being sick, and Gran, being her usual self, and said what she thought, then she turned, to Mabel, and said.

"By your quiet Mabel, you've never uttered a word, since you came in from work, I think you, and me, should have a bit talk." Mabel looked the picture of innocence, as she asked Gran,

"What do you want to talk to me about?" Gran said, in a reproachful voice

"You bloody well know, what's wrong with you, so don't come the innocent with me, because your problem hasn't started to show yet, but I know, it's under your bloody jumper, and if you can't face your breakfast, on a morning, tell our Ethel, then she wont make you anything, think yourself lucky, that your breakfast hasn't been wasted, as I've been eating yours, as well as me own."

Mabel didn't know what to say, she felt awful, as every one was looking at her, and every thing had gone quiet, but in a way she was pleased her worry, was out in the open, the only thing that bothered her at the moment, was if she was told to leave, where could she go? she knew she'd been a fool, now she was left to sort it out, she couldn't go back to her parents, it was bad enough living with them, before she joined the land army, her mother ,and Father ,had been against it, her Father was the local vicar,and they would never allow, her go back in this state, her mother put a smile on for the congregation, same as folk thought highly of her Dad, the vicar, but neither of them had time for Mabel, that's why she loved being at Ethel's, she had started to cry and soon she was sobbing.

Wilf ,looked at Frank, and Colin, "Come on lads, he said, as he rose out of the chair, this is woman's talk, lets leave them to sort it out."

Mabel looked appealingly, at Ethel, as fresh tears started again, Ethel's, heart went out to her, as she looked at Mabel's grief stricken face, Mabel had put her head in her hands now, as she rested her elbows on the table, her shoulders slumped, as all the energy seemed to drain out of her.

Please don't through me out? Mabel, begged Ethel, just till I can find some where to go, as you are all the family that I've got, as she motioned to every one around the table."

Gran said, "I told you we needed to talk Mabel, Linda, noticed that Gran's abrupt tone, had softened,as she told Mabel, you are not the first, left holding the baby, and you will definitely, not be the last." Ethel said who's for another fresh cup of tea? Jennie, Linda, and Susan, offered to wash up, as they were going out with the GIs, Linda, said to Susan, and Jennie, afterwards,

"It's true, what they say, it's the good girls who get caught, now look at me, I've had more feller's then hot dinners."

Jennie said, I don't feel smug, as it could have been any of us in Mabel's predicament."

"Aye," Susan said, "there is none of us blushing Violets,but I do feel sorry for Mabel, and I for one, will do all I can to help her, although I'm sure Ethel will help her, as she is a good sort is Ethel."

When there was just Gran, Ethel, and Mabel, left in the kitchen, Ethel said, "If you just go to work as normal Mabel, until you can no longer manage, or Rains, realise what's wrong with you, then we will work some thing out,but until then, we will carry on as normal."

Mabel jumped off the chair, and hurriedly put her around Ethel. Thank you for not throwing me out Ethel, Mabel cried, you as well Gran." After Ethel had scolded a fresh pot of tea, Wilf walked in with Frank and Colin, Ethel looked up at Wilf, and smiled,"If you were four miles away Wilf, you would hear this kettle boil, right you lads go and get some hot water, and get washed, then we will have you to bed."

"But its still light, Auntie Ethel, Frank insisted, and Eric that lives down the road does not go to bed as early as us."

"I don't care what Eric does, he has got nothing to do with me Ethel, told Frank, and Colin, in a no nonsense voice, but you have, so you will just have to put up with it, and you're going to bed." Ethel, went upstairs ten minutes after Colin, and Frank, and found, they were washed, and in bed, she had to smile, as she looked down on their sleeping faces, she thought to herself and they said they were not tired." Now she would go downstairs, and listen to what Mabel, was saying to Gran. Mabel had dried her tears, but her face was still blotchy, with all the crying, she was still terribly upset by the way she was squeezing the wet hankie.

"My mam was forty years old when I was born, Mabel said, as she was hiccuping, I had been taught, that little girls were supposed to be seen and not heard, my parents had each other, and did not include me, when I was in my teens, and my friends called round, my father would never invite them into the house, as he said they were no better then they should be,and when I went out with my friends, I put makeup on after I had left the vicarage, and rubbed it off before I went back in, it was a welcome relief to leave home, as my parents looked on me as a nuisance. I have, wrote a couple of times, telling them about my job, but I've never received a reply, people looked to my mother, as a pillar of the community, in times of trouble, but I know, she wouldn't even have me, her own daughter over the doorstep with the trouble, I'm in."

Gran said, "I bet you feel better now, it's out in the open?"

"I do Gran, Mabel tearfully replied, but in the long term, I don't know what I will do? As I can never keep it, as I'll have to go to work, and yet I know, I could never give it away."

Gran said in her no nonsense voice, "It's too early to start making arrangements yet, you have five months to go, and anything can happen in that time." Mabel had started crying again. Gran said, now what's matter with you? I didn't think you would have any tears left."

"I'm crying with relief Mabel, sniffed, as I don't know, what I would have done or, who I could of turned too, if you had told me to get out."

Ethel said to Mabel "I'm going to make you a cup of coca, with milk, then you can take it to bed, as you've worn yourself out with all that crying." Gran never been one, to miss something, to eat, or drink, said "

Make me one our Ethel, and then you can help me to bed." Ethel said,

"By the way Mabel, Do you want a cooked breakfast in the morning?"

No thank you Ethel, I don't think I could face it." Ethel then asked her, "What have you been doing with your breakfast?"

As I cook everyone's breakfast, Ethel remarked, then I go straight out to milk."

"I have been leaving it Ethel, I'm sorry for wasting it." Gran spoke up,

"Oh it wasn't wasted our Ethel, I ate it."

"So you have been having two breakfasts Gran, I can hardly believe it."

Wilf was sitting, laughing, "How did you manage two breakfast's? Ethel asked?" Gran said

"Well it was easy, I didn't have them both together, there

was an hour and a half between them." after what seemed a long night, Ethel flopped down in the chair opposite Wilf, everyone, that was in the house, was in bed, the lure of the GI s dances, were some thing the land girls couldn't resist, apart from Mabel,Prudence was snapping at everyone now, as she still hadn't received a letter from Bill. Wilf said "you look weary Ethel."

"Oh there seems to be such a lot of trouble, Frank, and Colin, are going to Margaret Emmerson's, tomorrow to pick up that icing sugar, they are both looking forward to getting iced cakes, but the main job will be icing Prudence's cake." Wilf said, "I think she has heard the last of Bill."

"So do I wilf, Ethel, sighed Gran, has said it now for a while, but if he doesn't show up, it'll break Prudence's heart." Wilf said,

"Come and give me a kiss Ethel, you know you want to, and I won't tell anybody, he said laughing." Ethel said

"I just might, as you keep me happy, every one else seems to have problems."Susan, Jennie, and Linda, came back home at eleven o clock, as they had the milking, to do at six o clock, the next morning, and as they opened the door, they saw Ethel, sitting on Wilf's knee. Linda said "I hope we are not disturbing anything?" Wilf answered, "No, not, at all." but Ethel's face was crimson. Linda asked Ethel, "If Mabel was alright?"Ethel said,

"She has worn herself out crying, but what's done, is done, she will just have to make the best of it, I just hope, Rain's don't find out what's wrong with her, or she will have no job, Oh dear we do live in troubled times Wilf"

188

CHAPTER 17

Next day as Frank, and Colin, made their way to Margaret's farm, they saw Linda, and Jennie, in the field hoeing turnips, and the boys were watching them for a while. Frank said,

"I bet those two are hot Colin, I know I am, and I'm not working in this heat." Colin said, "I know we won't be as hot as those girls, as we were sheltered coming down the lane, as it's like a tunnel, as the trees at both sides of the lane meet at the top, just then, the girls stopped hoeing, and tried straightening up, rubbing, the bottom of their back's at the same time, they looked over, and when they saw Frank, and Colin, they waved.

Frank, and Colin, liked doing these jobs for auntie Ethel, as they liked showing off their bogey, that uncle Wilf, had made for them to do Ethel's messages, It was a big square box on wheels. Ethel sold butter, and eggs, and on a morning, when she delivered the milk, with Wilf she took orders off people, then after morning school, Frank, and Colin, delivered the eggs, and butter, with the bogey. When Wilf, and Ethel, started delivering the milk, Ethel, carried the eggs, and butter, with her, but they had so many customer now that, there wasn't room on the handcart. Colin said,

"We just have to go over that little footbridge Frank, and then we are there, do you think Mrs Emmerson; will be pleased with this sugar?"

Frank answered sourly; she should be, as there is four stone of bloody sugar for her."Colin, looked at Frank, in horror,

"You have not to say that word Frank, because Auntie Ethel, said she would wash your mouth out with soap."

"I know that Colin, but I keep forgetting, cos when we lived with Gran, in London ,we could do what we wanted, and say what we wanted, and she didn't care." Colin said,

"She didn't care, that we were hungry neither Frank, or have you forgotten that? We have never been hungry at Aunt Ethel's."

"Oh I know that, and we'll never go back to Gran's at London."

"Well we couldn't anyway Frank, because do you remember,?when she told us, that we were going to to the country, to live but, we had not to go back to her after the war, as we were a nuisance, and she didn't want to see us again."Then Colin started to cry.

"It will be alright Colin, Frank told him, as he put a protective arm, round his brother. If we just behave ourselves we will stay with auntie Ethel, for ever and ever." after they felt that problem had been sorted, they went and knocked on Mrs Emmerson's door, her face lit up when she saw the sugar.

"Come on in boys Margaret Emmerson sang cheerfully,as she stepped aside to let the boys through, I have a glass of milk, and a piece of chocolate cake, ready for you two, I thought you wouldn't be far away." On the way home, as they were dragging the bogey, with the huge bag of icing sugar in it, Colin said,

"Its good isn't it Frank, Aunt Ethel, will make, us a chocolate cake now, and ice it."

"Yes but don't forget some of the icing sugar, is for Prudence's cake."

Gran said, "Prudence wont need a cake Frank, as she is only kidding herself that she is getting married,Gran said Prudence, will never see Bill, again. That will be good, won't it Frank? If Gran is right and Prudence doesn't get married, we will have that big cake to eat as well."

Frank carried the big bag of icing sugar, in to Ethel's kitchen, at the same time Gran, swivelled round to look, so she wouldn't miss anything,

"Were do you want this sugar putting auntie Ethel?" Frank asked as he humped the bag through the kitchen.

"Oh put it in the scullery, Ethel told them, and it didn't take you boys long to do that little job, and I bet Mrs Emmerson, gave you some chocolate cake," as the boys came back through to the kitchen, Ethel put an arm around each of them, and gave them a cuddle, Colin said, "Mrs Emmerson gave us a piece of chocolate cake; will you make some now as we have brought you some icing sugar?"

Ethel said, "It's baking day tomorrow so I will make you some." Gran ears pricked up at the sound of chocolate cake and she said, "That will be good; I could enjoy a bit chocolate cake." Ethel wondered who the worst was, the boys or Gran?"

Down on Rain's farm, Susan, and Mabel, was busy hoeing turnips, Susan turned around and saw Mabel, leaning on the handle of the hoe,

"Are you all right Mabel? Susan asked her."

"Yes I'll manage Susan thank's, its just so hot, but I'll have to work as long as possible, I have no idea how I'm going to do manage when I can't work, as I don't know what I will do for money, it's good of Ethel, to let me stay, now in this condition, but I can't stay there for ever, with no money, and I don't think they will want a crying baby in the house. Oh Susan, I wish I hadn't been so stupid, I've made such a mess of my life."

"Have you no relations you could go to Mabel?Susan asked her sympathetically, just till you've had the baby, I've been thinking, I could may be write to your parents, and see if they would at least, help you out with money, until after the baby's born, I thought they might help you if I wrote and explained."

"No Mabel shouted at Susan, almost panicking, it wouldn't help, they would just think less of me, then they do now, no Susan it's good of you to try and help me, but I have no way out." Susan rushed over, and put her arms around Mabel, as she started to cry,

"Come on Mabel, Susan soothed, we will think of some thing, the worst is over I think, with Gran, and Ethel, knowing about your condition, they will help you, Susan started to giggle,as she said, and best of all you have me." Mabel dried her eyes and smiled at Susan,

"I know you're a good friend Susan, but we'd better get cracking, or we'll both be looking for a job."

Back at Ethel's house, the heat from the kitchen was over powering, Ethel had the door wedged open, but there was no draught, to blow through to cool things down, as Ethel wiped the sweat off her brow, with her pinny, she had baked all day, having made twenty loaves of bread, and teacakes, all morning, then after she had cooked dinner, she had made fruit pies, also ham and egg pies, which were Wilf's favourite. and cakes, including four big chocolate cakes, which she had yet to ice, the fire was blazing, as she needed to keep the oven hot, so she could fill it, with a huge bowl of mince and onions, then she would add some dumplings, there was two huge bowls of fruit crumble to cook yet. Ethel walked into the scullery, to fetch a pan so she could boil the milk for the custard, on the fire, after the potatoes, and the vegetables were cooked, Eva, Prudence,and the four girls, were coming for tea. Ethel was just rubbing her hand across her brow, as Wilf walked in.

"By its warm, in here isn't it Ethel? You look as if you could do with a sit down, and I'll make you me and Gran, a cup of tea."

Gran said, "Our Ethel, has been on the go all day, she has rushed about like a blue arce'd fly."

"I know I have Gran," Ethel hurriedly tried to tell her, "but there are so many people to feed, but I suppose I shouldn't complain as there is a lot of folk in the cities starving."

Gran said, "I hope Prudence doesn't start about her bloody wedding again , as I can't abide her talking about America, as I know, she is only kidding herself, that she is getting married,and she is assuming she's going to have a happy life in America as she won't face the truth, that he won't be back."

Ethel said, it's very humid today, I think it'll break with thunder, and it's made it extra hot in here, with me baking all day." Wilf, looked fondly at Ethel, as he passed her a cup of tea,

"Tomorrow Ethel, I'm going to take you for a leisurely walk."

"Oh where are we going to Wilf?"

"Well you know, we arranged to pay old Sid, every six month for renting his fields ,well it has gone over quick, but it's due, this week, so I thought, we could go there together tomorrow,what do you think Ethel?" Ethel, enjoyed her hard working life with Wilf, and they had prospered more then Ethel, or Wilf, would of thought possible, Ethel said,

"It's a long time since we had to use your burial money Gran, to buy Buttercup, they all laughed,"

Wilf said, "I remember that bloody Joe, with his sarcasm, he would get a bloody shock, if he saw how it had turned out." Wilf, Gran, and Ethel, would have got a bloody shock, if they could have seen Joe, after he had been to see Eva, which was a long time since. Joe's girlfriends parents, had travelled a long way, to see what had happened to their daughter, as they had not heard from her for a long time, when she had agreed to live with Joe, she didn't know, that he was married, then when she had found out, he told her that he was divorced, and then she found out it was another pack of lies, and he had gone awol from the army, so they had no money coming in, and she was pregnant, she was sitting crying when her parents arrived, her dad hadn't reckon much to Joe, when he had first met him, so Joe ended up on his own, as she left with her parents, from then on Joe, had no job, no money, and no where to live, he couldn't pay the rent, on the house, he had started earning a few pounds where he could, but he had to be careful, as the redcaps were looking for him. They had nearly caught him the night before, so he thought to his self, I have to get away from here, so I'm getting on the next train, when the guard isn't looking, I don't care where I end up. His trousers were filthy, and his hair, badly needed washing, and cutting, his jacket was hanging on him, and his shirt was torn, he tried not to be seen, as he stood in the station, waiting of the train to come, no one from his past would recognise him now, as he had a long beard, and his face was drawn in, and he was scruffy, but he wasn't going to risk stopping here. The train was pulling in now, he would wait till some passengers got off, then he would hurry over before anyone stopped him, the carriages were packed, as the train set off, Joe thought about the time, when he'd worked on the railway, he used to prune his self in front of the mirror, before he put a foot out of the door, he was down on his luck now,and he knew, he looked like an old man, the motion of the train lulled Joe to sleep.Then he woke with a jump, as he felt a dig in the ribs, as someone pressed against him, to lever them selves out of the seat. Joe rubbed his eyes and realised every body was leaving the train; he would get off and see where he had ended up, as he made his way out of the station, he looked up at the sign, and then he had his answer. Portsmouth station, well Joe wasn't really bothered, as long as he could get hold of some money, and some where to stay, a man, and a woman ,were walking in front of him, the woman had a shoulder bag on, with her purse just showing at the top of the bag, Joe saw it, as he casually walked past he carefully picked the purse out of the bag, then he started to hurry, he knew if they had seen him they would of got the police, then he would have been in trouble for going awol, he would hurry in to the first pub that he came to, sweat was standing on his brow, then he would go straight to the bloody toilet, and dump this purse, there was more money in then he could of hoped for, when he went to the bar it was crowded ,a young soldier had just paid for his pint and gone to the toilet. Joe was never one to miss a trick, so he leaned over and picked it up, then made his way over to the over side of the room, he thought this is the way to ,get a cheap pint, he didn't mind sleeping rough in this warm weather, but he would have to find some where before the cold weather started, he noticed

some good looking girls had come in, he could of clicked with
them once on, but nobody would give him a second look now, he
supped the pint off but he was hungry,so he would go and look
for a cafe, he soon found one, with the window all steamed up,
and drops of water landing on the window bottom, a tired
looking waitress sauntered over,she said to him.

"What is it you want? Because we haven't a lot left,"so he
got a plate of greasy chips, and a sausage, which tasted like
sawdust, he thought he would make his way down to the docks,
after he had finished this and go and see if there was any
warehouses, that he could get in to tonight to get his head down,
he would call in at the dock pub first,as he could afford a few
drinks now, as he stood at the bar with his hand wrapped around
his glass, he looked across the bar, where there was a mirror
hanging, bloody hell, he couldn't believe how he had changed.
After Joe had a few drinks ,he was just supping his pint off, then
he was going to go some where for a bit sleep, an old bloke came
hobbling, over to the bar, his big toe was sticking out of his shoe,
he was filthy, the front of his jumper had umpteen meals slopped
down it. Joe thought the old feller must be in his late sixties, as
the bloke handed his glass over for a refill, the bar owner said,
"Are you feeling any better today Jack?" as Joe turned and
walked out.

Back in the countryside, Ethel said, this isn't getting the
tea cooked, sitting here talking, as she got off the chair, and
hastily sliced, another one of the loaves of bread, that she'd
baked earlier, the tea was ready to serve, as Prudence, Eva, and
the girls, walked in, followed by Susan, Mabel, Jennie, and
Linda, just behind them Frank, and Colin, appeared, and said,
"We've been waiting for you coming back outside uncle Wilf,
we've been watching Pippa, and we think , she is going to have
her piglets tonight, as she is rolling in the straw, and grunting."

"As soon as we have eaten our teas, Wilf said, we will go
and see what's happening with pippa."

"Can we come as well? asked Margaret," Wilf looked at Eva and she shrugged her shoulders ,well I don't see why not Eva thought, after they had eaten their tea and gone with Wilf, I might have been better off, watching the pig farrowing, then listening to Prudence's wedding plans, as she was for ever emphasising, about going to America.

Ethel just remembered, a letter had arrived this morning for Susan, and as Ethel, was apologising, to Susan, as she had forgotten all about it, it had reminded Eva,that there was a letter at home for Prudence, as Prudence was still rattling on about the wedding, and not getting a letter off Bill. Prudence was pleased,that Ethel, had managed to get some icing sugar, so that her cake would look nice, as she was taking the rest of her cake to Texas, with her, for Bill's family.

Ethel said, "We have Linda and Jennie to thank for that icing sugar, if they hadn't swopped, a bag of sugar, to Margaret Emmerson, your cake wouldn't have been iced."

Prudence looked round at every body and said "Did I tell you, Bill owns a big hotel in Texas, his brother mother and father are running the business, until we go over there, I will still let his family work for us, then when I'm over there, I will take over the day, to day, running of it, and I will, see to all the practicalities, until Bill is demobbed,although his family, might as well stay at the hotel with us, as I will ,need staff, and after all, they have been looking after it, all this time, so I wouldn't turn them out she said sympathetically, you must all come over to visit us, as I've said, there will be plenty of accommodation, I'm lucky, I have so much to look forward to, I never thought, I would get such a good honest man, like Bill." Susan didn't look very happy reading her letter, so Ethel, asked her if there was anything wrong?

"Well as you know Ethel, mam can always find some thing to complain about,Susan, told her, Dad is still not feeling well,and our Joyce, has left her husband and moved back in, with Mam, and dad, bringing her three kids, with her, all under five, I've never seen, the lasted baby,and mam is complaining about our Helen, as she is always going out, some where or other, and my auntie Sally, lives with them, she is dad's sister, she is a lot older then dad, her, and mam, don't get on, mam is thinking, I've forgotten about them, as I've never been back for a visit, I'll just have to write and tell her, I can't come yet, as we are busy." Prudence said,

"I thought you were always busy on a farm."

Mabel said; don't put off going home, because of me Susan." Prudence turned around and asked how it affected Mabel?

"Well Susan is doing my share of the heavy work, while I'm in this condition." Prudence said,

"I think it is terrible that boyfriend of yours, just going away and never giving you a second thought,it is not acceptable, did you not think about the consequence 's? I bet you didn't, at the time, well you wont be able to keep it that's for sure Prudence, said knowingly, and if you stay here, you won't dare, put your face out of the door, once people, get to know, what's wrong with you, people will call you all sorts, don't you think, you would be better off leaving here, before people get to know, could you not go back to your family?"

Mabel, looked at Gran, with grief stricken eyes, Gran said, "I am going to say this once, and then everyone will know where they stand, as she looked at Prudence, resentfully, first of all. She is among her family now, and we don't give a bugger what people say, and when the baby is born, it will be living here with us, I would of thought, that you had enough on your mind Prudence, wondering if that feller of your's, will ever be seen again, just think on, talks cheap, and by God, them Americans could talk." Eva looked at Prudence who was sitting lost for words, as Gran had protected Mabel fiercely, Eva got up, and then said, and "I will go and get the girls as she wanted to get out of the bad atmosphere."

Prudence said, "I will come with you Eva, as she pressed her hands down on the chair arms and levered herself out, then stood and looked at Gran with hands on her hips and said,

"Well I hope, you will still come to my wedding, although we have had a difference of opinion, or your new dress, will be wasted." Gran said,

"That's just where you're wrong, I haven't bought it yet, and I'm playing safe." Wilf was on his way round with the girls as Eva and Prudence opened the door, Eva had a sly smile on her face, where as Prudence didn't look very happy at all,Wilf thought better, then ask Eva what she was smiling about, no doubt he would get the full story later when he and Ethel managed to have a bit privacy,as soon as Wilf sat down in his chair the girls ran and kissed everyone , by, bye, as they were going home, after they had gone, Ethel asked Wilf,"Where are Frank and Colin?"

"Oh they have gone to play with some lads that they know, it's alright isn't it? Mind you, they are looking forward to that chocolate cake Ethel, but they are not on their own laughed Wilf, as he smacked his lips together."

"I'd better bring the dish out for you Ethel", Linda told her, "so you can start icing the cakes," and then Linda said, Will you do the first one Ethel? And show me how it's done, then I'll do the other three for you." "Do you think you could manage then Linda? Asked Ethel,

Gran said, "she is very insistent so she deserves to have ago, I don't care what it looks like, after its iced, I'll still eat it, what do you say Wilf?

"Oh you know me Gran, I'll not say no to a bit chocolate cake,"

Ethel turned to Linda and said smilingly, "You have plagued me, to ice these cakes, so you had better watch carefully. You will need to make two kinds of icing, one lot to sandwich the cake together, and a different mixture on the top."

"Well you can sit down and tell me what to do Ethel, as you have had a hard day,"

Gran asked, "Have you never done any icing of any description Linda?" Linda stopped emptying the bag of icing sugar in to the dish, and looked at Gran as she said,

"No I had never even seen bread made till I came here, and saw Ethel making it." Gran was shocked, and asked her, what did you do for bread cakes and such like at home?"

"Linda said, "Oh we bought it all at the shop, mind I wouldn't want to eat all that shop bought stuff now, that I know what home baking tastes like." Wilf was sitting listening to them, and then he said,

"If you lasses watch Ethel, she will make you in to good cooks like herself." Susan Mabel and Jennie were sitting watching the cakes getting iced Susan, said,

"Its strange, but life's so different living in the country, to what it is living in the city, all the girls agreed, they would never want to go back to living in the city."

"Yes," Wilf agreed, as he sat in the chair with his legs stretched out in front of him, and his stocking feet resting on the brass fender.Country life goes on at a steady pace, no one is ever in a hurry to go anywhere as there is plenty of time, and I've always said, the man that made time, made plenty of it."

"Ethel's face was wreathed in smiles, and she laughed at Wilf, and said," "Is that why you never rush?" "I have no need to rush lass." he said, and as Ethel walked past his chair, he slapped her playfully on the bottom.

"Gran," started to laugh at the girls and said, "You'll just have to find your selves a farmers son, then you can stay in the country, it'll be better going after something, that you might get, rather then going after a promised trip to America, that I don't think will ever happen."

"Mabel said." You know what you said about the baby Gran, did you mean it?" Gran said, "I wouldn't have said it, if I didn't, as you should know me by now Mabel, I never mince my words." Mabel, "rushed over and put her arms around Gran, and cuddled her as tears ran down her face."

"Later on, when Frank and Colin walked in, they were beaming, when they saw four chocolate cakes, fairy cakes and lots of other cakes on the table, Colin asked, "if they could have some cake with a glass of milk?"

"Yes," said Gran willingly" I will have some cake as well, put the kettle on Linda, as our Ethel looks worn out." As Frank, was stuffing the cake in to his mouth, he asked Ethel, if she would make these cakes every week?"

"Yes I will Frank."Ethel answered him with a smile, and these girls can do the icing."

"Wilf," looked up between mouthful and said, by its a bit of good cake that just cut me another slab, would you Linda? And I think Gran is holding her plate out for a bit more." Linda, had enjoyed doing the icing tonight, with Ethel instructing them on how it was done,they had all done it together.Linda, couldn't imagine her mother, or sister Jane ,doing any icing and they would never bake cakes, Linda had lean't such a lot about making dinners, and baking, as she had lived on fish and chips, jellied eels, and pies bought from the shop, her mother wouldn't know how to make bread, she knew she had made the right decision, on joining the land army, or she would never of met Ethel, she had made her mind up, that she would always live in the country know."

"Grace," came along to Ethel's the next morning, to tell her that Mrs Lee was very upset, as she had received a telegram, to say that Robert was missing believed dead."

"Gran hung her head, as she said. Well I'm very sorry to hear that, he is a very nice lad, but until we know for sure, there is still hope," The girls had all left for work, and Gran said, the news will keep until tonight, until young Jennie gets in from work, as she is going to be distraught, so we'll have to choose our words carefully, when we give her this terrible news."

CHAPTER 18

Down on the farm, Linda and Jennie, were blissfully unaware of anything happening to Jennies boyfriend Robert, the girls called the dog and went and brought the cows down for milking, after they had finished milking, and taken the cows back to the field, they went in for a cup of tea, and a bacon sandwich, which Margaret insisted, they did every morning. David,Margaret's,husband had been ill with a bad back, but he was alright now, the old man that had been helping them, was not coming back to work, which pleased the girls, as they were able to carry on working there. They saw David through the window, making his way to the house when the postman handed him a letter, David carried it into the house whistling, as he was a jovial man, he said to the girls , as he came in,

"I always hand the post to the boss, and do as I'm told." he said laughing. He was a very pleasant person. Margaret opened the envelope, and gasped, "On my God David, our Paul has been badly injured, he's in hospital, and we have to go to him." She had got herself in to a right fluster, "just take it easy Margaret."David told her it's no good fretting, until I think what to do." Margaret sat down with her head in her hands, and cried.

"Linda asked David," "Would you like me to bike to Tommy's, pub? As he has a phone and he could ring the hospital, and find out what's happening, as there is no point in speculating."

"Yes go straight away Linda thank you." David looked relieved, that someone had made a suggestion,

Gran sitting in her chair, could see every one coming and going down the road, she was a bit surprised though, to see Linda pedalling past, as if her life depended on it. "Ethel," Gran shouted, "Come here quickly." Ethel ran down the stairs, thinking that something was wrong with Gran, as she had been busy, putting clean sheets on the beds.

"Whatever's the matter Gran?" Ethel shouted,"You gave me a bloody shock shouting like that."

"Well go outside and catch Linda." Gran told her irritably.She has biked past here as if some bugger was chasing her, and see what's happening."

Ethel didn't have to wait long, before Linda came pedalling back down, she stopped when she saw Ethel.

"What is wrong?" Ethel asked Linda, as soon as Linda had stopped the bike.

"I have just been to Tommys, Linda told Ethel anxiously, and he has rang the hospital for me, as David, and Margaret received a letter this morning, telling them that Paul is in hospital, and they have told Tommy, that Paul has a lot of injury's, and also has had some of his leg amputated, I think Margaret and David will want to be with him, so I'd better go."

"Oh Linda I have some more bad news,Ethel told her unhappily, Grace called this morning and told me that,Mrs Lee has had a telegram saying Robert is missing believed dead, break it to Jennie as best you can when you get back to the farm. As Linda biked back to the farm, she thought what a day I'm having, and it's just started, Margaret and David were devastated, when Linda told them how bad Paul was, he had been in hospital a few weeks before the letter had arrived,

"Margaret," said "we'll have to go to him, but what about this place?" as she looked beseech at David, and unchecked tears ran down her face.

Linda said "there is some more bad news, Robert Lee is missing believed dead,"as Jennie burst in to tears Linda said, "I am so sorry Jennie, to be the bearer of bad news, but there was no easy way to tell you, as Linda opened her arms and Jennie went into them." A short time later, Linda said,

"I'm going to get some work done, as it wont do it's self,Oh by the way Linda turned and told Margaret, I saw Ethel on my way back from ringing the hospital, and she said is sending Frank and Colin down this afternoon,to help with the farm work." At dinner time Margaret and Jennie pushed their food around their plates, each thinking their own unhappy thoughts, where as Linda ate, as if she had never had a bite for a week, as she had worked hard all morning, as Jennie's mind was on Robert, and David didn't do as much as he usually did, as his mind was on his son Paul, by tea time Margaret had made arrangement to go to the hospital at Portsmouth.

Frank and Colin had called at the farm, their help was very welcome, as Linda felt as though, she was working the farm single handed.Frank and Colin had come on along way since they had arrived at Ethels as evacuees, they were big strong lads, now that they ate nourishing food and plenty of it, Wilf had made sure that they had some discipline, and they were no longer the cheeky boys, that Ethel had taken in to her home, although stability had helped. Back at Ethel's, house, "Wilf," said

"I know there is a lot of misery about Ethel, and maybe it's wrong to feel happy, but we can't make a better of it, so get ready and we will have a leisurely walk, and pay the rent to old Sid, for the fields." As they walked down the country lanes Wilf took Ethel's hand, as though it was the most natural thing to do, and she didn't snatch it back as he thought she might. As they approached Sid's farm, Ethel said," Doesn't it look desolate Wilf?" "Aye it does Ethel, if that lass of theirs had been out like she could have helped Sid more then she did, then he wouldn't have had to get rid of his cows."" Well I'm pleased we bought them are you Wilf?" "Aye I am lass he said." as he smiled fondly at Ethel. "Wilf' knocked on Sid's door, it was so quiet they thought there must be no one at home, and it was a lovely sunny day they had enjoyed their walk. Wilf said to Ethel, "We can always come back tomorrow." just then the door creaked open, just far enough, to see who had knocked on the door, just then Sid shouted,

"Who the bloody hell is it then? you stupid bitch, he came

to the door shoving Mary out of his way in his stocking feet, when he saw Wilf and Ethel he looked uncomfortable, as he put his hand to his chin and rubbed his whiskers absentmindedly, he didn't bother much now with his appearance,and the embarrassment in front of Wilf and Ethel ,was terrible to bear,as they were always clean and tidy,but, he had lost his cows ,his wife was dying, and that bloody bitch was expecting that Peters bloody kid. Wilf thought that Sid had forgotten they were there.

"Look Sid, Wilf broke into his thoughts, if we have come at a bad time, I will just give you this rent money, then we'll go."

"No sorry Wilf, Ethel, come on in Sid beckoned them." When Ethel saw Sid's wife Norah, Ethel thought that she had shrunk, and Mary, Sid's, daughter looked nervous, as she passed her weight from one foot to the other. Ethel turned and smiled at her, and then realised it wouldn't be long before Norah and Sid had a grandchild,

"Come on in then and sit down," Sid was saying,"As I don't see anybody now, so have you any news?"

"Oh well, there is plenty of misery around," "Wilf was saying,"" have you heard about, Robert Lee, and Paul Emmerson,?" after Wilf had told them all that he knew "Sid said,"

"I will go over and help on the farm, as they will need a hand and I'm doing nothing." Wilf said

"I'm sure those girls wouldn't refuse a helping hand, and David won't feel like doing much." Sid seemed to perk up a bit as he said,

"I will walk over after tea and offer David and Margaret an extra pair of hands."

"Well I'm sure the Emmerson's will be pleased, Linda and Jennie will also welcome some help Ethel replied."Down on Emmersons farm arrangements were hurriedly made, it was decided, that Margaret and David's daughter Judith, and her husband with the two children would move in to the farm house.it seemed a good arrangement, as Judith would carry on and feed Linda Jane and Sid, and her and her husband would be there, on a night to keep an eye on the place. Later that night after she had eaten her tea, Jennie went along to see Mrs Lee, Roberts's mam, as Jennie knocked on the door and walked in, Mrs Lee walked over to Jennie her arms out stretched, and then with arms around each other, they held each other and cried. Roberts's dad not knowing what to do decided to make a cup of tea, although he was awash with it, as everyone that had called today, had drunk a cup of tea, and he had one with them, as he didn't know what else to do. As "Ethel," said to Wilf later,

"Its hard to imagine there is a war on, and all these people getting hurt and killed, then she lifted her hand in a gesture of hopelessness."

The next morning, when Linda and Jennie arrived at the farm, Sid had already been there a while, and was learning against the byre wall having a fag, in the early morning sun. He shouted, "Hello," to Linda and Jennie, as they made their way down to him, the girls didn't know, if he was screwing his eyes up against the sun, or if it was the smoke off his fag, that was getting in his eyes.

"Are you lasses ready to go for the cows? Sid enquired, as I will walk with you." Linda stood still hands on her hips, and and faced Sid, as she said haughtily,

"I hope you are not, going to be following us around, checking up on us, as we won't put up with it."

"Oh no, Sid stuttered, its just old habits die hard, all me life I have risen early, and now I have nothing to get up for, he answered unhappily, as Wilf and Ethel bought me cows, as you know, then when Wilf and Ethel, called yesterday and told me about Paul, I offered to come and help you lasses." Linda felt sorry for him after what he had said, so she "invited him to come and get the cows with them."

"Yes why not? Sid said warily" all three of us can have a

walk, before we go and see David and Margaret." it didn't take the three of them long to do the milking, and after they had taken the cows back to the field, and done a few jobs, they still hadn't seen neither Margaret, or David, the girls told Sid that, "Margaret had not been outside since she had got the devastating news."

"Well what do you two think we should do? Sid asked, as we have to see them, should I go and knock on the door?" Linda and Jennie hesitated, not knowing if they should disturb Margaret and David, but as Sid pointed out, "we'll have to see them, before they go, so come on, he beckoned to the girls, we will all go together." as they went through the little garden gate, David saw them and lifted his hand and waved for them to come in. Margaret was in the kitchen frying eggs and bacon, the girls went to help her, as Sid went to sit with David, Margaret's face was red and swollen, her eyes were blood shot with crying, the girls were desperate to know what to say, as they felt very sorry for Margaret, at the same time Jennie was trying to cope with her own grief over Robert.

"We both feel very sorry for you and David, Linda told Margaret; we didn't know if we should call in this morning." Margaret turned and looked at them.

"You did right to come in, Margaret told the girls with tears in her eyes, as we are relying on you two, to keep this farm going, and you also have Sid to give you a hand. I'll give you both some money, before we go, as I don't know when we'll be back ,our Judith will be here, so come in as usual for bacon sandwiches, and a bite at dinnertime." As they were eating, Linda asked them where they would stay.

"Oh David has a cousin we can stay with,Margaret told them, but we have only met them twice, and we'll still be twenty miles away from the hospital, but its better then nothing, Margaret said with a sigh."as she put her hand in her pinny pocket, and brought out a hankie, as fresh tears ran unchecked down her face, Linda was wondering what to do, as Jennie got up and walked round the table, and then gently put her arms round Margaret. Linda noticed all the food had been eaten, so she got up and cleared the table.

Old Sid was sitting thinking, although Margaret was deeply upset and worried about her son, she still put a good meal on the table, even when he had called round yesterday afternoon, to offer to help, Margaret had invited him to stay for tea, he'd accepted with out hesitation, he'd told Margaret and David, that he would come along everyday with the girls, and do any job that needed doing, he didn't want paying, all he wanted was his meals, as Judith, cooked like her mother, Aye Margaret had trained her well,he thought, as it took his daughter Mary, all her time to boil water, when he thought about it Norah, his wife,had never taught her, as she had no idea herself, it was a poor house his, for grub, Last night Margaret had handed him a loaded plateful of dinner, it was piping hot, straight out of the pans, bye it had been a long time since he'd seen a good dinner.He was awakened from his reverie, as Linda nudged him in the ribs, and asked him "if he was intending doing any work today?"

later on, as the land girls were sitting having a chat, with Ethel and Gran, on Ethel's high backed chairs, round the huge table, that took nearly all the floor space, up in the kitchen, that Linda mentioned Sid, she said

"I think it's strange, he has a daughter our age, as she pointed to Jennie, and he has told Margaret, that he doesn't want any money for working, only his food, Is there some thing wrong with his daughter Mary?" As Linda finished speaking, Gran was sitting on the edge of her chair, trying to get everyone's attention.

"If I could get a word in edgeways,Gran said grumpily, I'll tell you all, what I said to our Ethel, all them years ago, I forecasted what would happen there. Norah is twenty five years younger then Sid, he used to live on the farm with his father and mother, after his father died he carried on farming, then Norah landed up here on holiday, she was a bonny lass, I don't know what she saw in Sid, maybe thought he had some money, which he had but the greedy bugger wouldn't part with it. Well he took a shine to her, his mother and everybody told him it would never last, her not being a country lass, but after her holiday they wrote to each other and eventually they got married, she was eighteen, he was forty three well from the day she moved in she never did a hands turn, Sid's mother did all the cooking and house work I don't think he ever got a decent meal after she died, he'd got his self a bonny lass, but he's had a empty belly ever since, Sid always wanted more bairn's but she didn't seem able to have anymore after Mary, mind you I've always said, just as well when you see how gormless she is, aye Sid's had plenty of misery she wouldn't do owt, and now she's ailing, she cant."

"Talking of food How far is tea off our Ethel, it's late tonight, and me belly thinks me throat's cut, I like me meals on time."

"I know you do Gran, Ethel answered her, but I have been very busy today, you would have something to moan about, if you lived in the city, you wouldn't have much food to eat at all."

"Yes so you keep telling me our Ethel, but I don't live in the bloody city, and I'm hungry now." "You don't look very well tonight Mabel, Gran said, and your not saying very much, are you hungry?"

"Oh I'm alright Gran just a bit hot like every body else."

"Well prop that door open Mabel, and let a bit of draught in."

"Are you sure, you won't be cold Gran?"

"No the only thing that's wrong with me is, I'm bloody hungry."

The next morning as the girls arrived for work ,they were surprised to see that David had already been and brought the cows in for milking, in answer to the girls question, "he," said,

"He had to keep, busy,or his mind would wander, and that

wouldn't do anybody any good, as he had to keep a level head, for his sake and Margaret's, also he didn't want to get under Margaret's feet, as she was rushing around, they were setting off later, Harold was giving them a lift to the station, but first he had some deliveries up at the hall, where the injured soldiers were staying, as it was being used as a convalescent home, and on his way back he is going to pick me and Margaret up, and take us to the station. He was telling Linda and Jenny, that Judith and her husband had moved in last night, it's good of them David said, to keep an eye on the farm for us, and I love my two grandchildren, but last night when the three week old baby was crying, my nerves were jangling.

David stood and thought back to last night with a sigh. Margaret had cried all night, he had reached over to try and soothe her, as her body was shaking and she was sobbing in to her pillar, he didn't feel very well, as he'd had no sleep, and they had a long journey in front of them, it was good of Harold to pick them up, with his horse and cart, it would save them a three mile walk, he would go in shortly, and have his breakfast, then he would get washed and changed, then he would have to sit round waiting of Harold, he could count, the times, that he had left the farm, he'd never had the need, he was most comfortable in his old cap, he had owned that cap now for a lot of years, and it had a few years wear left in it yet, he didn't see the need to get dressed up, as some folk did, this old jacket had more patches on then enough same as these trousers, but you didn't need now't fancy for milking cows, and mucking byres out. The hospital hadn't told young Linda much , when she had rang from Tommy's phone, he didn't know what was in store for them when they reached the hospital, he was frightened that Margaret couldn't take much more, he was in such deep thought, he'd not heard Linda saying, "breakfast was ready." she was standing looking up at him with her hands on her hips and then she linked arms with him, and lead him to the house, like a child, talking to him as they were walking into the house,once inside the house conversation was a bit stilted as no one felt like talking.

"Judith" said "Brian was given three rabbits last night, you girls can take them home with you." After breakfast the girls went back out to work, as David went to get washed and changed, as he was putting the collar on to his shirt, he thought Margaret put that much starch on his collars, that they would stand up themselves,　just as well she had put his collar studs away, or he would of forgotten where they were, when he thought about it he couldn't remember how long it had been since he had been dressed up. Margaret was on her way upstairs their old battered case lay ready on the bed, God only knows when we will get back he thought, as he picked up the case and made his way down the narrow stairs, passing Margaret on the way, as she let out a long shuddering sigh, her face was ravaged by tears ,as he went in to the kitchen his granddaughter Emma, ran over to him holding out her chubby little arms to be picked up, he carried her over to the chair and sat down with her on his knee, he thought this might be the only normality I might have for a while, as he sat and cuddled her chubby little body, close to him, Judith came over and put a mug full of scolding tea down on the table beside him.

"Drink that dad, as I don't know how long it will be, before you get another one." as he looked up at his daughter, he could see by her face she had been crying but it was her brother after all, she was smiling at him now,then she said,

"Dad you have run your fingers round the inside of your collar four times."

"I know Judith, but I feel so bloody uncomfortable with a shirt and tie on, I think I must have put weight on, since the last time I was dressed up, this collar is digging in to my neck, so is this bloody collar stud, I'm going to have to undo this top button, it'll not show with having this tie on." Margaret was in the kitchen now, getting her self flustered, checking this and asking

Judith if she can manage to see to God knows what. David would usually keep quiet as his domain was the out buildings, but feelings were running high, as they were all sad,

"Come on Margaret, let's walk outside and get a bit fresh air."David told her as he was ushering her out. "Harold will be here shortly, and every thing is left in capable hands, as both him and Margaret, put there arms around Judith and Emma and said a tearful goodbye, Harold arrived."

Judith watched her dad climb up on to the cart then put his hand out to help mam up, Judith thought they both looked deflated, but they had a lot on their minds, and a long journey ahead of them, Judith stood and waved till they were out of sight, although she could still here the clip clop of the horse. "Well she thought it's no good standing here, I'll have to start and make a midday meal, for the workers, and I have two babies's to attend too." As David and Margaret climbed down off the cart, David knew the next part of the journey wouldn't be easy for Margaret, as they had both only been on a train once in their lives, and neither of them ever thought they would have to do it again.

CHAPTER 19

The big engine was standing ready, with smoke pouring out of its funnel, readily,building up the steam, so they could set off on the next stage of their journey. David walked over the platform to the carriage, and opened the door, then he turned round and put his arm round Margaret's waist, to help her up the steps, and he felt her shiver,as he helped her to a seat, while he reached up to the rack in the carriage to store their case, He wasn't looking forward to this journey himself, the only form of transport they ever used was the horse and cart, they didn't see the need, to go galavanting off, they had all that they needed on the farm, they were nearly self-sufficient, somebody rang a hand bell, the engine puffed out a cloud of smoke, and they were off.

"David said to Margaret," "Just hold my hand lass, till we get there, then we will see what's to do about that lad of ours." as the train chugged on David began to wonder if they would ever get there, the train was starting to blow its whistle as they were pulling in to another station,David leaned over Margaret and rubbed the steam off the inside of the carriage window, so he could see out,then he turned and took hold of Margaret's hand and tried to reassure her that Paul would be alright,Margaret looked at David and said,

"I wish I had your optimism." as they had travelled a few miles down the line the carriages started to fill up with soldiers, they all had their heavy kitbags with them which took a bit of room up, it was hot and every body was smoking, some airforce girls got on, and had to sit on their cases, they were offered the soldiers knees, some of them gave a cheeky laugh and took them up on it. David was watching Margaret, he knew she was tormenting herself over Paul.David was thankful when they arrived at their destination, he would of liked to stretch his legs out in front of him, before he stood up, but there was no room,so they sat still till those, that had been sitting on their cases had made their way out. David got up holding on to Margaret's hand, and then he turned and said.

"Once I get off this train give me your hand and I will help you, as its a big step down to the platform,"as Margaret rose stiffly from her seat, As they set off, out of the station, they were amazed at the amount of people, as they had never been in crowds like this before, everyone was rushing around. Margaret said,

"Surely they all can't be in a hurry? We will never find your cousins in this lot she said anxiously."Margaret wasn't used to this amount of people and it overwhelmed her, David was in a sombre mood as he felt out of his depth,

"What are we going to do David?"Margaret tearfully asked him.

"I don't know Margaret, just give me time to think," he said, as he stroked his chin thoughtfully. Then they saw Maud, standing waving her hankie, they managed to make their way over to her feeling relived, after being pushed and shoved, Maud put her arms round Margaret, then around David, to welcome them.

"Billy is waiting outside, Maud told them, he borrowed a car, to come and pick you up, as we thought you would be weary, as you have been travelling all day." Margaret thought it was good of Billy and Maud to consider them. but she was dreading having to ride in a car, also the conversation was stilted as the couples hardly knew each other, they had only kept in touch through sending a Christmas card. Margaret exclaimed, "What a sight," as curtains blew in the breeze at the glassless windows, all the buildings had been demolished by German bombs, they both realised the war hadn't touched them, living in the country. "What a dismal place this was, David thought,"He was feeling thoroughly fed up with all this travelling, he had tried to cheer Margaret up a bit, on the way down, but now he felt depressed himself, then later on tonight, he would be face to face with their son, who had some of his leg amputated. "What the hell do you say to somebody who's lost their leg? He wondered, and only twenty years old and had all their life in front of them. now they had reached Maud and Billy's house, they got out of the car and went in to the house, it was a dingy little house in a very crowed street, when they had drove down the street, Margaret and David were surprised to see a group of woman, standing with their arms folded, all with cross over pinny's on, and headscarves rapped round their heads like turban's.When Margaret has mentioned it Billy had nodded his head and laughed as he said,

"They will be standing talking about someone; it's how the older ones pass the time of day, as the young women are either away in the forces, or doing war work in the factories." Margaret had always thought, that David's cousin lived some where better then this. Just then there was a rumble and the house shook, as a train whistled as it went over the bridge, at the bottom of the street, David saw Margaret shudder, and Maud saw the look of panic on Margaret's face, Maud,said, as she laughed,

"You will get used to it, as they go over day and night, this bridge carry's passengers and goods trains." Margaret had never known nothing like it and that dark brown wallpaper as you walked in the front door and down the passage was dreary, Maud had fried some sausage which tasted as if it was full of sawdust, and David thought the shop bought bread was like putty, not crusty like Margaret baked, when he had asked Maud, if she baked bread? She laughed and said.

"I've never baked bread in all my life, and I'm not starting now, beside's we prefer shop bought."David thought they must like condensed milk as well compared to fresh cows milk, witch him and Margaret had brought with them.Margaret was watching David, he wasn't the type of man for sitting around making small talk, and when he came in to the house at home,he would stand in front of the fire warming his backside, she noticed he was doing the samething here only he was standing in front of a empty grate, where as at home he would of been standing in front of a log fire, that was roaring up the chimney.

After tea Margaret wanted to go to the hospital, and as Billy had taken the car back to his friend, they would have to go by bus, it turned out to be a horrendous journey, Margaret felt as if she would never get there, they had been travelling for ages on the bus when the bus drew to a halt, the conductress informed them, that they would have to walk the rest of the way, as the bus did not go as far as the hospital. As they were getting off the bus, David turned and asked the conductress directions to the hospital. She said,

"You are not from round here are you?"

"No we are not." answered David.

"Well." the conductress said, "A word of warning for you both," as she tilted her head back and looked up at the sky, "it's a dry light night, tonight, a proper bombers moon, you still have a couple of miles to walk to the hospital, and then,when you come back tonight, down this road, if you turn to your left, there is a air raid shelter, when the planes come over tonight as they will,get yourselves into the shelter, and I hope that you find things as you would hope to, as I take it to be someone close that's in hospital."

"Well thank you for your help,David answered, and by the way it's our son that we are going to see." As they left the bus, and started to walk, David and Margaret both wondered what they would have to face. When they finally arrived there, an hour later, they were walking down the corridor towards the ward, that Paul was in, when a nurse stopped them and asked them, who they had come to visit? And they would have to produce their visiting cards, or she wouldn't be able to allow them on to the ward, this final hurdle felt too much to bear. David explained

"We have done a lot of travelling today, in order to see our son."

The nurse said "I'm very sorry, but there is no admittance to any ward, with out a visiting card, I will go and get matron, as they stood waiting, Margaret shed a few tears, and then she asked.

"What are we going to do David?"

"Well if I knew that, we wouldn't be bloody standing here now, would we?" Margaret had a sodden hankie in her hand, and she kept squeezing it, as she swopped her weight from one foot to the other, she was getting herself aggravated.

"We have lost ten minutes visiting now David", Margaret cried." "As it's ten past seven." just then a door opened, and a severe looking woman walked towards them, in a matron's uniform.

"Now I am matron on this ward, she hollered and I understand from my nurse that you are trying to visit your son, but you haven't got a visiting card." David coughed, and took a step towards her,

"Now look here matron, David tried to explain, we have travelled all day, to get here, where do we get the bloody card from?" matron looked grim faced, she pulled herself up, to her five foot eight ins height, at the same time putting her arms under her huge breast, and lifted them up.

"I will not be spoken to, in that tone of voice, on my ward,as she stood arms akimbo, and feet planted firmly apart, you should of sorted the cards out before you came here,making a nuisance of yourselves, and it is up to the patients to make sure that their visitors receive their visiting cards."

"How the hell can he? When he is lying in there with half his bloody leg missing,"David said angrily. While this was going on Margaret looked at her watch, and saw there was only five minutes left of the visiting time, she thought she would try and appeal, to the matrons' better nature,

"Please could we just pop in and say hello?"Margaret begged.

"No sorry visiting is nearly over, and I am not going to bend my rules, so if you go home and comeback tomorrow night, I will sort the visiting cards out for you." David said, "Miserable bitch." As matron walked away down the corridor. Margaret told him to be quiet or they might not get to see Paul at all, as they turned to walk back the way they came, Margaret was still sobbing into a soggy hankie, they passed the nurse that went to fetch the matron, she just shrugged her shoulders helplessly.

As they were walking back up the road they both thought all hell had broke loose as they heard a tremendous bang, planes engines were throbbing over head, the ack ack guns were firing back at them, flares were lighting up the road, a lot of the houses they had passed today were reduced to rubble, people were running into the shelters.

"Come on Margaret, David tried to shout above the noise, as he grabbed hold of her hand, we had better run as best as we can." they both knew they wouldn't be able to go very fast, as they were both over weight, as they got near the shelter, a air raid warden, with a tin hat on was waving his hands, and telling them to hurry up and get in to the shelter. As they entered the over crowded shelter, the smell of urine and unwashed body's hit their nostrils, babies were crying, mothers were bouncing them on their knees to try and pacify them, as David looked around he thought they must carry all their things around with them, some people had blankets thermos flacks sandwiches and God knows what else, there was another tremendous bang and the ground under the shelter started to shake. Margaret reached for David's hand, an old woman sitting near them started to pray, the older children started to cry, a woman who was sitting on the other side of David, had got her knitting needles out, and had started to knit, the click of the needles were setting David's teeth on edge, he noticed the wool went right back in to her pinny pocket, the same as Margaret's did, when she was knitting, as she kept the ball of wool in her pocket. David nudged Margaret, and said,

217

"Theses wooden slatted forms are uncomfortable," as he shuffled his backside to try and find a comfortable position, shaking the form as he did so earning himself a scathing look, off everybody else, a woman walked to a pail that was in the corner and relieved herself.

"Bloody hell, I've seen every thing now." David whispered to Margaret. A man started singing roll out the barrel, then one by one they all joined in and started singing the popular song's of the day,after all the song's had been sung, peoples eye lids were starting to droop, it was a long tiresome night.

Next morning as every one picked their bags up and began leaving the shelter, to go home and hope their houses were still standing, Margaret and David asked the air raid warden, if they would be able to get a bus from here? He took off his tin hat, and scratched his nearly bald head, as he thought,

"Well he said, there will be no buses running within two miles this morning. As he pointed with his nicotine stained finger, at the broken gas and water pipes, so you will have to walk." Margaret linked David's arm, and they both set off, neither of them had the slightest idea where they were going, as they walked they couldn't believe the devastation, possessions were exposed to public view, clothing was clinging to masonry, David's throat was gritty and croaky,they were picking their way over debris and boulders covered streets, they had walked so far up the road when the w,v,s,ladies in their van,stopped and offered them a welcome cup of tea, it helped to quench dry throats,after David had drunk two cups of tea, he took the tobacco pouch out of his pocket, and stoked his pipe up,he was soon blowing smoke rings in to the cold morning air. Margaret thought his pipe would ease his mood, as he liked a pipe full of baccy, first thing in the morning at home.

Back at Maud's and Billy 's house, they were both worrying about Margaret and David, as they were country folk, and were not used to a city, it had been a bad night, they had

218

been bombarded all night, the enemy planes had been busy dropping bombs, and all their crockery was smashed to smithereens, they had no glass left in the windows, and the door had been blown off its hinges,the sky was glowing red off all the fires, it seemed as if the whole city was on fire,the watermains were fractured, so there was a shortage of water to fight the fires, Margaret was really unhappy, but she knew it was no good wallowing in self pity.

It was two hours later,after they had walked most of the way, when a bus arrived to take them to the top of street, where Maud and Billy lived,as they made their way down the street, the same woman were standing arms folded,still gossiping. David wondered if they had been there all night. And he also wondered what greasy food they would be offered today?

It was dinner time back home,on David and Margaret's farm, Judith had taken over from her mother, so Linda Jennie and Sid, were still getting well fed, and getting all the jobs done on the farm between them, things were going better on the farm then what they were for Margaret and David at Portsmouth.

Back at Ethel's house, she was busy chopping carrots and onions up, as last night, Jennie and Linda had brought all the rabbits back home, that Judith had given them, so Ethel had got out the big jam pan, as it was the biggest pan she had, and it was huge, then she put the chopped rabbit in to it to simmer, before she added the carrots and the onion, last night after tea, Linda and Susan had skinned and gutted the rabbits with Ethel, as Jennie washed up, Gran told Mabel "to sit down." As Gran told Ethel later,

"That lass, has a bad look, and all is not well with her." Ethel said

"I keep telling her Gran, to take things easy, as she will not be able to keep going to work for very much longer."

Ethel looked deep in thought as she picked up the pan, then she explained to Gran. "If we all eat together, that huge pan will last three night's, I've also made two huge pie crust's, I've never had five rabbits all together before, I know we only got them because Margaret and David had to go to the hospital, and Judith couldn't use all of them, but we will." Gran looked over at Ethel and said,

"Aye I've always said, wastes not want not, and I've never been far wrong."

As Prudence finished her morning teaching, she decided to walk along to Ethel's, with Eva, and see if Ethel had iced her wedding cake yet, another fortnight and Prudence would be married, as she walked along with Eva, she felt on top of the world, even Gran 's sour tongue, couldn't marr her happiness. As they lifted the sneck and walked in Prudence couldn't believe the size of the pan on the fire, Ethel told them all about the rabbit's, and how she had made all the chocolate cakes, Prudence coughed slightly to get attention then asked,

"Ethel have you iced my cake yet? As surely it's more important then chocolate cakes." Gran looked across at Prudence, and said Aye,

"I reckon it could be the rise before the fall for you Prudence." Prudence who was standing up ready to go to the lav, spun round and said,

"What do you mean?"

Gran said, "time will tell." as Prudence made her way down the garden path, on her way she saw Wilf talking to Arthur the postman, on seeing Prudence he lifted his hand and waved a letter at her, Prudence could hardly believe it, as it had American post mark on it, the lav forgotten, she ran breathless, in to the house shouting,

"He has wrote to me, I always knew, my Bill would never let me down, Prudence said indignantly, he is dependable, Aye its one in the eye for a lot of folk, she said smiling."

Gran said, "If you are bloody meaning me, you are not bloody married yet." Prudence was so flustered, she tore the envelope open, and the letter fluttered to the floor out of her hand, Gran leaned over and picked it up, then,read it, she said,

"I doubt you are in for a shock Prudence." as Prudence leaned over and made a grab for it back, as Prudence started to read it, she cried out like a wounded animal, her legs buckled under her, and she dropped back into the chair as the springs groaned under all the weight.

Wilf walked in as all this was taking place, and wondered what was wrong, till Gran told him, Prudence was still sobbing, so Ethel made the inevitable cup of tea. Wilf said,

"Bill had a bloody nerve, a wife and kids at home, as if that wasn't bad enough he was seeing three different women, besides you Prudence,

"Well at least with his wife finding out about his entire woman, it has saved you standing in the church waiting for him," Gran said knowingly, "it wasn't one in the bloody eye for me neither, as I wasn't daft enough to rush out and buy a bloody dress, so it has cost me nothing, and when Colin and Frank come in later, we'll taste that cake."

Later as the girls were going for the cows, they saw a soldier walking down the lane towards them, Jennie said,

"I think that is John, Margaret and David's son."

"Well you could be right, Linda replied, as he looks the same as the photo that Margaret showed us." as they were about to pass him, he stopped, and asked

"Where have you two bonny lasses come from?" Linda who was never stuck for words, starting telling him about her and what was happening on the farm, his face dropped when they mentioned Paul, but after they had finished milking and taken some into the house for Judith. He said,

"I only have three days, but I will help you if you need me."

"No I think we'll manage," said Linda, as she looked round at everyone to make sure they all agreed, "as Sid is working with us."

"Ok then I'll see you girls tomorrow," he said smiling. Little did they know, that they would be pleased with a bit help from John.

Later as they were all sitting round the table enjoying the rabbit stew, everyone had loaded plates, as Ethel had put plenty potatoes on their plates, as well as the stew. Gran looked up and smiled, as she was loading her fork up,

"By this is good Ethel, I was ready for it, as I haven't had much all day." Wilf started to laugh,

You have eaten all day Gran, everytime I've been in, you have been eating something." as Gran carried on shoving the food into her mouth, she thought there is two bloody miserable faces round this table, and they are both of their own making, Mabel should of known better, and Prudence was too old to have fancy dreams. Just then there was a knock at the door, and Sid poked his head in.

"I hope I haven't come at a bad time, but when I got home, I found that Norah had passed away." Ethel got up from the table, and offered Sid a seat, and a cup of tea, everyone that had some thing left on their plate had stopped eating, apart from Gran, as she said afterwards, when Ethel asked her, why she had carried on eating?she said,

"Well me starving myself isn't going to bring her back, and besides I was looking forward to me tea." Sid refused the tea and a sit down, and stood ringing his cap as if it was a dish cloth, to reveal his bald head.

"I was just wondering, if you would do the baking for the funeral tea? Ethel lass, as you know my Mary, is no bloody good, she was lying on her bed when I got home, didn't even know her mother had died downstairs, she is a waste of bloody time." Ethel didn't think she would have time, but didn't say so to Sid, Eva or one of the girls would help her, between them they would sort it out.

CHAPTER 20

At Portsmouth, Margaret and David,were having a bad time of it, as they made their way back to the hospital, after they had eaten a bag of chips, that Maud had brought in for tea, they were both tired, weary, and worried about Paul, they had been so near to him last night and yet they were not aloud to go and speak to him, after finally getting there, and collecting the visiting cards, the young nurse was showing them down the ward to where Paul lay, looking aimlessly at the ceiling, at the sound of his parents voices, he asked them.

"Why have you come?" without taking his eyes off the ceiling. Margaret laid her hand on his arm, as she looked into his troubled face. He snatched his arm away. David knew, it wouldn't be easy, but he didn't think it would be this bloody hard.

"Look Paul", David said, "We have come all this way to see you, the least you can do is talk to us, I know it's hard for you, but once we get you home."

"Don't mention bloody home to me, he shouted, because I won't be coming, why do you think I never sent visiting cards? Because I didn't want to see you, and as for knowing how I feel, you! Haven't lost a bloody leg." a voice from the next bed asked,

"Is there was anymore visitors on their way in? as I'm expecting my mother or sister, my girlfriend will not be coming anymore, not now, that she has found out that I'm blind in both eyes." Margaret's heart went out to him,

"How old are you son?" she quietly asked him. He gave a laugh, which had no mirth in it.

"I was twenty yesterday."He told Margaret unhappily. David saw the sadness in Margaret's eyes, as she looked round the ward at all the horriffic injuries. David spoke to Paul,

"Don't put your mother through this Paul, we both want

the best for you, so don't shut us out you don't know how hard it is for us, sitting in a bloody shelter all night." the lad in the next bed started talking again. David was answering him as there was no one else there, then ten minutes before visiting time was over, this woman with a headscarf on and a coat that had seen better days, came hurrying towards them, as she got near, the blind lad held his arms wide, and she went into them and gave him a cuddle, Margaret heard him say,

"I thought you were not coming tonight mam." and she answered

"I will always be here for you Ronnie." at the end of visiting time, David and Margaret went to see the matron, they were relieved to see that it was a different one to the night before, she warned them ,

"It will take time for Paul to learn to live with it, but after the stump has healed, he could be fitted with an artificial leg, he has had, quite a few injuries, but given time they will mend."

As they stepped out of the hospital door the sirens started wailing, making such a horrible noise, David reached for Margaret's hand automatically,

"Come on Margaret," he shouted above the noise, "let us find another shelter."Margaret was getting more despondent,they saw the silver barrage ballons bobbing about on long wires, when they went in the shelter.There was a lot of ashen faced people sitting in the shelter, they all nodded listlessly, as David and Margaret made their way into safety. Margaret was terrified as the enemy aircraft droned overhead, they could hear the bombs finding their targets, Margaret put her hands over her ears as a building near by crashed to the ground, the air was thick with smoke, as the shelter door blew in. "Margaret screamed", some of the older people started to cry, babies screamed after being roused from sleep,then darkness engulfed the shelter as the lamp went out,people were calling to each other, and walking about in a daze,the a r p man tried to tell people "to sit still." As whole streets had been wiped out, the guns were retaliating, making a huge noise, the city was on fire, but the water mains had been fractured, so they were short of water to fight the fires that were burning out of control. It had been a long frightening night, as at last the all clear sounded. David and Margaret got stiffly up on to their feet, Margaret was rubbing her knee, as David was trying to straighten up, and rub his back at the same time,after being in the same position all night, when they came out of the shelter, the following morning, they realised the ballons were no longer bobbing about, as they had screamed down to earth, in the night, after being caught in the crossfire and ignited.

Next morning at the farm John, Margaret and David's son, was up and about when the girls got there, and he had already been for the cows, he agreed with the girls that it was hard for Sid, finding his wife dead, but he had gone to the pub last night, and come out legless.

Grace was worried about Mary, with her being a midwife, she felt it was her duty, to keep a eye on the girl but she wouldn't open the door in answer to Grace's knock. Grace was telling Ethel later on in the day,

"I just don't know what else I can do." Grace was saying,

"I heard that you and Eva were doing the baking for the funeral, where is the funeral tea held?"

"Mary,"SIDS daughter, was sitting with the door locked, she knew Grace meant well, but she couldn't be bothered with her at the moment, she had a lot on her mind, and her Dad was drunk all the time.

"Wilf is trying to catch Sid, sober,Ethel was explaining to Grace,as we have some fields rented off him, and we thought that Sid might sell them to us, as he wont need them, and someone else might try buying them.

"It's a shame about Norah," Grace remarked, "she is your age, isn't she Ethel?" Gran said,

"Well she hasn't been killed with work, as she never did a

hands turn." Grace thought Mrs Brown, had her own views on everything and wasn't very sympathetic.

When Eva came along she had news of her own, Mark was coming at the weekend, he had a weeks leave, Eva and the four girls were looking forward to it, as Prudence got more miserable, as the date that would have been her wedding day got nearer.

Margaret and David felt as if they were wasting their time, they had been at Maud's three days now, and were no further forward, they had never been in bed and Paul had never spoken to them, David was trying to keep happy to jolly Margaret along, but it was starting to tell on him, they had been to the hospital three times, and never arrived back at Maud's the same way, it was a wonder they hadn't been injured, bloody great craters in the road, ambulances and fire engines tearing round, buildings on fire, and they were living on chips, or jellied eels .David was hoping Sid and the land girls, were managing all the work on the farm. The matron had told them, that, "Paul would have to be moved shortly, to make way for badly injured people, the hospital had done all they could, but she would know more tomorrow after the doctor had been round, maybe he could go home, or to a convalescent home. Margaret was going to try and get him to talk tonight, she was sick of having a one sided conversation, when she looked at Paul, she could cry for the fun loving son that went away, and look how he had come back, but tonight she was going to tell him,

"They were going home, he would be moved in three weeks time, and the doctor had said when they were sure that the leg wouldn't get infected, so he had three weeks to make his mind up, if he wanted to come home. When she reached over and took hold of hold of his hand he didn't pull away. His mother and father would never know, what he had been through, or what he had seen, but when he thought about it he couldn't take it out on them, he had been thinking all day about his parents, his life on the farm, but how could he face people with half a bloody leg missing? Oh God he was a bloody cripple, his life was over, he wished they had made a proper job of him, then he wouldn't have been here to suffer, the same as all of them poor buggers in here. Just then, a tear slid out of the corner of his eye, and the next minuet he was in his mothers' arms crying like a baby, while she patted his back and made soothing noises. David reached for his hankie, and blew his nose noisily, he felt they had broke through that wall that Paul had built round him, and given time things would work out, but he knew there was a rough road ahead, as they walked out of the hospital, after promising Paul, that they would come back tomorrow. as they left wailing Minnie was making that horrid noise, but they both felt happier now then they did, when they had first got here, they made straight for the shelter, it was so full of people they were bursting out of the door,

"I don't want to have to stand all night Margaret wailed." Right, David answered,

"lets walk to the next one then, as they were getting out of the city centre, they saw the woman again, going to supply tea again to the rescue workers, David and Margaret were trying to dodge the shrapnel, that was raining down on them, seeing David and Margaret, out in such horrendous conditions, they stopped and offered them a lift, the woman with the mobile canteen asked them, where they were headed? As they could shelter a while in the van, when David answered Dean Street, one of the women looked away while the other one asked if they had family there. David said,

"Yes we have cousins there, that is where we are staying." well the woman said.

"That's where we are heading, we have been told that the street has had a direct hit, there was no sign of any survivors, but don't worry as they are digging there now." Margaret sucked her breath in and started to cry.

"I want to go home David, I can't take no more of this." They rode to Dean Street with the woman, and all that was left was a pile of rubble but it had to be searched, the men were digging,they kept stopping, and listening intently,for cries or moaning that might be heard from the demolished buildings incase anyone was still alive under the masonry, unfortunately there was no one. The woman driving the van told them,

"There is some centre's open for the homeless where you could go, If I was you I would get in to one of them for the night." They seemed to walk all night. Margaret knew it was no good wallowing in self pity, but this was a nightmare, the planes seemed to be going, now that they had dropped their load, there was fires burning, the air was thick with smoke, the dock's had been hit again.

"We will head towards the station,David told Margaret, and then later on we will go to the hospital, and leave a message for Paul, after they finally arrived at the train station,they were shocked to see people asleep on the platform,the waiting room floor was covered in sleeping people, one women who was getting out from underneath her blanket, told David, "it was a nightly occurrance, people bedded down where ever they could.David and Margaret waited until they thought it was a decent time to go to the hospital, then they caught a bus,as they were gazing out of the bus window, they were saddened, to see peoples possessions exposed to public view, building that were still standing had ribbons flapping out of the glassless windows, yesterday the ribbons would have been someone's curtains. When they finally alighted off the bus, they were going to see matron, they had arrived later then expected as the bus made some unscheduled stops, and there had been a lot of diversions.

They finally arrived at the hospital, and after explaining to the matron, she allowed them ten minutes with Paul, he told them, he would come home when he was allowed out, as he didn't fancy a convalescent home, and he promised to write to them, there was hugs and tears, then they headed once more for the station, and the train to take them home.

As they were finally sitting in the compartment, relief flowed through them, neither David nor Margaret would ever forget this trip, they were country people who very rarely left the farm. David turned and looked at Margaret,

"Cheer up lass," he said "we are going in the right direction now; we will be in our own bed tonight." Margaret was still coughing, the soldier who was sitting opposite, offered her some sweets to suck, they knew, that they looked scruffy, Margaret's good coat smelt of smoke and it was dirty, David's suit had a hole in the knee and his white shirt had spots of soot on it, off all the fires, the soldier sitting opposite looked very clean and tidy.As Margaret sucked the sweets the cough eased a little. The soldier was very pleasant and as the journey progressed, Margaret said to him

"We have been to the hospital to see our son, and we have been caught in the bombing, that's why we look so untidy." Mark said

"I am going to visit my two little girls, who are evacuees, and are staying with a lovely woman who has twin girls." The rhythm,and the swaying of the train was making Margaret and David tired, they'd had four nights without being in bed, they tried to fight it, but they couldn't stop their eyes from drooping. When they awoke it was to the sound of doors clashing, they were back at the local station, and the soldier was still there smiling at them.

"By you two have had a good sleep," "Mark told them," "it seemed a shame to wake you."Just as the three of them were coming out of the station yard, Harold was waiting with his horse and cart,

"Come on you three,"Harold shouted over to them, "lets be having you, this is the third bloody train I've waited for today,"

"How did you know we were coming back today then?" David asked Harold. Margaret turned to the soldier and asked,

"Where are you going?" Harold started to laugh,

"Get on that cart Margaret, this lads called Mark, and his two little girls are staying with Eva, Ethel's daughter."

"Oh I thought I knew you from some where." Margaret hurriedly said.

"How did you know we were coming back Harold?" Margaret wanted to know.

"Well your Judith was getting worried, Harold explained so she asked Linda to go to Tommy's and ring the hospital. The matron said, you had called in to say ta-ra to Paul, and you were catching the next train, so Ethel sent young Colin and Frank down, to tell me to pick you up." Margaret said,

"Oh but it does feel good to be nearly home, you can come in and have a cup of tea Harold and we will tell you all about it," then she turned to Mark and said, before you go back to your unit,bring Eva and them little girls down for tea."

As soon as David and Margaret arrived back home Linda and Jennie came in for a cup of tea, and to see how they were bearing up. David asked,

"Where's Sid at? Is he not coming in for a cup of tea?" then he chuckled, and said, "I hope you lasses haven't frighten him off." Jennie said

"Oh he has only been here once, Norah died while you were away, and now he just sit's in the pub."

Later on that night Wilf said, "I'm going along to Tommy's, it seems to be the only place that Sid goes to now, and we need something written down, may be a long term contract, with those fields Ethel." Gran asked,

"Do you think he might sell you them fields?"

"I don't really know Wilf replied."

"Do you want me to tell him to come and see you Ethel? Wilf asked her, as the funeral is the day after tomorrow, and no one knows where the tea will be held." As Wilf walked in the pub he saw Sid leaning on the bar, and then someone beckoned Sid over, so he turned and sat down with them. Wilf ordered his half pint as he wasn't a big drinker, and debated how he could get a private word with Sid, he didn't have long to wait, then Sid was back at the bar ordering another drink. Wilf asked him,

"Will you sell me those fields, which me and Ethel are renting off you?" Kevin who farmed near Sid, was standing at the bar, and he said,

"Are you selling your fields Sid because I would buy them off you?" Ernie who was standing behind, asked Sid how much he wanted for his fields? Sid was standing at the bar chewing his bottom lip, he turned around and faced everyone holding out his braces as he rocked backwards and forwards he said

"Well I have never been a man for speeches, but as you all know it's my wife's funeral the day after tomorrow, I've nothing to stop around here for now, as you all know, I sold all my cows to Wilf here. My daughter is having a kid to God knows who, so I have just decided to sell the bloody lot tonight, and it will go to the highest bidder, seen as you own the pub Tommy, you can take the bids. Lizzy came through to the bar and asked Tommy, if Sid was drunk? Tommy said,

"No he just wants to sell the farm, and there is quite a few wanting it." The night progressed, and as Wilf left the pub he wondered what Ethel would say, to being the new half owner, of Sid's farm. Sid told everyone in the pub, that he was,

going to live near a relation of Norah's, and that bitch,being his daughter Mary, could go and look for Peter, or any bugger else that would take her."

The following day, Sid arrived at Ethel's with the deeds, Wilf had the money ready, and it was also agreed they would have the funeral tea at Ethel's. Sid handed Ethel some money for baking. Margaret Emmerson had sent a 5lb piece of ham over for the sandwiches. Ethel asked,

"How is your Mary keeping Sid?" Sid was very off hand,

"Oh I don't know, and I don't think she is coming to the funeral." Ethel thought he seemed unconcerned, so she said,

"Mary will be about her time for having that baby." Sid shook his head,

"I don't know, and I don't care, she has carried on without a thought, for me or her mother, so she has made her bed, so she can lie on it, as I'm moving away." At the same time, as Sid, her dad, was at Ethels, Mary was thinking about her unborn baby, it would be in her way, and she had never seen Grace the midwife, as she made her mind up as soon as it was born she was going to go far away from here, and leave it behind, as she didn't want it.

Night time arrived and Mary felt the pains were getting worse, next morning found Mary in a bad way, she could hardly stand the pain, her dad had never looked in on her to check if she was going to her mothers funeral,he had just shut the house door, on his way to the church. It was her mothers funeral day, but she wasn't bothered, but as the day wore on she wished she had somebody to help her, or just to go for Grace, she wished she hadn't been so clever, ignoring Grace,Mary made her mind up in between pains, that she would try and get downstairs and crawl up the narrow lane. she knew that nearly everyone would be at the funeral, but if she could just hear anyone about she could shout, it was hard work trying to get downstairs, then when she got the front door open, she had to rest, as this baby was coming now, and there was no one there to help, it took all Mary's strength to crawl up the lane. She was tired and bleeding heavy, but Mary never made it any further.

After the burial, Sid went back to Ethel's house for the funeral tea, but he didn't stop long, he couldn't wait to get along to Tommy's. As Gran remarked,

"They are a funny family, Mary hasn't even come to her mothers' funeral, and Sid hasn't bothered going home to check on Mary."

232

CHAPTER 21

As Sid stood at the bar drinking his final pint, Mary was drawing her last breath, lying in the lane, and she hadn't delivered her unborn child. When Sid in a drunken state, later staggered down the lane, he tripped over Mary, he swore, bloody sheep, or something laid on me lane, then in his drunken state, he decided to go back and shift what ever was on the lane. He thought at first it was a bundle of rags, till he bent down and had a proper look, and then he jumped back and cried out in shock, when he realised it was Mary, and she was dead. He picked her up with tears in his eyes, and carried her into the house. She was dead, Oh God he wished he had been home earlier, she had needed help, and there had been no one there for her, he sat with his head in his hands and cried, then he finally made his mind up, he would go along to Margaret Emmerson's as he needed someone to turn too and talk to him. He had just buried his wife today, and now his daughter was dead, trying to give birth to that bloody kid he thought with hatred, supposed to be that bloody Peter's. When he reached the farm he realised the Emmerson's were in bed. And when he thought about it he had nothing to say, and nothing to live for, so he didn't knock Margaret up, and with his mind made up, he didn't go home to his dead daughter neither.

Wilf was just saying to Gran and Ethel over their last cup of coca that it had been a good turnout Gran said

"There is plenty of that ham left as well, she said, as she belched."Wilf said

"We will have some more of that tomorrow Gran." Next day dawned hot again; there had been no rain for weeks,

"By we are getting a good suntan Jennie," Linda remarked.

"Yes but its bloody hot, working in all this heat, but you

like it hot don't you Linda?" They were walking in to the byre with the cows, when Margaret and David heard their startled screams, they both ran towards the byre,as the girls were running out, it was then that they saw Sid's legs dangling from the rafters, he had hung himself with his belt. David said later to Margaret,

"It was a hell of a shock for those lasses, finding Sid hanging."

"Yes I know David," Margaret agreed with him, "I just hope, it hasn't put them off going in the byre to milk, as it will take some time to get over, something like that." "I suppose a double funeral will be to arrange now." "Margaret said knowingly."

Along at Ethels, they were very surprised and upset on hearing the news about Sid, Wilf was annoyed, he said,

"If Sid was intending doing something as bad as that, he could of found some where different then the byre, where he knew Linda and Jennie would find him, but he never gave anyone else a thought, when he was a live." Wilf concluded. Gran said

"Sid and Mary couldn't live together in life, but they have gone together in death." The following afternoon a car pulled up outside Ethel's house, Wilf who had been working out in the field, came to the wall to see who it was, and he told frank and Colin to be quiet, so he could hear what was being said. Two women got out of the car and the man driving it sat still, the woman knocked on Ethel's door and waited, for Ethel to answer, Wilf could wait no longer, so he walked round the car and asked the man who they were? And what they wanted?

"Well we are relations of Sid," said the man, "and we were told, that Mrs. Harrison, had seen to the funeral tea for Norah, so we thought she might do the same for us," as Wilf raised his eyebrows and sniffed, the man said. "We would pay her of course." Inside Ethel's kitchen, the two woman were telling Ethel why they had come, one of the woman said,

"It must be hard for you Ethel; I don't know how you manage, with that old woman to look after." Gran spun round in her chair and shouted,

"I might be bloody old, but I'm not bloody deaf, standing there with all your airs and graces, I've been listening to you two, and I know who you are you are, Norah's cousin, you used to come up here just after Norah married Sid," the woman that Gran was pointing her finger at said, "yes that's right." as her face flooded with colour.

"Aye I never forget a face, you were a right flighty piece, and now you come up here with your fancy friend," just then it seemed another thought had come in to Gran's head. "You remember her don't you Ethel? "Hilda that's you name isn't it?" Hilda was wishing she hadn't come, as her friend didn't know about her past, and if they stayed much longer, it looked as if she would find out, as the old bat was going to tell her.

"look Mrs Harrison I'll leave you this money, and I will pay you the rest what ever I owe you, on the funeral day, as she emptied her purse, then turned and lifted the sneck, then grabbed hold of her friends arm, and hurried her out. Gran started to laugh,

"By you have made a bit of money out of her our Ethel, talk about paying someone to keep their mouth shut." Ethel said,

"Well I wouldn't have said anything to embarrass her." Gran said,

"Aye may be you wouldn't our Ethel, but I bloody would, she stood there all la –di-da, I hadn't forgotten her." Wilf was still leaning on car when the women came back out of Ethels.

"What are you doing about the dog and the hens? Hilda asked, as she stared at Wilf. "You bought the farm, so they are your problem."

Wilf walked back into Ethel's looking glum, "Them miserable buggers, have just left Sid's dog, and the hens on the farm, I will go now, with Frank and Colin, and bring them hens back. I don't know what to do about the dog, as it's only a pup, it's not very old."

"Can we have it uncle Wilf? Frank and Colin chorused together, Ethel said "You can't leave it down there, but we have enough here Gran said,

"Let them have it,do you not remember that day Sid called with the pup? Jess and her got on alright, as she is only a young dog." As Wilf and the boy's made their way to Sid's farm, or Ethel and Wilfs, as it was now, they could hear beauty, as that is what the boys called her, she was howling, as they reached her, she was still tied up where Sid had left her, she was wagging her tail and nuzzling in to the boy's, as they untied her. Wilf said,

"That dog is very hungry, put her on the barrow, and she can have a ride back", after they had caught the hens, and got back to Ethel's, beauty got a good feed then went straight to Gran. Frank asked Gran,

"Do you like animals? They seem to like you."

"Oh I do Frank, I like them better then a lot of bloody people."Gran said with feeling.

Ethel was standing in front of the fire stabbing the potatoes with a fork, to see if they were cooked, as the rabbit stew, was simmering on the fire, alongside the potatoes, as she straighten up, she pressed her hand in to the bottom of her back, and said to Gran.

"I will have to do some baking tonight for the funeral tea." Linda was the first of the girls through the door, and heard what Ethel had said.

"I will help you Ethel, Linda offered, we will as well, said Jennie and Susan, but Mabel dose not feel up to it." Gran looked round, as they all walked in, and on seeing Mabel's face, said,

"After tea you go to bed Mabel, you will be comfier, because by the look on your face, it'll likely be a few days before you are back on your feet again." Mabel protested feebly, and refused the tea that Ethel offered her. Gran said,

"Go on Mabel get yourself to bed." Then as Ethel was serving the stew and potatoes out Gran said to Jennie,

"After tea run and ask Grace to come along, and if she is not in, then tell her husband, that Grace must come along, as soon as she gets in." Ethel thought no wonder my backaches as I have two dogs to lean over now when I'm cooking, as Gran sat beside the fire, and the dogs' lay together at Gran's feet. As they all sat down to tea everyone's mind was on Mabel, and Ethel knew that she couldn't put the baking off tonight, as soon as Jennie ate her tea, she stood up scraping her chair back from the table.

"I will go now, and see if Grace is in." as she reached Grace's house her husband answered the door, after Jennie explained to him why she was there, he said.

"I will tell her as soon as she comes home, but she is at a birth, so I don't know how long she will be." Jennie thanked him then set off back to Ethel's with a heavy heart, as Linda walked back in to Ethel's, Wilf and the boys were going to move the hen houses around, so they could make room for the one they had just brought from Sid's.

Just when Ethel thought, she couldn't cope with any more people, Eva Mark Prudence and the four girls arrived, when Mark was told that Wilf was busy with the hen house he went straight back out to help him, Linda and Susan had their sleeves rolled up ready to start and bake with Ethel. Jennie couldn't settle, she was standing wringing her hands and telling Gran, that "Mabel was having niggling twinges." Gran said,

"She will have more then that, before this night is over, and its bloody chaos in here." "Prudence said sourly."

"I wouldn't like to be in her predicament tonight, with a smug look on her face." Gran said,

"A lot of folk wouldn't of wanted to be in yours neither last week, when Bill's wife, wrote and told you, her husband couldn't marry you, after you made such a bloody fuss. I know what she wrote, as I picked the letter up, as it fluttered to the floor, you were well and truly took in with him, as his wife said he was engaged to three other woman as well as you, and all your fancy talk about going to America, you were all show off, till that letter came, and I know exactly what it said, as I read it twice to make sure." Everything had gone quiet. Eva said,

"I didn't have time to make my clothes for the wedding, Just as well the way it has turned out." Ethel looked at the girls, as they were starting to bake, and asked if they could manage while she went back up to Mabel? Gran waved Ethel away,

"You go up and see to that lass Ethel", Gran told her, "and I will keep these lasses right." As Ethel went back upstairs, Gran turned to Prudence and said,

"I will tell you some thing else, "Mabel is young, she will be able to get on with her life and find happiness, at your age Prudence, I doubt if you will." Ethel was gently rubbing Mabel's back, as Mabel turned a tear stained face to Ethel, and asked,

"What is wrong with me Ethel?"

"Oh Mabel, Ethel answered, as she held Mabels hand, "you are so innocent, your losing the baby."

Downstairs Wilf, Mark and the boys, had walked in, they strode over to the fire, rubbing their hands together, then holding their palms to the flames, Wilf sat down in the armchair, on the opposite side of the fire to Gran, saying "its nippy tonight," as he eased his boots off, then stretched his feet out, and rested them on the fender. The boys sat on the prodded mat, in front of the fire stroking the dogs. The girls were baking under Gran's supervision. Wilf was surprised how quiet Prudence was, but he supposed there must be a reason for it, and no doubt he would find out after off Ethel. Just then Ethel came walking downstairs, she had left Mabel moaning loudly, her pain was excruciating, and she was writhing on the bed. Ethel was thinking things couldn't get any worse, when Grace walked in. Ethel nodded her head at Grace to follow her through the kitchen, as Ethel hurriedly told Grace, what was happening, Ethel could see by the look on Grace's face, that she was surprised, to find out about Mabel, as she had no idea that she was pregnant. Upstairs Mabel was clutching Jennies hand, as Grace and Ethel walked in to the room Mabel was rolling about on the double bed, she cried out as a piercing pain gripped her, Ethel picked up the damp cloth and rubbed her sweating forehead, Grace rolled her sleeves up, and began to examine her. She looked round at Ethel, and said.

"We will have to try and staunch this blood, or I fear she will be in a bad way." As Ethel looked at Mabel's face, it was the same colour as the white pillar, and her bedraggled hair was plastered to her head with sweat. Downstairs Gran was sitting watching, Linda and Susan baking. prudence offered to make everyone a cup of tea, she put a hand on each of the chair arms, and levered herself out, at the same time, her skirt rose up above her fat dimpled knees, revealing her long knicker legs. Colin nudged Frank, and they both started to laugh, as Linda was leaning in the oven taking some fruit pies out, Gran looked at them and said,

"I will have a bit of that pie with me cup of tea." Eva said,

"It's not long since you had your tea Gran."

"Aye I know, but these two haven't done much baking, and someone has to taste it." Wilf not being one, to miss some thing to eat said,

"I will taste it as well Gran, because it smells good." Wilf saw the look on Colin and Frank's face and said, "Aye you two lasses, we'll all have a bit, wont we boys?"Gran said,

You lasses all want to take notice, of what's happening upstairs, don't you lot be left up the bloody creak with out a bloody paddle." Prudence trying to get back in to Gran's good books said,

"There is never a dull moment in here, is there Gran."

"No there isn't." Gran answered nastily, "But you had your moment last week." Prudence thought, she had better make a cup of tea, as Gran and wilf, would drink tea all day, and no doubt Ethel and Grace would like one, as they had been upstairs a fair while now.Linda was still busy baking, so Prudence settled the kettle on the red hot coals, and took the tea caddy down off the mantelpiece, and spooned the tea leaves into the big brown tea pot. When the tea was scolded, Prudence asked Linda, to run upstairs with the tea for Ethel and Grace. Gran looked at Prudence, and asked her,

"Why can't you take it up? Linda has enough to do, and I was just going to ask her to make a nice meat pudding for supper." Linda said,

"I don't mind taking the tea upstairs Gran, but I don't know how to make a meat pudding,

"Take the tea up first Linda," Gran instructed, "then I'll tell you."As Linda entered the bedroom, the smell of blood hit her nostrils, there seemed to be blood everywhere, Ethel was leaning over the bed helping Grace, but she turned and smiled at Linda, the continual bending was making her backache, and she kept rubbing her back with her hand. Jennie looked up and saw Ethel rubbing her back, and looking so tired, she said,

"Come on swap places, have a sit down Ethel."Downstairs, Wilf looked at Gran and said,

"I don't think this commotion is going to over very soon and its woman's work, so I will go now, and Colin and Frank can stop with me for tonight." Frank wanted to know what was going on, and said,

"I'm all right; I'll stop here, what is wrong with Mabel?" Gran looked at him and growled,

"No you won't stop here, and mind your own bloody business." Frank knew not to push Gran too far, so he turned to Wilf and asked,

"Should we go now uncle Wilf?" at the same time Eva Mark and the girls, decided to walk along with Wilf,after Eva had been back upstairs and made sure they could manage

240

without her,and promising to come along in the morning to help if necessary.

Upstairs the Tilley lamp was hissing, giving off a comforting light, Ethel had just fuelled them all earlier on in the day, as Harold had delivered a two gallon container of paraffin. Ethel had just been on her way out again, when the coal man arrived, and said he had a ton of coal for her, Ethel had never had as much coal delivered before, but her and Wilf had a lot of pigs breeding now, and the butcher had killed four for them last week, so Wilf had struck a deal with the coalman, Ethel came out of her reverie, as she realised it was going to be a long night, and everyone was worried and upset about Mabel. Gran had her own memories, which she kept to herself, but it didn't stop her thinking about it now. Her own daughter had laid up there and bled to death giving birth to Ethel, she just hoped the same fate wouldn't happen to Mabel. Linda and Susan had done all the baking, Gran had smiled and said,

"You have both done well, and that pie tasted good, you two lasses have saved our Ethel a lot of work, I'm pleased about that, as some times our Ethel is worn out."

Upstairs the bedroom was so hot, and there was a sickly smell of blood, Jennie was rubbing her eyes with her hankie.

"Are you all right?" Grace asked her patting her knee.

"I'm all right, just a bit tired but I expect everyone else is as well." Jennie sniffed. Just then Mabel started groaning again, she, was tired, she felt as if her strength had been sucked from her, it was now, three o clock in the morning. Gran was still sitting in her chair; Linda had helped her down to the lav earlier on, as Gran said,

"I can't keep me legs crossed all night,and I have a feeling it could go on all night." they could hear Mabel moaning in distress, then she seemed to find a bit of energy from some where, and gave a huge push, as the tiny baby slithered out of her body, Mabel was exhausted. Grace picked it up and rapped it in a cloth, she would take it away with her, as the next two hours passed by, Mabel seemed to recover a bit, and as she slept soundly upstairs, everyone was starting work with out a wink of sleep. As Ethel tiredly, stirred the oats in the milk, Wilf arrived, Gran had told Susan the night before, and to soak the porridge in the big pan, so it could stand overnight then it wouldn't take long for it to cook this morning. The boys had walked back along to Ethels, with Wilf, they were asking Ethel if they should go and collect the eggs?

"No have some porridge first,Ethel told them, then while uncle Wilf and me milk the cows, you two can feed the hens, and gather the eggs, then after we have delivered the milk, you can both help uncle Wilf see to the geese, and the pigs, while I fry you all some egg and bacon."

Ethel knew that she would have a hard day, as Mabel was in bed, so she would have her to see too, and she would have to have a decent cloth to cover that table for the funeral tea tomorrow, she was thinking about Sid's farm, or her and Wilf's as it was now. Wilf had said when he offered to buy the fields off Sid, he had never expected him to sell the lot, but as he later explained to Ethel,

"He didn't have a lot of choice, or time to make his mind up properly, because if he hadn't bought the lot, then him and Ethel would have had nowhere for the cows. But just now Ethel didn't know what to do with the house, just as Susan couldn't tell MR Rain, what was wrong with Mabel, or when she would be back at work.

Susan felt so tired, her eyes felt sore, MR Rain was still standing lecturing her, going on about land girls taking time off, when there was nothing wrong with them Susan thought, if he only knew how wrong he was, Susan was like everyone else, who was at Ethels last night, no one had been to bed, it couldn't be helped, everyone was relieved that Mabel had pulled through.

Across at Margaret and David Emmerson's farm, Margaret was getting every thing ready, for Paul coming home, she wanted his bed bringing downstairs, and as David told Linda and Jennie, it would be a week or two yet before he was home, he just wished Margaret would stop fussing, as David knew, it wouldn't be easy, having Paul home, a young fit lad going away to war, coming back a man, with half a leg missing, and he dreaded to think what sights he would of seen, it was arranged David and Margaret would go to Sids, funeral, and Jennie and Linda, would stop and see to the farm, it was only right as the girls hadn't known Sid long.

As Frank and Colin walked down the lane dragging the bogey, Colin asked Frank,

"What are we going to Mrs. Emmerson's for?"

"I don't know," said Frank, "we don't always get told much, Gran always says, do as your told, and don't ask questions."

"Well the last time we came here, it was for the big bag of sugar, Colin said knowingly, and then he asked, why did we have they to sleep at Uncle Wilf's last night? And why is Mabel in bed today?" Frank was getting annoyed; he stopped walking and looked at his younger brother,

"I don't know shouted Frank do I? So shut up about it." when they reached Margaret's door, they could see her bagging cakes pies and biscuits, she looked up as she heard them at the door.

"Come on in",Margaret invited," I have made these for auntie Ethel, I thought it would help her, for the funeral tea,now take care with all these cakes, we don't want them broken, do we boys?" Colin had just started to tell her, that Linda and Susan had baked all night, when Frank gave him a kick on the shin, after they had loaded the bogey up, the boys sat and ate a lump of chocolate cake each, while Margaret wrapped the biggest lump of cheese up for them, that they had ever seen to take back to Ethel. Margaret thought she would send a big lump of cheese, as Ethel would have enough of her own ham, as someone had told her that Ethel had four pigs butchered last week.

When the boys finally arrived back at Ethel's, she was sitting in the chair enjoying a cup of tea, with Wilf and Gran, and as the boys started to unload the bogey, Ethel scrambled wearily to her feet, at the same time Wilf, was out of his chair, Wilf was concerned for Ethel, as she looked tired, and on top of mabels carry on, she had a funeral tea to attend too,

"Come on lass sit down ,you look all in, we'll put all this stuff on the table then we will sort it all out after you have had your cup of tea." when the tea was served Linda offered to carry it upstairs for Mabel to save Ethel's legs, and Gran said,

"Mabel didn't eat much for her dinner, if she doesn't eat, she will never get her strength back." everyone seemed to be having a early night, as they had never been to bed the night before .Wilf, Gran and Ethel were having their nightly mug of coca, Wilf stood and warmed his backside in front of the roaring fire, before he sprawled his self out in the chair. Wilf looked at Ethel sitting drinking her coca,she would make him a good wife, and he did love her,If only she was free of that bloody Jack.Wilf cleared his throat and looked directly at Ethel, and asked,

"Why don't you try and contact Jack, and divorce him? Then we could get married." Gran had been listening, so she turned to Ethel and said,

"Well our Ethel I agree with Wilf, if you leave it any longer you'll be too old." Eva Mark and the girls had been along to Ethels earlier on in the day and enjoyed it, but now, Eva was getting herself in to a temper over Joe, her ex husband, she had agreed to a divorce, and it all seemed to be going well, then this morning she'd received a letter from his solicitor, telling her that he had moved and never left a forwarding address, so things were at a standstill, and now she desperately wanted to be free of him. Ethel, Evas, mam, was pondering her problem on how to get in touch with Jack, Evas dad, so she too could have a divorce, little did she know, she would see Jack, sooner then she thought.

CHAPTER 22

Jack was sitting in a dockside pub, wondering what he could do for money once Betty was gone, the woman he lived with, and had her working for him, as a prostitute. He was doing all he could to send a bit of trade her way, but she was sleeping a lot now, and all the flesh had dropped off her, in her sleep she would mumble ,about her son, who she had given away when he was born, she had called him Philip. Jack knew he didn't have long left to live, he wasn't as bad as Betty, and he didn't want to be left on his own, he made his mind up, he would go and see Ethel, after all this time, and she was still his wife. That old Gran would of passed away by now, he thought,so he made his mind up, he would go the day after tomorrow,but first ,he would empty the little tins, that Betty kept on the mantelpiece, with money in for rent and other bills, he would also have a word with that feller, who was always in the dockside pub, and ask him, to keep sending customers to Betty, just incase Ethel had passed on, as he would want some money to come back too, as Jack made his drunken way home, he met two drunken seamen, who were looking for a woman, so he took them back to Betty, she was still in bed, so Jack told them to get in with her, but to pay him first. Betty opened her eyes and begged Jack to send them on their way,

"Please Jack don't do this to me," she begged him, "I'm ill." But Jack just sneered at her, and told the seamen to take no notice, of her, as they were in bed with Betty, Jack emptied the tins, he made up his mind he would go now, as he was walking out of the door, he could hear Betty moaning she was in pain, but he didn't care, as he walked along by the docks, he met the bloke again, Joe he thought he was called ,Jack stopped him and gave him, some money and Betty's address, and Joe agreed to send some customers along to her, he might even call and see Betty himself.

Jack got to the station, he sat down on the wooden slatted bench, and promptly fell a sleep, no one gave the old white haired man a second look, the following morning, when the train pulled into the station, Jack was off the seat, and clamouring to get on the train as the service people were getting off. Once on the train he made straight for the toilet, he would have to keep hidden, as he was not going to buy a ticket. Jack never realised how many people used the train toilet, or how often, he was tired of going in and out. finally after travelling all day the train whistled, and pulled into the final station, he got off the train, he had done it, he wasn't daft like every bugger else, buying a bloody ticket, he set off along the road, a motor bike and sidecar passed him, "I could have had a lift off that bugger he thought." Tommy thought who is that white haired tramp? Jack knew he couldn't walk three miles in one go, he would have to have a rest, he would go over the field and sit against that haystack ,and open his bottle of whisky, he smiled to himself, he'd had to hide in the train toilet to afford this bottle of whisky, but he would enjoy it. After drinking the full bottle, he snored till next morning. When he first woke up he didn't know where he was. Then he remembered, and set off up the road to see Ethel. Gran was sitting in her chair, alone in the house, when Jack lifted the sneck and walked in, Gran had seen someone coming up the road, but she hadn't recognised Jack. She shouted,

"Who the hell are you walking in here like this?" The dogs raced over snarling at him, one held him by the leg, while the other one pulled him down on the floor by his arm, and that is how Ethel and Wilf found him. Gran didn't know who got the biggest shock, Ethel and Wilf, or Jack, on seeing Ethel and Wilf together, and Gran still alive. Jack said to Ethel.

"You are still my wife, and I have come here to stay."
Gran said savagely,

"You will not stay here, if our Ethel doesn't want you too, as it's my bloody house, and the way I look at you, and your colouring, you haven't got long left in this world, so you need'nt think, you are coming here, to be looked after, and we are not paying for a bloody funeral." Ethel thought, just as well he didn't turn up yesterday, when Sid and Mary's funeral tea, was eaten here. Ethel would not of known Jack, he used to be a thick set man, with dark hair, his threadbare clothes, were hanging on him ,his eyes were sunk and Gran had seen straight away that he had a deathly pallor, it was a shock to see his head of white hair. just then Frank and Colin came in, and asked Ethel.

"Do you want the butter and eggs delivering Aunty Ethel?" Jack just snarled at them, who the bloody hell are they? Selling butter and eggs, they must be making money like hay Jack thought. Ethel was standing wringing her hands.

"You are not stopping here Jack, I don't want you back."

"And who's going to stop me?" Jack laughed.Wilf moved closer to Ethel, and put a protective arm around her.

"I will Jack; I will not have Ethel upset,"Warned Wilf. Jack got up off the chair, and on his way out he said.

"This isn't over yet." Jack decided to go and see Eva, surely she would have a soft spot for her dad, as Jack walked along to Eva's, he thought if Eva wouldn't help, him he didn't know what he would do, he thought he would knock on the door and wait of Eva answering it, as he knew she probably wouldn't recognise him, he got a shock when the door opened, and Prudence, stood there starring, at him.then she hollered.

"What do you want? We don't feed tramps," as she stood blocking the door way, with her feet apart, and arms folded. Jack hesitated, before he asked,

"Does Eva still live here? As I'm her father,"

"Yes she does", answered Prudence, "but she is not in,"

"Well can I come in and wait?"Begged Jack, as he had nowhere else to go,

"No you can't"Prudence told him harshly. "If you want to see her, you will have to come back when she is in." Then

Prudence slammed the door, with such force, it rattled on its hinges. Jack thought bloody woman, he wouldn't be treated like this, he knew, it was too early for opening time, but as he walked past the pubdoor it was open, so Jack walked in, and finding no one in the pub, as Tommy was in the cellar. Jack went behind the bar, and helped his self, to the two bottles of whisky that was on the shelf, he knew this coat with the long pockets would come in handy. He had pinched it off the bloke, who had left it on his chair, when he went for another drink, at the dock side pub. He put a bottle in each pocket, and walked quietly out and up the road, as he sat on the roadside, with his back against the wall he took the top off the bottle, he would have a drink, till he decided what to do, but Ethel need'nt think, that she would get rid of him that easy.

All day Ethel was a bag of nerves, her stomach was churning. Gran kept looking at Ethel.

"I bet that buggers gone along to the pub, our Ethel, because he could never walk past, he always had to be in a pub, he has always been a heavy drinker, I suppose the pub was beckoning, he will be in a nasty mood at closing time." Wilf looked at Ethel,

"Why don't you eat your dinner Ethel? Rather then shove it round your plate, you needn't worry, I'm not going along home tonight, I'll sleep in that sideboard bed, so that I am here, if he decides to, call back." Wilf had hands as big as shovels, he made a fist with one hand, and hit the other hand with it, and then we will see if he fancies his chances with me,"he told Ethel and Gran. "I will make sure that he doesn't pester you, by the way I think tulip is getting ready to have her calf, we'll have to keep a eye on her, are you listening to me Ethel? Don't sit there worrying, as I will see him off, if he comes back here." Gran looked at Ethel,

"I thought Mabel, was getting up today after dinner, go and see what she is doing Ethel." Gran said to Wilf, after Ethel had left the room,

"We will have to try and keep Ethel's mind off that bugger, as she is really worried."

Just along the road Jack was getting up off the roadside, he had drank half the bottle of whisky, he would go back to Eva's, and see if he could get some money off her, if he could get past her, that had filled the doorway up, when he had called earlier.This time, Eva answered the door to his knock, she knew it was him, as Prudence had described him,and told her that he had been while she was out,even so,Eva scarcely recognising Jack, when she answered the door to his knock got a shock at the state he was in; as he looked like an old tramp.

"What do you want? Eva stared at him; I didn't think I would ever see you again"

"Well what a way to welcome your dad," he said, as he staggered and nearly fell in, past Eva. Can I come in? I have come all this way to see you."

"No you haven't"Eva retaliated, and you stink of drink, you can come in for half a hour, then we are all going out, so you will have to go, as he staggered in, and sat down near the table, prudence got up, and snatched her purse out from under his nose, and put it in her pocket. Jack looked around, as he sat in Eva's house, he thought, things must be looking up for her and Joe, as the shabbiness had gone from the house, he wondered if that fat bugger was a relation of Joe's, thinking about Joe Jack thought he'd better ask Eva, for some money now before he came in.

"I came to see your mother Eva, Jack told her sorrowfully, but she dose not want me, so could you give me some money? And I will get the train back." Eva knew if she didn't give him some money, he would never go. So she stood up, to get her purse.

"I will give you this, she said as she took a few coins out of her purse, then go, and don't come back."she warned him, he was smelt of drink, and he could hardly stand up, as Jack staggered out of the door, Eva locked it,"Bloody good riddance, to you." She said to Jack's retreating back.

As Grace biked along the road towards home, Jack was staggering towards her, if she hadn't of swerved, she would of rode in to him, she was still trying to place him, when she called at Ethel's, to see how Mabel was getting on. As Grace walked in through the door, Gran was in her usual place and Mabel was sitting in the other rocking chair at the side of the fire.

"How are you today Mabel? Grace enquired,I thought I would call in and make sure that you are all keeping well, especially you Mabel, as grace patted her knee, Mabel said,

"Thank you Grace, and all of you, as she looked at Gran and Ethel,for all you did for me I do appreciate it," as she sniffed and rubbed her eyes, with the back of her hand, as she was filled with gratitude. Grace took a closer look at Mabel, and said

"Don't upset yourself, it is over now, and you have paid for your leaning,"Grace was pleased to see that Mabel had got her colour back, and she was looking well. Ethel had the big brown teapot in her hand,

"We are just going to have a cup of tea Grace; I will pour you one out."

"Oh thank you Ethel, I could do with one to quench my thirst, I have been out on my bike, and a tramp walked right in front of me," Ethel said,

"I don't suppose you recognised him, it was Jack, he has already been here making a nusance of his self, Wilf is going to stay here tonight, incase Jack comes back, which known him he will." Grace was shocked,

"Are we talking about the bloke with the white hair?"

"Oh yes Grace, its Jack, it was a shock for us as well, I never expected him to come here again."

"Well I would never have believed it."Grace gasped. After Grace had drank her tea, and talked a while, she got up and put her empty cup on the table, then looked across at Mabel, and asked,

"Are you really feeling alright? As you are looking better,

you would tell me if there was any problems wouldn't you?"

"Oh yes thank you Grace, for coming along the other night, and, staying all night,"

"Oh you have Ethel to thank for looking after you Grace smiled,I'm just pleased, you pulled through,"Grace said, as she squeezed Mabels shoulder affectionately, "well I 'll be off ta-ra."Grace called, as she walked out through the open door.

After they had eaten their tea, the land girls, apart from Mabel, who was still sitting in the rocking chair talking to Gran, said, they would stop in tonight incase Jack came back. Wilf said,

"No need I'm here, you lasses go and enjoy yourselves, If Jack has any sense he'll keep away from here." later on after Gran and Mabel had gone to bed, Wilf helped Ethel to make the bed up, as Ethel put the eiderdown on the bed, she was looking so serious, that Wilf grabbed hold of her and pulled her down on the bed beside him.Ethel started to laugh,

"You keep trying don't you Wilf?" Ethel giggled.

"One of these days I will put a smile on your face."Wilf told Ethel, as he wrapped his arms around her, "and we will wake up together next morning."

Mean while back at Portsmouth, Joe had been sending fellers, round to Betty's, he thought he would make some easy money, so he took the payment, and sent them to Betty's. When they saw the state that Betty was in, they went to get their money back off Joe, so his head was constantly going from side to side incase any of them caught up with him. Betty's breathing was down to gasp's, she knew she didn't have long left.

Along at the dock side pub, four young seamen were looking for a woman, someone pointed Joe out to them, "go and see him," the lads were told, "we have seen him, sending fellers to a woman that lives near by." Joe couldn't believe his luck, when these lads were offering him money, for Betty's services. When the young service men arrived at Betty's, they were angry with Joe, one of them said,

"Who the hell, could do anything with her?" they turned to go, just as Betty mumbled, Philip, one of the lads turned round and looked at the pitiful woman, that was laid on the bed, with her eye's closed, she was mumbling, the seamen opened the door to go, but Philip turned back,

"We can't leave her like this, he called out to the others that had come with him, he walked back over to the bed, as the other three walked away, one of them looked back in and said,

"don't waste your time on her, she is only a old prostitute, she probably has the pox." just then Betty was moving her hand, and muttering drink, so Philip picked up the old cracked cup without a handle, and held it to her lips, then as she laid back down, Philip took hold of her hand, and as a tear ran down Betty's face, she tried to tell him, she had a son once, but she had to give him up, Philip thought the other lad's would think he was soft, if they could see him holding this woman's hand, but she needed comfort, as he could see she hadn't long left, and he knew what it was like being left on his own, many a night, he had cried himself to sleep in the children's home, he wished he'd had a hand to hold some times. It was starting to get dark, so he found a bit of candle, and lit it, so he had a flickering light, he sat and talked quietly to the old woman, she seemed to be a lot calmer now, but she hadn't spoke for a while, then when he was wondering what to do, as the candle was nearly burnt out, her hand went limp. Philip got up and placed her hand on the dirty blanket, just as the candle burnt out, he turned and looked at the bed again, as he opened the door to go, he thought,

"I comforted an old woman, in her last hour of need." he would never know, that the hand he had held was the hand, of his own mother.

At Ethel's house, it was two o clocks in the morning, as Ethel crept quietly up to bed. Wilf had finally got his own way, and put a smile on her face, but they didn't dare wake up together, Ethel thought, just as well Gran is a deep sleeper, and she came to bed at nine o clocks. As Ethel lifted the blankets and slid in quietly, Gran said,

"Don't tell me, it has taken you five hours to make up a bed; I know what you have been on with." Then she turned over, taking the blankets with her, Gran thought our Ethel is as bad as them lasses, they are all sex mad.

Along the road, Jack was lying drunk next to the hedge, he still had some money left off what he had got off Eva, and a full bottle of whisky, when he thought about Eva, there had been four kid's at Eva's, she must have had another two, since he had gone, he didn't bother to ask, or to speak to the kids, he didn't like kids very much.

Next morning when they were all eating breakfast, Ethel kept lowering her eyes, and smiling when Wilf looked up at her, she knew she was acting like a school girl, but she felt embarrassed, she also wondered what Gran would say. The only thing that was making her unhappy, was thought's of Jack, she didn't believe that he had gone away, and the cheeky bugger never bothered once about his daughter Eva, but he went looking for her to give him some money,he always did cadge, she had a feeling that Jack was not far away, and he was a nasty piece of work, and now that he knew that she had a little bit of money, he would stick a round, until she gave in, and give him some. Oh God she loathed him, she'd had to scrimp and scrape all her life, to make ends meet, and she'd had to work hard for her money.

"Well do you want some or not our Ethel?" Gran's voice brought her back out of her thoughts.

"Sorry Gran, I was thinking."

"You haven't got time, to sit and think about that bloody Jack," Gran said sourly.Wilf had been sitting with the teapot in his hand.

"While you have been sitting thinking,"Gran said frostly, "Wilf has been saying, that tulip and primrose, will likely calve today, so it'll be a busy day." After everyone left, Wilf went back to see to the cows. Frank and Colin to school, Mabel walked round, to collect the eggs for Ethel, as Gran said, a short walk wouldn't hurt her, in fact it would do her good.

"Cheer up Ethel," Gran didn't like to see Ethel upset, "that bugger, Jack, will go back, in his own time, he always has done." Eva walked along after dinner and said,

"I have not seen dad anymore, but I didn't expect I would, as I gave him, money, the day before."

"Well you are dafter then I thought you were our Eva ,as he never gave you, or your mam, a second thought,"Gran was shouting, "I would like to hit him, with this bloody stick." Eva sat down, and asked "how is Mabel?"

"Oh she is a lot better, she has walked round to gather the eggs," Gran said. She is a long time Ethel thought,

"I had better go and see if she is alright", as she walked over the stile leading to the field, she could see Mabel and Wilf, standing in the shed, watching Tulip giving birth to her calf. Wilf turned on hearing Ethel, and smiled at her, as the hither was getting an all over wash off Tulips long tongue, she was trying to latch on to her mother, as her first thought, was food.

"Do you think Primrose will calve as quick Wilf?" Ethel asked him.

"I would say, she will of done before morning." Said Wilf knowingly.When Linda Susan and Jennie came in at teatime, they asked if Jack had been near today. Linda spoke up,

"Oh with a bit of luck he might have got sick and gone away." Ethel shook her head, and said,

"No he won't, and I'm frightened of him,"

"That is why, I'm sleeping here to protect you Ethel, so eat your tea, as I'm enjoying mine." Linda said,

"We will stop in tonight, if you want us too Ethel?"

"No you girls go to the dance; you have looked forward to it all week." As the night war on the girls got ready, Wilf thought it was taking them a long time, and said as much to Ethel. But Ethel laughed at him, and said,

"You don't understand girls, do you Wilf? they have each others hair to do, then they have to draw the seems up each others legs, as none of them have any nylons, and after all that they all share their clothes so they have all that to sort out." The girls rode rode their bikes to the dance, as the transport didn't turn up, Mabel was looking tired, and said,

"I think I will go up to bed Ethel, as I do feel tired,"

"Aye I will go as well, if you will help me our Ethel."As Gran started to get out of the chair, Wilf put both his hands on his knees, and pushed his self, out of the chair,

"Well I will just go and check on primrose", Wilf said, as he left the house whistling. No one knew that Jack was watching what was going on, as he was crouched down behind the wall. Ethel was upstairs helping Gran into bed.

Jack walked in, and took the lid off the coca tin, that Ethel always kept her money in, and emptied it in to his hand, then straight in to his pocket,even in his drunken state he knew there was a lot of money in it, he was in such a hurry, and his hands shook with drink, he dropped the empty tin on the floor, and it rolled in to the corner, he walked out of the house, looking about him, making sure, he hadn't been seen. But Frank and Colin were walking up the road, and saw him coming out of Ethel's, and he walked drunkenly up the road. They all so saw uncle Wilf, in the field so they both jumped over the stile, and ran over to him,

"Can we sit with you Uncle Wilf, Just till Primrose has her calf?" asked Frank and Colin.

"Well you can stop a while, then auntie Ethel will want you both in bed," Wilf told them.

Ethel walked back downstairs, unaware that Jack had been in, and stolen her money, and intended coming back, as he thought to his self as he walked back to the pub, "that bitch needs a good hiding," the land girls were not having a very good night, first the transport didn't turn up, so they had to bike, then when they got there, the dance had been cancelled. Linda said,

"We have biked here; we might as well go in that pub for a drink." Meanwhile back at Ethel's, she was sitting down, having been on her feet all day, wilf Frank and Colin, were waiting of Primrose having her calf, because as Wilf said,

"She wasn't far off," and he had calved plenty of cows, the trick was to sit quiet and they would calve easily."

Along at the pub, jack decided he was going to finish his drink, and go and give Ethel a good hiding .That bugger behind the bar, and his wife, had never bloody spoke to him, he knew they didn't like him, because they were all in with Ethel. Jack walked to the bar, and banged his empty glass down, then walked out, letting the door bang shut behind him.

Ethel got out of the chair; she wondered if the boys were with Wilf? she parted the curtains and looked through the window.When the door banged Ethel jumped,and was terrified as Jack staggered in, leering at her, Ethel turned round and saw his face,scowling at her nastily,her stomach was churning,her hands had started to shake, she all so noticed the coca tin lid on the sideboard,she knew then he must have been in, while she was upstairs, and pinched the money.He made a grab for Ethel, smacking her hard across the face, Gran heard her cry out, and tried to get out of bed. The land girls were on their way home, as they had gone to the pub for a drink, and they were bored, so they decided to go home, and leave their bikes, and walk along to Tommy's .Linda had already shouted,

"Should we bike along to Tommy's? Or take our bikes home." Jennie shouted back,

"Come on girls, we'll take the bikes home, as I'm getting a stiff backside, we have been on these bikes long enough." Gran was shouting of Mabel to get her out of bed, But Mabel was sound asleep, so Gran banged on the bedroom wall with her stick, Mabel opened her eye's, and threw the bedclothes off ,and ran through to, Gran, who was shouting,

"Help me down the stairs, that bugger, is hitting our

Ethel." Jack was hitting Ethel's face, with his fist, making her nose and mouth bleed. Ethel was seeing stars, the dogs started barking and going for Jack, Jennie on hearing the dogs, knew that something was wrong, just then the boys were on their way in, Jennie shouted at them to go for Wilf. The land girls walked in, as Gran lifted her stick with both hands, and brought it down on Jack's head, and then the girls grabbed him, and dropped him down on the floor. Ethel pointed to the empty coca tin, so the girls said they would take the money out of his pocket, as he rolled on the floor the girls pulled his trousers off, he had nothing on underneath. Gran gave a cry out, as she poked him with her stick,

"Look at his dick," Gran shrieked, "the dirty bugger, has pox and his dick is covered in scabs." Jennie was just taking the money out of his pocket when Wilf came puffing in, he bent down and punched Jack full in the face, then he picked him up and told Frank to open the door, then Wilf threw him down the path, as Jennie threw his trousers out after him. Ethel was trembling, and sobbing, her face was covered in blood, it was two hours and two cups of tea later before Ethel stopped shaking.

Jack had crawled out of Ethel's garden, and then spat his teeth out; he'd had a full set of teeth when he came here, now he had none at all, in the front. That bloody feller that Ethel had taken up with was a bloody animal, Jack thought he would need some stitches in his head, as it wouldn't stop bleeding, where that old bitch had hit him with her bloody stick, and them bloody lasses, were bloody mad, he would never go back there.

Next morning Jack was back at the station, as the train pulled in, Jack quickly boarded the train, then went in to the toilet, he felt ill, his head was still bleeding slightly, after two hours of being fastened in the toilet, Jack thought he would risk being found with out a ticket, and went in to the carriage, which was full of service people, one of them looked up when Jack walked in, and asked him, if he had been in a accident? Jack sensing he might be on to a good thing, said,

"I was robbed beaten up, and left for dead, I don't know how I've managed to get this Far." so one of the lads took off his cap, and said,

"Let's have a whip, round, I think it is awful what this man has been through."The train was full of service men and women, they all started to shuffle about, reaching in to their pockets, and bags to find a few coppers, to throw in to the cap, that the young soldier was passing around. Some of the soldiers were giving him a fag, some of the people had been home on leave, and had sandwiches that their mothers had made for them, they shared with Jack. When Jack finally got off the train he felt better, he could hear the coins jingling in his pocket, he made straight for the dock side pub, he would have a few drinks, and buy that lad a few drinks for sending Betty customers, then he would go home to Betty, and collect the money she had made for him, as he opened the pub door, he saw him straight away, and went over and bought him a drink for looking after things for him. Joe thought he would play it safe, and take all the free drink, then after tonight, he would have to use a different pub, because once this bloke went home to Betty, he would find out that he had kept the money. Jack was buying the drink all night for them both. Jack got so drunk he couldn't walk on his own. Joe thought he had better take him so far home, so he decided to take him along the dock side, then he would leave him, as they set off arms around each other, Joe thought, "when we get around the next corner, I'm leaving him," although they were holding each other up, just then two young sailors came running towards them. Joe quickly swung round, so they wouldn't recognise him, as he had took money off them, and sent them to Betty's, as he swung round, he dragged Jack with him, and Jack tripped over Joe's feet, Joe couldn't hold him, as he slipped in to the dock, dragging Jack with him.

Three weeks had passed since Jack had gone, Gran watching out of the window shouted,

"Eva Ethel, come here, the police are here." just then they knocked loudly on the door, as Ethel opened the door, she was asked if she was Mrs Harrison? And they were also looking for Mrs Anderson. The older police officer said,

"He was sad to inform them, that" "both men had fallen in to the dock, and drowned." Gran sitting listening shouted,

"Thank God for that, they won't be bloody missed." after the police had left, Wilf having seen them arrive, came to see what was happening. After he was told, he said,

"Right Ethel, we will see the vicar, and we will be married, we have waited long enough." Gran said,

"I will buy a new dress, this is the happiest day of my life, this is all I've always wanted, to see our Ethel settled with a good man," Gran laughed, and said, "I couldn't have got a better man, for Ethel, if I'd picked one myself." when they told Prudence she didn't look very happy, Gran said,

"Surely you wouldn't begrudge our Ethel happiness, would you Prudence? just because yours didn't happen." the next three weeks seem to go very fast for Ethel, as she planned her wedding to Wilf, finally it had arrived the night before the wedding, and as Ethel climbed the narrow stairs to bed, she thought "I'm getting married in the morning, and I might have a little secret of my own to surprise Wilf with.".